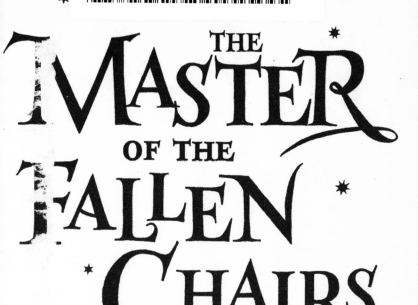

THE MASTER OF THE FALLEN CHAIRS

Praise for *The Master of the Fallen Chairs*

'For page-turning adventure…*The Master of the Fallen Chairs* is just the thing. A newcomer to writing for this age group, Porter plays a good hand before finally coming up trumps as his story heads to its powerful close'
Nicholas Tucker, *The Independent*

'Mysterious deaths, shifts in time, magic, suspense and a talking auk – [I was] hooked'
Philip Ardagh, *The Guardian*

'an engrossing tale'
Kate Kellaway, *The Observer*

'A rip-roaring read of adventure, mystery and fantasy... A fabulous cast of fascinating characters make this irresistible'
Julia Eccleshare, *Lovereading4kids.co.uk*

'A highly original and exciting debut children's novel… Consistently dark and sinister, the author manages to evoke a spine-chilling atmosphere throughout, whilst creating a gripping story and spinning threads for future novels in the series… Sure to become a future classic, I can't wait for the sequels already!'
Shelley-Anne George, Waterstone's Southampton, on the Waterstone's website

THE MASTER
OF THE
FALLEN
CHAIRS

HENRY PORTER

ORCHARD BOOKS

ORCHARD BOOKS
338 Euston Road, London NW1 3BH
Orchard Books Australia
Level 17/207 Kent Street, Sydney, NSW 2000

First published in hardback in Great Britain in 2008 by Orchard Books
First paperback publication in 2008

ISBN 978 1 84616 625 9

A CIP catalogue record for this book is available from the British Library.

1 3 5 7 9 10 8 6 4 2

Printed and bound in Great Britain

Orchard Books is a division of Hachette Children's Books,
an Hachette Livre UK company.
www.hachettelivre.co.uk

Acknowledgments

Thanks to Liz Elliot who first heard this story in
1984 and has encouraged its writing ever since.
Also to my friend Gilbert Adair who was
with us when Iggy was born.

I owe a debt of gratitude to Pamella Merritt for her
intelligent reading of each successive version of *The
Master of the Fallen Chairs*. Thanks to my father, Harry
Porter, for telling me about a game involving candles
that was played at Birlingham before the era of health
and safety regulations, which I have called Slipcandle.
Thanks to Quintus for his Latin, to Ivo and Rachel
Dawnay for the Bridge of Tarle, to Alex and David
Campbell for showing me the Watchman stone, to my
agent, Tif Loehnis, for her many clever suggestions, and
to Ann-Janine Murtagh for the elegance of her editing.

In memory of Christopher Trevor-Roberts

For my Godchildren,
Bronwen Carter, Rachel Cockerell,
Milly Dawnay, Sophia Margerison,
Benjamin Porter and Harry Seymour.

And also for Alexander Porter, Oliver Porter,
Lily Kamp and Henry Kamp.

Contents

Chapter One

Advent
1962

He came on the shortest day of the year between the storms that carried the smell of the sea twenty miles inland and the great snow of that winter. But before his arrival there was an equally mysterious disappearance.

Bella Brown went missing without a word to anyone. She was my friend and she worked in the house. A few of her belongings vanished with her, which led police to believe that she had run off with someone. This didn't seem likely because Bella was extremely shy: she barely looked anyone in the face and when she came across me in my first weeks at Skirl, she found an excuse to hurry away. Those that knew her continued to imagine that she had suffered a terrible fate, perhaps crushed by a falling tree in the storms, or something even worse.

Around this time, there were a number of sightings of a stranger in the valley, a sinister type, bundled up against the weather in some very odd clothes indeed. The police came to search a broken-down barn but found no trace of him – no footprints in the mud and no sign of anyone camping out there. Amos Sprigg, who looked after the sheep, swore that he had seen a pile of old sacks rise up and a man emerge covered in dust, as though a bag of flour had been tipped over him.

Someone – maybe the same character – was glimpsed hurrying across moorland at the head of the valley, then a day or two later, standing at the edge of a spinney, observing the house. He seemed to be covered in hides and a big black hat. This time, Amos was joined by Simon Vetch, a big ruddy-faced cowman. Armed with an axe handle and pitchfork, they crept up to the spot, but the man slipped away into the murk of the winter afternoon long before they got there. The police were telephoned again and a constable came but Amos and Simon couldn't agree about what they had seen and the officer, who still had several blocked roads to deal with, wondered aloud whether they had been at the cider. They shook their heads and stumped off. Both of them knew that someone – or something – had been out there: they *knew* and the dogs *knew* and no damned policeman was going to tell them different.

After that an unease settled on Skirl, the ancient home of the Drago family which was owned by my cousin and guardian, the Colonel. It was a huge, despondent place, hidden from the world in the deep U-shaped valley made by the Skirl River. Few people came to visit, but when they did they rarely noticed the house until they rounded some large laurel bushes and found themselves staring up at its sightless windows, startled by the size of the place and its brooding silence. The forest of ornate chimneys that stood high above the roof were mostly smokeless, the stone of the building was covered with ivy, lichen and moss, and the courtyard on the eastern side, where carriages once drew up and servants sprang from the doors with lanterns and umbrellas, was choked with weeds and saplings.

At the centre of Skirl was another very old building founded 600 years before, maybe even more – no one knew. In some places you would come across bits of old wall that were made out of a much darker stone, and there were doorways that had been bricked up and painted over.

15

One house lay within the other, like the kernel in a nut. When I was bored I would try to work out exactly where the ancient house had been, but its shape and plan somehow always eluded me. Every time I followed a stretch of that dark stone, which sparkled with tiny crystals of feldspar and was damp to the touch, it would abruptly disappear behind a newer wall. It was as though the old house didn't want to be discovered.

There was no hint of this secret house when you entered Skirl, as I did for the first time one beautiful day in July, just eight weeks after my mother's death. She had died a week after my thirteenth birthday in May, and I was at boarding school in England when they told me. And now I was at Skirl, not in Kenya on our farm, and nobody had said how long I would be staying or if I would be there forever.

This is perhaps why it made such a deep impression on me when I walked through the front door and came to a huge hall, at the end of which was a staircase that divided and rose through three floors past windows of mottled glass. I remember letting my case drop to the floor and gazing up those stairs and wondering at the number of rooms in such a house.

Later I would discover two more floors but these could only be reached by one of the many other stairways that threaded through different parts of the building.

To the left of the hall was a drawing room and the dining room, to the right more reception rooms, a snooker room and many smaller chambers that were packed with clutter, and furniture covered in dust sheets. I felt there were more rooms than any single person could visit in a lifetime. Each time I went exploring I discovered new rooms and passageways, and these were all hung with pictures of every description – landscapes, portraits, studies of flowers and animals, mythological scenes, battles and slaughter – but because it was so dark it was often difficult to make them out, especially the higher ones.

The kitchen was at the back of the house, along with the pantries, storage rooms, servants' quarters and a laundry that had once served a household of up to fifty or sixty people. Here the stone floors were worn and at a lower level than in the rest of the house, and in some places you could see drainage channels carved into the stone, which meant that this might have been part of the old house.

There was never a building with more stairways, galleries, hidden thoroughfares, corridors that doubled back on themselves, dead ends and doors that led nowhere. The place was alive with noises – the wind whining through the doors and windows, the creaking of tired wood, things flapping and juddering in the breeze high up in the house, the clank of pipes and gurgling of drains, the scratching of mice, the tolling of clocks at different times and, more sinister, the fits of unfathomable whispering and scurrying that sometimes filled the darker corridors for a few frantic seconds.

Skirl became gloomier and more mysterious as the winter fell upon the valley, a universe that seemed to expand without limit into the night. I spent most of my time in the kitchen, in the company of Tom Jebard, who looked after the place and was the only person who knew every inch of the house and did not get lost, and the cook Alice Camm, an unstoppable talker with a fascination for disasters. Earthquakes were her speciality, closely followed by plagues, thunderbolts, hurricanes, volcanic eruptions, meteors, freak waves and the mysterious disappearance of ships. She saw an omen in everything and during those dark December evenings, she often muttered that the storms and the disappearance of silent, sweet-natured Bella Brown heralded much worse to come.

And she was right.

Just as the last light faded over the moorland in the west, a stranger came to the front door. He walked up, bold as brass, tugged at a handle and sent bells trembling in different parts of the house. Jebard stirred from the kitchen where we were sitting and looked up at the bell quivering on the spring contraption above the door. The two terriers, Applejack and Trumpet, a spaniel named Thistle and an old sheepdog named Black, all searched his face. His eyes narrowed, his hands rubbed his worn brown corduroys until a second ring came and he pushed himself out of the chair. The dogs needed no further invitation and raced off through the house, followed by Jebard and me carrying a storm lantern, which saved us the bother of feeling for light switches on the way.

By the time we got there, the terriers were snorting and scratching at the bottom of the door. Jebard handed me the lantern, picked up a heavy stick, turned the lock and began to draw back the bolts with his free hand. Then he took the lantern back and held it up high. 'Now you stand back, Kim. I don't want you hurt. If there's trouble you're to go and find someone to tell.'

'Who?' I asked, thinking that if there was trouble, Colonel Drago, who lived in his rooms a long way off in the house, and Alice Camm, would be no use whatsoever.

'Never you mind,' he mumbled. 'Just you tell someone. You run to Simon's cottage. That's what you'll do.'

The light swept over a figure padded with layers of coats and jackets. His boots were wrapped in cloth and his hands were gloved and folded in front of him. By his feet stood a perfectly cylindrical kit bag balanced on its end. We could see nothing of his face because it was hidden in the shadow of a peaked fur hat, which had large earflaps. With my head still full of Bella Brown's disappearance and the stories of a stranger skulking around the place, it occurred to me with a thrill that perhaps there was no face beneath the hat.

'What you want here?' demanded Jebard roughly.

There was no answer.

Jebard moved back a little and brandished the stick. 'If you've got nothing to say for yourself, you'd best be off, or we'll telephone the police.

Do you hear? We don't want your kind here.'
He began to turn into the house, but the dogs had
shot from the doorway, down the stone steps,
and were running round in circles, barking
hysterically. 'Shut up, the lot of you,' he shouted,
then peered at the stranger again and pointed to
a brass light-switch inside the door. 'Let's have
some more light on this gentleman, Kim. Is it
you that's been watching the place?' Jebard
demanded, peering under the peak of the hat.

Still no answer came.

I turned on the light. The dogs came back up
the steps and began sniffing around the man's feet
and bag with interest. He glanced down and
made a sort of mewing sound to them. They
cocked their heads and moved away. Then he
reached up and undid something at his neck. The
earflaps sprang outwards and he removed the hat.
A wide, flat face was revealed. His head steamed
gently in the cold air: strands of damp black hair
were stuck to his forehead. He gave us a broad
smile; his eyes almost disappeared, his nose
wrinkled and his lips parted to show an even set
of teeth which seemed astonishingly white
against his dark skin. He nodded with an odd
familiarity, as though he had known us for a very
long time, then he performed an elaborate bow

in which the hand holding his hat drifted out behind him.

He advanced two paces and spoke, 'Igthy Ma-tuu Clava. My name is Igthy Ma-tuu Clava.' He repeated it again as though it was explanation enough for his arrival, and nothing more needed to be said.

'I don't care who you are,' growled Jebard. 'There's nothing here for you. Understand?'

The man smiled again. 'It's very cold. I would like to come in, if that would not displease.' His voice was high and there was a kind of shine to it. I couldn't place his accent, but his English was quite good.

'You can't stay here. We don't let any stranger into the place just because of a bit of cold,' Jebard added with a slightly menacing note. I could see he was trying to work something out.

'I am not stranger. I brother of this house. Look, I show you now.'

He removed a glove, opened his outer garment and began to search among the layers underneath. After much fumbling, he found what he was looking for and, giving me a wink, pulled out a small brown paper parcel, which he offered to us. Jebard took it. 'You will see, I am your brother,' said the man.

Jebard managed a weak smile. 'Whatever you are, sir, you aren't that. My only brother, Bert, s'been lying in the churchyard these twenty years, and a good thing too most would say.'

'In manner of speaking, I am your brother,' the stranger insisted.

The paper had come off easily and now Jebard was looking down at a Bible with soft leather covers that had curled back at the corners. 'What's this supposed to mean?'

The man was humming. 'It is the book which came from Skirl many years ago. It will prove who I am.'

'It don't prove nothing,' said Jebard.

The man's eyes came to rest on me; he seemed to be considering something. 'You are not my brother,' he said, wagging a finger at Jebard, 'but I think this small man is my brother. What is your name?'

'Leave the lad out of it,' said Jebard.

'Kim,' I said.

Jebard shot me an angry look. 'Where did you get this Bible from?' he asked the man

'From my father before three.'

Jebard shook his head. 'What's that mean?'

The man shook his head as though Jebard was being extremely slow. 'His name was Clava.'

Jebard held the book up to the light and read the inscription. 'To Clive Endymion Francis Drago, on the occasion of reaching his twenty-first birthday. From his loving father, Clive Drago, 4th April, 1855.'

The man leaned forward to place a finger on the first name. 'This is my father before three and this,' he said, touching the second name, 'is my father before four.' He nodded enthusiastically several times.

Jebard shook his head.

'I think he's saying he's a member of the Drago family,' I suggested.

'I know that, but it don't mean it's true, do it?' said Jebard. 'This Bible has been out in the world for over a hundred years. Anyone could've got hold of it and dreamed up a tale to make monkeys out of us.'

The man was now looking up at several large snowflakes swirling in the light above him. 'Nevertheless,' he said, wrinkling his nose as one or two landed on his face, 'I am Igthy Ma-tuu Clava, son of Clava, son of Clava, son of Clava.'

'That don't get us nowhere,' said Jebard. 'I've told you now – there's nothing here for you.'

The man began to feel in his clothes again and produced a small bag, which he held in the flat

24

of his hand. He undid a leather tie with a sharp tug. 'I have money. Look, see this money.' With each shake of the little bag a gold coin fell into his glove.

Jebard picked one up and examined it. 'Is this really gold?'

'Yes, these are Victoria's gold sover-reens.' He showed me the head of the young queen on one side. 'See, I am rich.'

Jebard was silent for a few moments. 'You say these are sovereigns. Where d'yer get them?'

'Father before four. He gave them to father before three and he gave them…'

'Yes, I understand that,' said Jebard testily. 'You say father before three was Clive Drago of Skirl House?'

'Yes.' Igthy Ma-tuu Clava nodded sympathetically as though it must be very hard being as stupid as Jebard. 'Then you will let me pass and come inside to warm myself,' he said, returning the coins to the bag.

The sight of the sovereigns shining dully in the light seemed to have altered something in Jebard. Curiosity replaced suspicion.

'Why've you come here? What's your business?'

'To meet with my brothers; to bring greetings,' the man said simply.

Jebard shook his head and looked down to the ground. The cold had drained his jowly face of blood; his eyes were busy with calculation. I knew he was thinking that turning this man away might get him into more trouble than allowing him in, especially since I had seen the sovereigns. 'Well,' he said, raising his head and looking from beneath his brow, 'it's five mile to the nearest village...and...well, they speak of snow tonight.' He paused to add weight to what he was going to say. 'But get this straight, Mister Mactullaver, or whatever you name is, you've got no brothers here – no relations of any sort. I mean...look at you, man.' His eyes ran over him. 'The master of the house – Colonel Drago – will speak to you when and...*if*...he sees fit. You'll have a roof tonight and a bowl of soup, but then you'd best be on your way, soon as you've said what you've come to say and the weather's cleared.'

Igthy Ma-tuu Clava smiled and gave another bow, then put his hat on with the flaps sticking out and hoisted his bag onto his shoulder like a sailor. There had never been any doubt in his mind that he would be allowed into Skirl.

Chapter Two

The Numinous Labyrinth

When I came to Skirl at the end of that terrible summer term, all I saw were the possibilities for exploring the house and the farm. I roamed the hills above the house, made kites and flew them from an ancient tomb called Sennak's Mound, watched the light playing across the landscape that lay like a map beneath me. I scouted out the woods in the valley and recceed the waterfalls and deep black pools of the Skirl River where, using some old oil drums from the farm, I built a raft. I dived from it and used it to catch trout with a worm on a hook and lay on my stomach peering at the tiny fish suspended in the amber patches of sunlight. When I'd had enough of exploring, there were collections of insects and wild flowers to be made, plans to be drawn of rockets and planes and a bigger and better raft with a sail and revolving paddles.

I found myself an old canvas shoulder bag with a leather strap and many pockets. Into it I put all I needed for a day outdoors – pen knife, magnifying glass, string, matches, a book of British insects called *Bugs for Boys*, hooks, weights and a line, a compass from the First World War which was cracked but just about worked, and finally sandwiches and a bottle of Alice's homemade lemonade.

Striking out with a couple of the dogs in tow and the bag across my back, I was happy enough. Colonel Drago seemed content to let me run free as long as I came in for supper at six o'clock and read for at least one hour a day.

My mind teemed with projects and plans for expeditions, and during the long daylight hours I just about managed to forget my mother's death. Because my surroundings were new and I was so far from Kenya – so far from where she had been alive – the loss was somehow less to me during the day. But at night when I went to my room in a distant part of the house, it was impossible not to remember her going like that – so suddenly, without the slightest warning of the sickness that would take her. How could she leave me?

But before I went to sleep every night, I talked to her. I had a framed black and white photograph of us together. I picked it up and told her what I had been doing and what I planned for the next day, hoping that she would somehow hear me.

The odd thing was that when I looked at the picture, I could hear her voice. I remembered its low and amused tone. I remembered how she used to play with my hair and say that I'd inherited what she called my wild, gypsy looks from her mother, Florence Drago. I studied myself in the picture and wondered what she found so funny about me. Skinny and tanned with a mop of dark brown curly hair, no shirt and bare feet, I squinted up at the camera held by my father. Mother and I were laughing at the puppies that had been born a few weeks before to Nuba, a farm mongrel, and mother had taken off her sunglasses and thrown her head back. I examined her face a million times and wondered what she was thinking at that very moment and what she would think the next and the one after that.

How I could have been so happy without knowing it amazed me. Kim Arthur Drago Greenwood looked exactly the same as he did in the photograph because he had hardly grown in the year since it was taken, but he was very different inside. That boy in the picture was like a distant relation.

Autumn had come, the winds had strengthened and on one particularly squally day of driving rain, Alba Hockmuth arrived. She was another cousin of the Colonel's, from somewhere in the middle of Europe, and she took up residence in rooms on the first floor at the front of the house. Not far behind her came Quake, the man who was appointed my tutor.

My future had been decided. I wasn't going back to school because my father couldn't pay the fees, and I wasn't going home either, for a reason that no one would tell me. At first I couldn't get to the bottom of it, then a few weeks later, by which time I loathed Alba Hockmuth and Quake more than anyone I had ever met, I overheard Alba say that my father was a drunkard and would have to sell up and leave our farm in Kenya – and that I would never go back.

I felt my face redden with shame and anger and ran to the kitchen to find Alice, but only Bella Brown was there.

Until that moment we had hardly exchanged a word.

'They don't know him,' I blurted out and I told her everything.

Bella put down the pan she had been scraping and came to me, wiping her hands on her apron. 'They're wicked people them two,' she whispered fiercely. This was quite unlike the Bella I knew. 'You don't go believing anything they say. Hear me? Wicked, wicked people! You'll be on your way home after Christmas. You'll see, Master Kim.'

Bella moved back to her bowl and darted a smile at me.

Alba Hockmuth came and went mysteriously in a long black car, and for the first four or five weeks I only glimpsed her in the distance, a cold imperious figure immaculately turned out – always in high heels and tight-fitting suit which exaggerated her tall, powerful build. The Colonel was seen less and less about the place and it seemed that she had taken over the running of Skirl, though nothing was said. I understood there would be no appeal to the Colonel on her decisions, which were transmitted through Quake with threats of privation and punishment.

Quake devised a timetable of lessons and homework that allowed me almost no free time. So that I wouldn't be distracted, he confiscated my

31

precious bag and placed it high on a bookshelf, which he thought was out of my reach. But it wasn't and I used it as much as I wanted when he wasn't there.

Quake – full name, as written in *Kennedy's Shorter Latin Primer*, Harold St John Xavier Quake – was a retired boarding-school teacher in his mid-fifties. He liked coming up to the big house, especially when Alba was there, and always appeared in polished brogues, a patterned waistcoat with a gold watch-chain and a silk handkerchief that blossomed from his pocket.

'He fancies himself, does that Mr Quake,' Alice murmured to Bella once, 'though heaven only knows why.'

I saw what she meant. He had a pale complexion with sunken grey cheeks and dark patches under his eyes, a long thin nose with a bulbous end, skinny ears that were streaked with broken veins, lank hair that fell across his forehead, and fingers that were stained yellow from cigarette smoke. His eyes and nose watered a great deal and he dabbed at them with a stained handkerchief which he pulled from his pocket and examined with intent. When he thought I wasn't looking he would gaze at himself in the glass of a bookcase, adjust his hair and adopt a noble pose by raising his chin and looking down his nose.

I did badly at most of my lessons, worse than ever at school, which meant that Quake was always punishing me with smacks across the hand and extra work. In the last days of November, my body rebelled against him and his regime of work: a boil developed under my arm then another came on my shoulder. They hurt so much that I couldn't sleep, and the hours of homework that Quake forced upon me were out of the question. Alice summoned Dr Champkin from the village, a kindly man with a red face and small, gentle hands. He glanced at Quake, who was saying that he had met many malingering boys in his time but I was the worst he'd come across, winked at me and gave me two weeks off lessons.

Quake evaporated like a bad smell, saying that he was going to stay with his mother in Dawlish. It seemed unfair that a creature like Quake still had a mother while I didn't, but in a strange way it made me feel superior to him.

Because Alba was also away I was left to amuse myself and run free, although Alice thought it better that I didn't go outside because she didn't want 'them boils getting filled with dirt from the farm.'

So I set about exploring the house just as I had done the valley, though I was not nearly so sure of myself once inside. It had almost magical powers to trick me. Not once did I come out of its dark interior the same way as I'd gone in. Because of the way the newer house surrounded the old house, it was possible to think you were on one particular level but then you'd take a step or two up or follow a gradual slope, and find yourself on a completely different floor with lots of rooms you'd never seen before. There were one or two routes that I never got the hang of, so I learned to skirt round them. Yet even when in the winter half-light I took the corridors that I knew and trusted, it was easy to be confused by doorways and corridors that looked the same, and I still managed to get lost.

Once I tried unrolling a huge ball of twine so that I would find my way back. But it ran out and when I retraced my footsteps, I found that it had mysteriously come loose from the chair leg I had tied it to and gone halfway up another corridor. As I began winding the string into a ball, my eyes strayed to a portrait of a young girl in a grey dress with a broad white lace collar. She was slender and pale and she wore a maid's cap of such fine material that you could see her hair through the mesh of the linen. Though she looked like a pilgrim child, mischief danced in her grey-green eyes and a smile flickered in her funny oval face. Around her neck was a string of tiny pearls and beside the bodice of her dress was written *'aetatis suae 12'* which meant that she was aged 12 when the picture was painted. She looked much younger and smaller than the twelve-year-olds I knew. There was no name on the frame and no clue about her identity in the painting. I stared at the impish expression for a few seconds and wondered who she was. But then the winter sunlight slid from the corridor and the picture all but disappeared into the shadows.

At this moment there was a faint fizzing in the air around me and to my astonishment, the end of the string rose vertically about two feet from the ground and then fell down as though it had been picked up and dropped. I gathered it up as fast as I could and tore off down the corridor.

That was the first really odd thing I saw at Skirl, although at the time I told myself that a gust had seized hold of the string, which certainly wasn't impossible in the draughty conditions of the house. I came to think of the other noises I heard as the creaking joints and wheezing of a very old person, but if I had been honest with myself I would have admitted that there was a profound disturbance in Skirl which was always most intense near the remains of the old house. These noises weren't made by anything I could see in the real world. Once I heard paper being crumpled. This was followed by the frantic gasp of air rushing into a vacuum. Another time the sound of a feathery kazoo pursued me down the corridor that led to my bedroom.

I wondered if I should mention all this to the Colonel but then thought better of it. Besides, the opportunity never seemed to present itself. Occasionally I saw him shuffling about, an old man dressed in a baggy tweed suit, with a look on his face which made you think he had stared into the pit of hell. His mouth was clamped shut, his right hand trembled at his side and he walked with a heavy clumping tread which told us when he left the rooms where he lived at the top of the house. He didn't seem to notice me, or anything else for that matter. When I said hello he looked surprised. 'Ah yes, Kim,' he said. 'Treating you well, are they? Good, that's the spirit. Carry on there.'

* * *

A few times I came across Jebard but more often it was Bella Brown who would turn up in the oddest places – places that weren't used much and had long been given over to dust and slow decay. We became friendly during the second week without Quake and she came to sit at the end of my bed and talked to me in a confidential manner, as though we were in a very crowded place and she didn't want to be overheard. She plied me with questions about my rambles through the house, at first innocently but then she began to ask me in a pointed way if I had seen anything out of the ordinary. I told her about the string, which didn't seem to impress her much. Alba and Quake were more interesting to her. Where did Alba go when she was away, she asked? Had the Colonel said anything about her? Did Quake know her before he came to Skirl? When they were talking about my father, did I hear them say anything else?

I couldn't help her with any of it. I asked why she wanted to know. She shook her head and gravely told me to keep her informed of anything unusual.

The next day, I took myself off to the Long Gallery. This was a place I had been told never to enter by Jebard because the Drago family records were kept there, and also because of the many cases of curiosities which he didn't want me getting into. I disobeyed him very soon after arriving at Skirl. There was so much to look at – collections of tropical beetles and butterflies, a treatise on the martyrdom of saints with scenes of gruesome torture, ceremonial shields from Africa, a bow and a quiver of arrows from New Guinea, mysterious brass tools, a display of old musical instruments, two cases of surgeons' knives and bone saws (one with traces of blood on it), a tin bath in the shape of a shoe, a misshapen skull from the island of Java and, most beautiful of all, a drawer of beads made from turquoise, amber, garnet, obsidian, bone, tortoiseshell, glass, shell, quartz, amethyst, rock crystal, coral, and pink and white marble.

Instead of a flat ceiling, the room had a barrel vault, which was decorated with plasterwork of Tudor roses and briars. A row of square windows with mottled glass along one side of the gallery filled the place with a pearly grey light. There were no shadows in the Long Gallery and it possessed the best light in the house for looking at pictures. There were many minute studies of flowers and insects, apparently by the same artist, which I admired more than I could say.

And hanging from rods along the entire length of one side, were tapestries of people playing games – bowls, archery, tennis, blind man's bluff, skittles and a strange sport where peasants with grotesque faces hurled sticks at a goose tied to a post.

At one end there was a chest that was covered with a frayed rug. On this stood a huge stuffed black and white bird, which had a very large beak, small wings and powerful webbed feet. It was labelled: 'The Extinct Great Auk or Garefowl.' Underneath was written: 'He of little wings.'

I don't know why, but every time I saw this sorry item it made me smile. I went over to the bird and, for the first time, wondered what was in the chest beneath it. With a little effort I shifted the bird back and pulled the rug away so that I could open the lid about six inches. A stale, woody smell hit my nose as I slipped my hand inside and began to feel about. There was nothing except a book that was pressed against the side of the chest, which I would have missed if my shoe hadn't lost its grip on the floorboards, causing my hand to hit the side. The book was slim and covered in a cream-coloured hide which felt like dried candle wax. I shook the worst of the dust off then undid the leather ties that held the covers together, and read on the first page:

The Lines of Tarle & Skirl: The Numinous Labyrinth.

I ran through the book and saw there was little text but many diagrams and maps, most of which meant nothing to me. In the centre were several grids of letters – sixty-four squares, each with a letter written in, and not all were from our alphabet. I thought these might be codes because no recognisable words leapt out at me – except in one, where I made out Ahrinnia H. amongst the squiggles. Without a key it would be useless to try to decipher the rest. At the back of the book a much bigger map of the Skirl valley had been sown into the binding. I unfolded it carefully because the paper was cracked along the folds. Beneath the heading *The Ancient Lines of Tarle* were two wide arcs that were marked by dotted lines. They started just above Sennak's Mound, spread either side of the valley, crossed the hills in front of the house and came together again at a point on the River Tarle some way below an ancient bridge known as the Tarle Steps. Right in the middle of this uneven oval shape was a scratchy little drawing of the old house. I wondered if the lines marked ancient boundaries of some sort but this didn't seem to make sense because they cut through fields and woodland and one sliced a cottage in half.

But that was all the time I was going to have with the book. Footsteps were echoing in the clear, still air of the wooden staircase that led up to the long gallery. They were made not by the flat shoes worn by Alice or Bella, or Jebard's boots, but high heels. There was a locked room off the landing halfway up the stairs. If the footsteps did not pause there they would certainly be destined for the Long Gallery.

I spun round, looking for somewhere to hide. The best place – indeed the only place – was behind the games' tapestries furthest from the door. There was a gap of about eight inches between the tapestry and the panelling. If I flattened myself against the wall and held my breath, I might not be spotted. I slid into the space and positioned myself so that I could peer out from a tiny hole in the tapestry.

A few seconds later, the footsteps arrived outside the Long Gallery and the door was flung open. Alba Hockmuth stood in the doorway. Across her shoulders she wore a black coat with a hood trimmed with fur. Beneath this was a dark red skirt, a string of pearls and a thick black leather belt. She seemed taller, thinner and somehow stronger than I remembered. Her neck seemed long and sinewy and in the curious light of the Long Gallery, her skin appeared as white as parchment. She held her head high. It was almost as though she was scenting the air and needed only to wait a few moments before she would know where I was hiding. Then she moved into the room with a slow, deliberate step, peeling off her gloves, finger by finger. She stopped and slapped the gloves impatiently against one hand.

'Come on out. I know you're in here,' she said quietly.

I closed my eyes and didn't move.

Suddenly there was a loud clattering followed by a thud from the direction of the chest. I couldn't see what had happened but Alba took several paces away from my side of the room and went over to inspect whatever had fallen. She muttered something then, to my complete surprise, gathered her coat closer around her shoulders, looked round once more and marched from the room, banging the door behind her. I waited a good ten minutes before creeping out.

It was then that I saw what had caused the commotion. The stuffed bird had fallen across the chest and then onto the floor. It now lay on its side, looking rather forlorn. I picked it up, brushed its feathers and put it back, wondering how on earth it had travelled so far.

That evening, Bella came to me later than usual. She was tense and her reserve had returned. She listened closely as I told her about finding the book with the diagrams and maps, and said she would very much like to see it. I told her I would show her where it was the next day.

'That old bird certainly saved your bacon,' she said with a glimmer of a smile.

'Yes, but how did Alba know I was up in the Long Gallery?' I asked.

'She didn't know you were there. She does that, you know. She checks the place when she comes back. She and that Quake are having dinner in her rooms tonight.'

I groaned at the mention of the name.

She got up and squeezed my hand. 'Goodnight, Kim dear. We'll go and look at the book tomorrow.'

'What's "numinous" mean?' I said.

She paused to think. 'Something like *mysterious. Awe-inspiring.*'

I was about to ask about all the noises in the house but she put a finger to my lips and told me that she had to go. 'Dream well, Kim. Promise me now: you dream well.'

Those were the last words I heard her speak in the real world.

Chapter Three

Arrest

When the outlandish figure of Igthy Ma-tuu Clava appeared at Skirl's front door on the snowy evening just before Christmas, I saw him as a relief to the brooding misery of the house and my sadness at losing Bella. But just from looking at him in those first few minutes on the doorstep, somehow I also knew that my life had changed forever.

We made our way from the front door to the kitchen – I held the lantern high while Jebard took up the rear, still with his club. Our visitor, or Iggy, as I now thought of him because to pronounce Igthy as he did with a click at the back of his throat was impossible, looked around as the light glanced across the pictures on the walls.

'Keep your eyes ahead of you,' said Jebard menacingly. 'There's nothing to interest you here.'

Alice was nowhere to be seen in the kitchen, though there was a distant clattering in one of the pantries, which meant that she was busy with the obsessive sorting and polishing of cooking pans that were rarely ever used. Jebard went to the opening of the passageway and called to say that she should stop what she was doing. This met with a stream of unintelligible protest. He shrugged and turned to me. 'I'll go and fetch the Colonel,' he said. 'You'll be all right here, Kim. Mrs Camm isn't far away.'

I nodded. Iggy didn't bother me at all. In fact, now he was standing in the kitchen light, I was even more fascinated by his appearance.

'What do you like to do, Brother Kim?' he asked, placing his hat on the table and brushing the earflaps.

I shrugged, feeling a little shy.

'Come, tell me.' He smiled and his eyes shone with warmth. 'What does Brother Kim like doing?'

'I'm good at making collections of things,' I said. 'I'm interested in science, insects, astronomy – anything but Latin and history, which I hate.'

'Do you know the "speeding of light"?'

'What do you mean?' I asked.

'The speeding of light. How fast goes it?'

'Oh, I see, *the speed of light*!'

'That's what I said.' he said.

'No you didn't. You said the "speeding of light", which is not correct English. The speed of light is 186,000 miles per second.'

'Such speed,' he said, evidently satisfied with the fact – or with me, I wasn't sure which.

I sat down on the bench by the table and looked at him. 'Why have you come here?'

He considered this and felt his clothes again. 'To see you and see more brothers and bring greetings from my island and from the people of my islands.'

'What are your islands called?'

'Ro-Torva Islands.'

'The Ro-Torva Islands,' I said. 'Where are they?'

'In the sea, Brother Kim. In *sea*.'

'Yes, but which sea? Which ocean?'

'All sea joined together. I know this because I came on boat all the way on *one* sea.'

'Yes, but there are names for different parts of the sea – the Atlantic Ocean, the Indian Ocean, the Pacific Ocean...'

'Your name is Kim. Your arm is not called by other name. Your leg is not called by other name. It is all Brother Kim.'

During this he had begun shedding layers of clothes. First came the gloves, two coats, several jackets and a scarf, then he unwound the leggings which had bound his calves and boots. They were sodden and caked in mud, and he laid them on the iron rail along the front of the kitchen range. Finally he stepped out of the waterproof trousers and stood in a collarless emerald and blue tunic of rough silk, which was very creased. Beneath this were an orange shirt with long tails and a skirt which had been hitched up under the waterproof trousers, but now hung down to a pair of black army boots.

'Best clothes,' he said, pleased by the effect he was having on me. 'Now tell me where your mother is. And your father?'

I hesitated and looked away. 'My mother...she died last summer...in Africa. My father is still there. We have a farm in Kenya. We grow coffee and a thing called sisal and we've got some cattle. It's a big place. I'm staying here but I will go home soon, I hope.'

His expression changed and he nodded sympathetically, but before he could say anything there was a noise from the passageway and a moment later Alice appeared, bearing a tower of saucepans balanced on a tray. Not until she reached the centre of the room did she notice the stranger. She stopped in her tracks, goggled at him, put down the pans and made for a drawer of kitchen knives where she seized the largest one. 'Where's Tom Jebard?' she whispered, her eyes darting around the kitchen to see if anyone else was there.

I explained that everything was all right and that Mr Jebard had given permission for Iggy to stay the night because of the cold. 'He's gone to find the Colonel,' I said.

'No, he *must* not be disturbed,' she said, her eyes widening. 'The Colonel is to be left alone.' She paused. 'Is this the man who's been skulking about the place, hiding and spying on us?' she asked.

'He can't be the same man,' I said. 'He's only just arrived,'

'How do you know that?' she asked darkly.

Iggy seemed to be listening to something else. He had put his head to one side and his eyes concentrated on the darkness that lay beyond the open door.

'What's the matter with him? Can't he speak?' said Alice.

Iggy turned to her with the intensity fading in his eyes and gave her his widest grin. 'Have you made plum pudding for brothers and Igthy Ma-tuu Clava?'

She looked at me. 'What's he talking about?'

'He told you his name,' I replied. 'It's Igthy Ma-tuu Clava and I think he's asking if you've made a Christmas pudding for the family.'

'What family? Anyway, what business is it of his? There's no call for it here. The Colonel doesn't like Christmas. That's his orders. There's not enough people for Christmas pudding. And if you make Christmas pudding, well, I mean to say you've got to start in November to make proper Christmas pudding. Everyone knows that. Not four days before Christmas.' Alice always gave several reasons for something, which followed no particular order other than the one in which they occurred in her mind. But Iggy's question was so odd that it calmed her and she laid down the knife to gawp at him. He gave her one of his bows, as though to acknowledge her admiration, then folded his hands on his chest and, rolling his Rs a good deal, exclaimed, 'Round the ragged rocks the ragged rascal ran his rural race.'

'Whatever does he mean?' asked Alice.

The performance was not over. He inhaled deeply and followed it with, 'The black dog danced on a barn floor barefoot.'

50

'Tongue twisters.' I said.

'Yes, but please, Brother Kim. My tongue is not twisted. Look!' he stuck his tongue out to show us how long and straight it was.

'He's mad,' said Alice. 'He's a lunatic, that's what he is. Whatever made Mr Jebard fall for this nonsense?'

Then we heard voices coming in the distance. It was Jebard and the Colonel. Instead of waiting for them to reach us, Iggy moved to the door with incredible speed and slipped into the passage. A minute or two passed. Then the Colonel could be heard exclaiming, 'What the Dickens? What's going on here?'

Alice and I hurried from the kitchen to find Iggy with the Colonel and Jebard at the bottom of the main staircase, which was usually a place of cavernous gloom, and was now lit by a chandelier made of stag antlers. Iggy was in the process of bowing deeply. He straightened with the words, 'Lord Drago. I am Igthy Ma-tuu Clava and I bring greetings from the people of Ro-Torva, to my brother Lord Drago.'

'I don't know what you're talking about. My name's Colonel Philip Drago. I'm not a lord and...'

'But you are lord and master of this place and the people herein?'

'Well, yes, if you put it like that I am. But that doesn't…'

'Then I bring greetings from your brothers in Ro-Torva to everyone in this house.'

'Will you please let me finish what I'm saying,' said the Colonel crossly. Iggy nodded obligingly. 'What do you mean by coming here like this? State your purpose.'

'Purpose?' said Iggy. 'To see everyone in this house. That is purpose.'

'Well, there's only us here. My cousin Alba is away, I believe, though she comes and goes like a bat at dusk, and one never knows.'

Jebard gave a small nod, which the Colonel didn't seem to notice.

'No,' said Iggy. 'Around us all are peoples looking at Iggy now.' His hand swept the hall.

The Colonel shook his head, mystified. 'You mean the people in the pictures? Well, yes, I suppose you might say that. But they're all long dead. I don't have time for pictures myself. Though there must be hundreds, maybe thousands in the old place.'

But Iggy wasn't looking at the portraits. He pointed over the Colonel's shoulder and up the staircase, jabbing his finger in all directions.

'I don't know what you're saying, man.'

Jebard and Alice looked around. They seemed to know what he meant. I knew, too, having heard the scampering in the corridors and felt the rush of air and the sensation of things brushing past me in the dark.

But apparently the Colonel did not understand. He shifted his weight on to his good leg and sank a hand into his pocket to retrieve a tobacco pipe, which he began to prod with a three-pronged instrument. While doing this he contemplated Iggy. He coughed and sucked the air through the pipe, examined it and aimed a watery eye at Iggy. 'Jebard here mentioned a Bible, which seems to have come from this house. Would you show it to me?'

Iggy nodded and said it was with the rest of his possessions in the kitchen. We left the hall, each one of us aware of the great silence that had descended on Skirl.

In the kitchen, Iggy held the Bible open and went through his explanation. The Colonel looked on, nodding, but made no comment. Eventually he said, 'And this came to you when your father died?'

Iggy shook his head. 'No, my father alive. He gave me this book and told me to spread greetings with our brothers.'

'And Jebard tells me there were some coins,' said the Colonel. 'Where did they come from?'

'From here also with father before three.' He jerked the bag of coins from inside his tunic and poured them onto the table in a neat line, his eyes dancing with pleasure. The Colonel held one of the thirty gold sovereigns up to his eye then gave Iggy a sidelong look over his glasses. 'These are worth a lot of money, maybe thousands of pounds.'

'Certainly,' said Iggy.

There was the sound of a car pulling up on the back drive and very shortly afterwards the bell rang at the back door. Jebard glanced at the Colonel and went to answer it. A few moments later, two policemen came in carrying their caps. Both nodded to the Colonel and one said to Jebard, 'This is the gentleman you were speaking about?' They regarded Iggy with suspicion. 'May we ask where you've come from, sir?'

Iggy looked at the Colonel and then me. 'Ro-Torva Islands.'

'Do you have any form of identification, sir? A passport perhaps?'

He shrugged and went over to his bag and rifled in it for a few moments, then brought out some documents, one of which he handed to the sergeant. 'Passport.'

The sergeant looked at the little blue booklet and haltingly read out Iggy's full name.

'You appear to come from the Ro-Torva group of islands. Is that some type of colony, sir?'

Iggy nodded. 'My brother he is king.'

Jebard cut in to say Iggy called everyone his brother and that no special significance should be given to this claim. I realised that he must have phoned the police when he went to get the Colonel.

'How long have you been in this country?' asked the first, a constable.

'Only a very short time.'

'You see, sir,' said the sergeant, gravely, 'a man answering to your description was reported in the area acting suspiciously over recent weeks. We are anxious to trace this individual because at about the same time a young woman named Bella Brown went missing. We would like to ask you a few more questions about your movements.'

'My movements?' asked Iggy. 'My movements very good indeed.' He flapped his arms up and down and raised each leg once.

'Quite the comedian,' said the sergeant. 'Perhaps

we'll continue this conversation at the station.'

This meant nothing to Iggy and he simply beamed at them.

'If you don't mind, Colonel,' said the sergeant putting on his cap. 'I think we'd better look into this further. We'll have him down to the station and make some checks on our friend here.'

'Is that really necessary, officer?' asked the Colonel. 'Jebard did right in phoning you, given the disappearance of Miss Brown, but this man seems harmless enough.'

'Better to be on the safe side, sir. We've had no word of Miss Brown.'

'Well, it may be that she simply left without giving notice. I don't think there's any question about that. Her things are gone.'

'Let's hope that *is* the case, sir. The lads on the farm don't think it's as simple as that.' With this he motioned the constable to pick up Iggy's bag. Iggy snatched up his hat and moved to the table to shovel the sovereigns into his purse.

'We'd better take these along too,' said the sergeant.

'I'm sure they're his,' said the Colonel.

'We may as well see if anything like this has been stolen in the area.'

Iggy was led away looking extremely surprised, though not particularly concerned, placed in the back of the police car and driven off to the local town.

Chapter Four

Quake

So, Iggy had come, and even though he didn't stay in the house that night, something profound had changed in its mood. There was a sense of dark contemplation. As I climbed to my room, I kept telling myself that there were bound to be noises in an old house, and that the shimmering I sometimes saw in the distance – just like the heat rising from the plains in Kenya – was a trick of the light. But that evening, the hubbub affected almost every room and passageway. And there was a new form of disturbance – the inexplicable fidgeting of objects. Chairs squeaked across the wooden floors, doors banged and folds of curtains were suddenly twitched, as though the material had been plucked by unseen hands. I blocked my ears to the noise with screwed up handkerchiefs and buried myself under my pillows, wondering about Iggy and who he was until eventually I fell asleep.

Next day, there was no sign of Iggy and no telephone call from the police station. The morning was very cold and grey but there was still only a light dusting of snow on the ground, which meant that Quake would be able to make his way to Skirl for three lessons – Latin, maths and geography.

I had breakfast in the kitchen and scowled at Jebard for ringing the police. Then Quake arrived and I followed him to the first floor library where a single log smouldered in the grate, giving off no heat at all. The lesson went as usual, with Quake walking up and down in the cold light shouting, 'No, boy! What tense is that verb, boy? What tense? Future perfect tense! Future perfect!' He banged the table and did the usual tweaking of my ear until I managed to get it right. When we moved on to maths he had no excuse for his bullying. That was the one subject I was good at and sometimes I was quicker than he was at calculations and he had to pretend that he had been distracted by my slouching, or that I had 'an insolent look in my eye'. If there was anything in my eye, it was pure hatred.

The geography lesson began and I asked

whether he had ever heard of the Ro-Torva Islands.

'Stop trying to divert me with futile questions, boy,' he snapped.

At that very moment, Iggy walked through the library door dressed as he had been the previous evening and wearing his fur hat.

For a short time Quake looked aghast but he recovered quickly. 'This is a classroom, not a railway station. What do mean by interrupting my lesson? And who are you anyway?'

Iggy introduced himself. Then Alice appeared at the library door. 'Begging your pardon, Mr Quake. I couldn't prevent him from coming up here. He wanted to see the boy. There was no stopping him.'

'Who – what the devil is he?' said Quake, sizing up Iggy with his most superior look.

Iggy approached Quake and peered at him, as though he was a specimen in the zoo. Quake backed away and demanded an explanation from Alice.

'I've been chasing him all over the house,' she said. 'He'll be the death of me.' She placed her hand to her heaving chest to emphasise the point.

'What's he doing here? Who is he?'

'The police say he's to stay at Skirl until they've

finished their enquiries. They talked to the Colonel and he says that's all right so we've got him for Christmas, although Lord knows how we're going to feed him. I mean, what does a man like this eat?'

'Plum pudding,' said Iggy helpfully.

'Is Miss Hockmuth acquainted with the facts?' asked Quake.

'Miss Hockmuth's gone away again, sir, and there's no telling when she will be back.'

'Why were the police involved? What's this man suspected of doing?'

Alice gave a very confused account of Iggy's arrival, the Bible, the coins and what the Colonel asked and how Jebard had phoned the police to be on the safe side. Quake blinked his irritation.

Suddenly Iggy said, 'Brother Kim come with me.'

'Leave the boy alone,' said Quake, his voice rising. 'He's to stay for his lessons. We have not finished yet and he is in *my* charge.' He seized me by the arm and led me to the table where he forced me down in front of the pile of school books. 'You will have detention for this. I am certain you arranged this interruption. I will not suffer disobedience and slovenly behaviour from you, young man. Do you hear?'

'I wasn't being disobedient, Mr Quake,' I said. 'Nor slovenly.'

'Now get on with your work,' he said, placing a finger on a diagram of different cloud formations and turning to Alice. 'That will be all, Mrs Camm. Please take this person away with you.'

Iggy shook his head and sat down across from me. 'Stay here with Brother Kim,' he said, flattening his hands on the table. I noticed the gold bangles on his wrist and a snake's-head ring on his right forefinger, which I was sure hadn't been there before.

Quake gulped air for a few seconds. 'I will not...I will not tolerate this intrusion. Mrs Camm, call Jebard!'

'Mr Jebard's up at the farm, sir.'

Quake looked around and caught me smiling. In one movement he picked up my copy of *Kennedy's Shorter Latin Primer*, the cover of which had been altered by some other boy that Quake had taught so that it read *Kennedy's Shortbread Eating Primer*, and slapped me across the back of the head. But just as he raised his arm, Iggy reached forward and touched my hand.

I felt nothing of the blow. Nothing whatsoever. I looked at him incredulously. How could he have drawn the pain from me? He smiled across

63

the table, rose, and gave me a nod of his head to say that I should follow. Without thinking, I got up too.

Quake shouted, 'Sit down this minute!'

'Not right to hit Brother Kim,' said Iggy rather formally. Alice nodded her agreement.

Sensing he was beaten, Quake moved to the table. 'I will not be treated like this! I will not allow my work to be a interrupted by a...by a savage. And let me assure you that Miss Hockmuth will be apprised of the facts of this incident, and she will have something to say about it, I have no doubt.' He barked out the numbers of the exercises I was to do for the following Tuesday and stalked from the room.

I grinned as he retreated. Quake had forgotten that Tuesday was Christmas Day.

Content that Iggy was merely eccentric and not a danger to me, Alice went hurrying back to the kitchen with the words, 'Stay out of trouble. You don't want *her* hearing about anything else.' Alba was disliked by Alice as much as anyone else at Skirl because of her temper and the unquestioned power that she now wielded. Several times she muttered that she never quite understood who Alba was and why she had been given so much influence at Skirl.

I had no time to contemplate what Alba would or would not do to me once Quake had spoken to her. Iggy had set off in the opposite direction and was calling over his shoulder, 'Come along, Brother Kim. We have very little time. I will lead the way.'

We took one of the staircases at the back of the house to the first floor and entered a narrow passage, at the end of which there was a window-seat where the light streamed in. Iggy sat down, raised his legs to the seat and crossed them.

'Come, Brother Kim, we have many topics to discuss.'

I sat and looked up at him. 'What topics?'

'Number one: ghosts. Number two: Brother Kim.'

'What about ghosts?'

'There are many here,' said Iggy, waving his hand. 'And Igthy Ma-Tuu Clava must find their secret. The secret of this place and why there are so many ghosts and what they plan to do and who is leading them and why. This most important place and most important events occur in this place. My purpose is to inquire into nature of this place and the forces that allow so many strange things to continue without impediment.'

'There *are* ghosts here,' I said. 'I see things moving and they make a noise.'

Iggy looked down at me. 'And Brother Kim is not afraid?'

'Sometimes when I'm alone in my room I am. Bella – my friend who's gone missing – used to come there in the evenings and talk to me and that helped.' I suddenly thought what a friend she had been to me and how I missed her. Before she disappeared she said she was going to see if she could move me into another room. Suddenly something struck me. 'But how do you know about these things, Iggy? You only arrived yesterday.'

He considered this and looked away. 'Clava told my father before three and he told my father before two and he told...' He stopped, seeing that I was tiring of this list. 'They say these things to me and I come here to inquire about the ghosts. I have map. See!' He took out the Bible which he had shown us the night before and removed a flimsy sheet of paper. The light from the window passed through it so that I could see dotted lines, symbols and some words written at the top.

'The Lines of Tarle!' I exclaimed. 'The same map is in the book I found. Do you have the codes as well?' He looked at me with interest. 'They're in the book too. Shall we go and find it?'

'Later, Brother Kim,' he said, returning the map to the Bible.

'What are the Lines of Tarle?' I asked.

'A crack in time,' he said. 'And at centre of the crack in time is house.'

'What do you mean?'

He did not answer but looked at the ring on his finger.

'Is that magic? Is that what made the pain go away when Quake hit me?'

He touched it with his index finger. 'Yes, but Iggy has only very small magic. Not big magic like important place here.' He looked around then down at me with a kindly expression. 'And you, Brother Kim. How is it being Brother Kim?'

'OK, I s'pose, though this house gives me the creeps. It was all right in the summer but now it's changed and, well, I'm getting a bit…'

'Lonely without friend Bella?' he suggested.

I didn't reply but that was the word I had been shy of saying. There was more I could say about Skirl closing in on me and about how in the last few weeks I had felt the loss of my mother so badly that I thought I would go mad. Then when Bella Brown vanished I knew in my heart that something bad had happened to her because she wouldn't have left without saying something to me, or explaining in a note.

Iggy nodded as if he understood all my thoughts without me having to speak them. 'Now Igthy Ma-tuu Clava is here and he has important investigation to make and it is his wish that Brother Kim also makes investigation.'

'What kind of investigation?' I asked. 'Is it something to do with the map?'

He made an odd gesture that involved raising one shoulder then the other and pouting. Instead of answering he said, 'Brother Kim is brave?'

'I don't know. Once there was a black mamba in my tent in the garden at home. That's a snake, one of the most poisonous in the world, and I threw some clothing over so it couldn't bite me. If I hadn't done that I wouldn't be here with you.'

'A snake,' he said with feeling. 'You are surely brave. There will be many things on our journey in the Lines of Tarle but no snakes...I am hoping.' He uncrossed his legs, sprang to his feet and placed a hand on my shoulder. 'But Brother Kim is brave because his mother died and that is worse than anything, and here you are talking to Igthy Ma-tuu Clava with sadness in your heart but courage in your eyes. Come, brave Brother Kim, our work must begin.'

He seemed to know the layout of the house better than I did. And after tearing down many cold echoing corridors, we came to a large room on the west of the house that contained one or two pieces of heavy, dark furniture and some pictures. The windows were spotted with grime, and dead flies and spiders had accumulated on the sills.

Iggy went to the far corner and pointed up to an old painting that I had never noticed before, probably because there was only enough light in the room to see it properly at this time of day.

It was a picture of the house at Skirl, looking down from the side of the valley. I could see that great care had been taken over the windows and stones of the building, the chimneys and the plan of the roofs, but the house was out of all proportion to the rest of the landscape and the various animals in the fields were either too large or too small. The cows that grazed on the hill were smaller than a white hare that ran across the fields being chased by three large hunting dogs. A pair of ravens, the size of eagles, were perched on the garden wall, and in the foreground there was a rather odd detail: a white garden table stood surrounded by delicate white chairs, which had toppled over in a gust of wind. The chairs lay scattered about the grass on their sides or up-ended. There were eleven like this. Only two remained standing.

The more you looked at the painting, the more there was to see. A moon hung low above the hills, although you could tell it was midday by the short shadows cast by the sun. At the front of the house on the top floor a window was open and a curtain flapped in the breeze. Near the bottom of the canvas – where the artist had written 'Skirl House' – a man appeared to be swimming in the river. Looking closer, it seemed as though he might have been in trouble in the roaring torrent. A little way up the river, a woman in a bonnet stood on the bank with her hands waving frantically. Beyond her were the Tarle Steps, which I knew was a prehistoric bridge made of huge flat stones that were laid across the river. Jebard once told me that the stones and twenty breakwaters positioned at intervals along the bridge were so heavy that no flood had swept them away in thousands of years. By the steps was an old man with a stick, who was standing by a fire looking out of the picture, completely unaware of the drama going on upstream.

A look of intense concentration had entered Iggy's eyes.

'Why are you interested in this picture?' I asked. 'What's so important about it?'

He shook his head silently.

'There's nothing to it – just the house and a lot of crazy detail.'

He made an odd seesaw movement with his head, then pulled the Bible from his tunic and began thumbing the pages until he reached the book of Exodus. He ran his finger down a page to the words 'the' and 'master', which had been circled in brown ink. I shrugged. That didn't seem much of a clue. Then he showed me the book of Leviticus where the words 'of the' and 'fallen' had also been circled. Finally in Luke Chapter One the word 'seats' had been underlined.

'Seats is chairs, I think,' Iggy said, clapping the Bible shut. He was pointing to a small brass plaque on the bottom of the frame, which read 'Master of the Fallen Chairs'. Below this was painted an inscription in Latin: 'QUI MAGISTRUM SELLARUM DELAPSARUM MAGISTRAVERIT SUPERERIT UT REM REFERAT.'

'Can you make this into English for Iggy with *Shortbread Eating Primer*?'

I shook my head. It was far too difficult.

'Same words on old paper,' he said, removing the map from the back of the Bible and squinting at it. He pointed to the figure of the old man. 'We go and talk to this old man at bridge.'

'There won't be an old man there. This was painted years ago. Even if there ever was an old man there, he must be dead.'

'No,' said Iggy. 'Old man will be there, waiting for us. He has big magic and we need to borrow big magic because we need to save our lives.'

'How do you mean?' I said. 'Who is threatening us?'

I got no answer. So I looked up at the painting, wondering if Iggy was totally mad. 'Who made the map? Is it a copy?'

He nodded. 'Clava made map. In Clava's Holy Book.'

Just then a very peculiar sensation began to creep up my back, which made me want to turn round. Iggy must have felt the same thing, because he glanced at me and then revolved slowly on the balls of his feet to look behind us. He murmured something in his own language and put his hand to the snake's-head ring.

I stole a glance but saw nothing. When I looked again, my eyes were drawn to a slight movement in the dust on the floor by the wall. Some marks were appearing, traced very slowly by a finger that I couldn't see. I realised that it was taking a great deal of effort to make these marks. Every so often there was a pause before the movement started again. Iggy crept forward. I followed and saw that the marks formed words. Without thinking, I read them out, 'Who put Bella in the wis...' We waited and very slowly, at the rate of about one letter every thirty seconds, the words 'wishing well' were formed followed by a question mark. Then there was no more movement in the dust and the strange sensation all over my skin disappeared.

'Who put Bella in the wishing well?' I whispered. 'What's it mean?'

'What is a wishing well?' asked Iggy.

'A well is a place where you get water and a wishing well is a place where you throw in coins for good luck.'

'You pay for water?'

'Not exactly – it's a superstition. People believe their wishes will come true if they make an offering of something valuable.'

'They pay the gods of the waters?'

'I suppose so,' I said. 'But what should we *do* about the message?'

'Where is wishing well?'

I shrugged. I'd never heard of one at Skirl. 'Perhaps I should ask Jebard or Alice about it.' I stopped, suddenly overwhelmed by what we had seen. 'Did a ghost really write that?'

He nodded nonchalantly. 'Of course, Brother Kim.'

'But a ghost...'

'Yes, Brother Kim, it is telling us where she is.'

I gasped. Chairs squeaking across the floor and curtains twitching were all very well but a message being scrawled in the dust was different.

'Perhaps the wishing well is on the map,' I said.

'Not on map,' he replied without even looking at it. Then he started for the door and I followed. As we left the room, I glanced back at the message and was not surprised to see the words in the dust being slowly wiped away.

Chapter Five

The Tarle Steps

Back in the kitchen we said nothing about our experience to Alice and Jebard, but I asked them about the wishing well. Jebard brushed the tip of his nose and sucked his teeth and said that there were many wells he could think of, but none was known as a wishing well as such. Most of them were blocked up or lost in the undergrowth. He mentioned that the water from some of the old wells was known to have healing powers and that back in the Middle Ages people came from miles around to drink at the wells. But the family put a stop to it and the wells disappeared.

Alice set lunch on the table and stood back with her arms folded, to watch Iggy consume some cheddar cheese and celery. This was all he would eat, having eyed the ham, hard-boiled eggs and thick brown soup she had offered him with suspicion.

'We've got a strange one here, Kim,' she said, as though he wasn't in the room.

Iggy wrinkled his nose at her and mentioned plum pudding twice, then after a little while he rose, burped loudly and with evident pleasure, and methodically began to put on his coats and the waterproof trousers. I went to get my duffle coat, gloves, hat and boots and my bag, which I had hidden in one of the outhouses.

'Where are you two going now?' asked Alice when I returned. 'You'll catch your death out there. It's biting cold. They say snow is on its way and we don't want anyone else vanishing, do we Mr Jebard?'

Jebard was of the opinion that Alice fussed too much and so tended to contradict her worries. I had learned to get what I wanted by allowing Alice to conjure some improbable disaster and waiting for Jebard to disagree. And his was always the final word. She would give in with the phrase, 'On your back be it' when she meant to say, 'Be it on your own head.'

'We're just going for a walk to the Tarle Steps,' I said. 'I know the way.'

'If you want to go all the way down there, that's

your business.' He turned to Iggy. 'As long as you look after Kim and don't go getting him drowned in the river, that's all right. You be back here before nightfall, mind.'

I looked to see if any of the dogs wanted to come, but only Black raised his head with any kind of interest, then he let it fall back to the warm floor in front of the range.

We set off down the drive, then cut up into the woods and climbed to the high ground where the pale light grazed the top of the winter trees. Rooks floated above us and then folded their wings and plummeted into the valley below, crying to each other on the wind. We looked through the beech trees down at the house – exactly the view in the painting – but it was too cold to linger so we pressed on. I was just wondering why the artist had distorted the landscape to fit the Tarle Steps into the painting – after all they were several miles from the house – when Iggy stopped in his tracks and raised a gloved finger. 'This is winter,' he said.

'Yes,' I said, wondering what was coming next.

'In the picture the trees have no leaves.'

'Yes,' I said.

'Then why is a man swimming? Why are summer chairs in the garden? It's a confounded mystery!'

'You're quite a detective,' I said a bit sarcastically, since I was annoyed that this hadn't occurred to me.

We left the hills and followed a track along the Tarle River, which eventually joined the Skirl River ten miles downstream. About half a mile along, the river widened into a great shallow pool and it was here the ancient people had built their crossing. The slabs laid across the river were enormous; some of them were ten feet long, and each was wide enough to allow two people to pass. At no point was the structure higher than a couple of feet above the water, so it was more like joined up stepping stones than an actual bridge. In all, it was about 100 feet long.

Apart from the hurrying of the water there was not a sound to be heard. The wind had died and the trees stood stark and silent above us.

'See, there's no old man here,' I said.

'If we make a fire he will come,' said Iggy with an infuriating certainty.

This was too much for me. 'There's no one here! The old man in the painting died long ago, if he ever existed at all. He can't be here!'

'He waves to us in the picture.'

'I don't believe you,' I said.

Iggy knew exactly how to make a fire. He built

a neat cone of dry wood around a core of old bracken and dead leaves. I asked him where he had learned this and whether he had been to school.

'Of course I went to school and then I attended the University of the Southern Seas.'

'I have never heard of that,' I said. 'Is there really such a place?'

'No one there has heard of you but it doesn't mean you not exist,' he said. 'Now we make this fire.'

I gave him my matches and he struck one, letting it fall in the tinder, which caught light easily. Soon the fire was roaring and snapping and sending a little stream of sparks into the trees.

'Matches made in heaven,' he said and winked at me. We took off our gloves and warmed our hands. Iggy felt in a pocket and pulled out a hunk of cheese wrapped in greaseproof paper, which he had saved from lunch. He broke it in two and we ate it, staring happily into the flames.

We must have been distracted by the fire because we did not see the man until he had reached halfway across the Tarle Steps. He was dressed exactly as he was in the painting – in britches, brown leather boots, a leather jerkin, a long green overcoat and a large black hat.

Around his neck hung a pair of spectacles, and he carried a long wooden staff. I froze. After the morning's experience, I immediately assumed he was a ghost. But Iggy nodded to me with a reassuring smile and laid a hand on my shoulder.

The man moved nimbly across the remaining slabs and came to a halt at the end where he drummed his stick gently on the last stone. He was very tall – over six foot six inches, I guessed.

'Every man who starts a fire,' he said, 'believes he's the master of that fire, but soon enough he becomes its slave, feeding its appetite with more and more wood, hurrying to the sound of its dying hiss.'

The man's breath was showing in the cold. This was no ghost.

Iggy gave him his deepest bow. 'Igthy Ma-tuu Clava, Lord of Ro-Torva.'

'Pleased to meet you, I'm sure,' said the man with no pleasure in his expression whatsoever. 'And you, young man? Who are you?'

'Kim Greenwood, sir,' I replied.

'I've been expecting you. I saw you this morning and I knew you would come.'

I couldn't help myself. 'You saw us this morning! How?'

'Don't interrupt.'

'But how did you see us?'

'You saw me, didn't you? So it is quite natural that I saw you.' His tone was testy and a little bored.

'But you're in a painting – we're real.'

'How can you prove that? How do you know you're not being squinted at, peered at and examined by all manner of common folk in some far-off museum? How do you know that, Kim Greenwood?'

'I can't prove it,' I replied, 'except to say that usually I know when I'm being watched. I know when my tutor, Quake, is watching me from behind. I can feel it on the back of my neck.'

'Ah, Mr Quake, yes, a low character. There's more to him than meets the eye, but I am sure you know that.'

'I don't know anything about him,' I said.

'Something of a past, shall we say.'

'What did he do?' I asked.

But the old man had lost interest in me and was fixing his gaze on Iggy. 'Now you're an interesting one. When I saw you I thought to myself, there's a chap who has travelled from some foreign part to save his neck. I am correct in that supposition, am I not, Mr Ma-tuu Clava? You've come to save your pretty neck...and maybe the boy's too,

81

if you can. That's why you appeared before the painting and tried to work out the mystery of all those fallen chairs. There *is* no mystery about the fallen chairs – they are death. That's what they mean – death. There are just two more left standing and waiting to be toppled over by a little gust of wind. He snapped his fingers twice and then blew on them. 'Puff puff! Just like that. Extinction, annihilation, nothingness. That's what awaits you two lads!'

He took one step down towards us. I noticed his hands were huge and bony. 'Have you paid?' he asked.

Iggy didn't answer.

'Cat got your tongue?' said the man nastily. 'Chewed it up and spat it out, did he?'

Iggy said nothing. Evidently he was going to leave me to do the talking.

'*Well*, have you paid?' the man demanded.

'Paid who?' I asked.

'Have you paid the *Watchman*?'

I was confused. 'Who's the Watchman?'

'I am the Watchman, naturally. There is a notice clearly stating that you must pay.'

'Where?'

'Over there by the fallen tree. The upright stone.'

I turned round. I couldn't see any stone. 'Where?'

'Look, boy! Use your eyes!'

I spotted something sunk in a patch of wet ground. It was exactly like an old gravestone. I ran over and read the words that had been etched deeply into its surface in very old lettering:

'My name is Watchman, heir am I still watching day and night welcoming all persons that comes heir to pay with silver and cross to the other side.'

I had no money. I called out to him, 'Will gold do? My friend has gold.'

'Gold is better than the rubbish they leave there – the trippers who come with their *filthy* children to *picnic* and *paddle* in this sacred place, leaving their *mess* here and the *clamour* of radios and cars hanging in the air like *bad odour*s. Cretins! Morons! Peasants! Tourists! The worst of humanity! But let me tell you that one or two of those fools that dare to cross my bridge without paying get a very nasty little shock.' He looked down at me. 'You seem to be worried, young man. And well you might be. But I don't hurt them. They always get to the other side without harm.' He laughed to himself. 'But then they notice something's wrong. The weather's changed; there are different sounds and smells in the air. Sooner or later it dawns on these imbeciles that they are in the right place *but in the wrong time.*' He laughed maliciously. 'Oh, you should see the look on their stupid faces when they're confronted with a band of mediaeval ruffians or a cave bear. It's quite a treat I can assure you. Oh yes, it really makes life worth living, if you know what I mean.' He paused and leered at me with a grin of broken and stained teeth. 'I picks 'em up and puts 'em down in another time. And they *never ever* comes back.'

During this speech, Iggy had walked over to the stone and placed three gold sovereigns alongside the grimy sixpences, threepenny bits, pennies and farthings.

'You don't seem to like people much,' I said, then immediately regretted it.

'Don't like people! That's an understatement, laddie. If you had seen human nature as I have – the killing, the cruelty, the filth in man's mind – you wouldn't like people much either. Your time is the worst I've seen in many centuries – the greed, the spreading yourselves out, the spoiling of all things beautiful and natural, the snatching and grabbing, the dirt and noise you make, the casual and wanton brutality. Man neglects the world in this time of yours. He despises and destroys things that he does not understand. As long as he's filling his fat belly and feeding his ugly offspring, he doesn't care.' He sighed heavily. 'But why do I bother to say these things to a stupid young boy and a man who pretends to be a half-wit? Let us get on with the business in hand. You have paid, so you may now ask questions, unless you want to go to the other side.' He leered at me.

'No, thank you,' I said quickly.

'Then they must be good questions or I will not bother with them. If they bore me, I will not hesitate to terminate this interview and return to a more salubrious time.'

Iggy stepped forward and bowed again. 'Brother Kim will ask the questions. He is very clever. He knows the speeding of light.'

'If he does he's halfway to understanding something about this universe. But somehow it seems unlikely to me.'

I coughed and turned to Iggy, thinking that he should be doing the talking if he wanted to borrow some *big magic*. But he gestured that I should go on and did that weird thing of retreating into himself.

'Are you the artist who painted the picture?'

'What a pathetic question! You must do better than that.'

'Do you know what the Latin inscription at the bottom of the picture says?'

'I have already told you about the meaning of the chairs. It merely underlines the point. *"Qui magistrum sellarum delapsarum magistraverit supererit ut rem refera"* means, "He who masters the Master of the Fallen Chairs will live to tell the tale." It contains an amusing play on the word "master" using the *late* Latin word *"magisterare"*, which has a syncopated – that is shortened – form *"magistrare"*, which means to rule, direct or command. You see the point? If you master the clues of the painting you may live.'

'You seem to know a lot about the painting. Will you help us with the clues?' I asked.

'Certainly not, you must use your own meagre intelligence to work them out by yourselves, but I will tell you this – there are people who want to stop you. Men and *women* who have black hearts.'

'Who?'

'That would be telling, wouldn't it?' He looked impatiently about the woods. 'If you haven't got anything else to ask me, I am anxious to return to the particularly beautiful summer where I have chosen to spend my time – without your picknickers, trippers, trash makers and teenagers with their little radio boxes. Besides, this winter of yours is not good for my chest.' As if to emphasise the point, he cleared his throat and a rattle came from deep inside his lungs. 'It's the damp, you see,' he said, pulling a yellow handkerchief from his coat pocket and coughing into it.

'Are you really a time traveller?' I asked.

'That's a question of principle, not detail,' he replied. 'I am, as you so crudely put it, a time traveller, but it is a more complicated business than you imagine. I am blessed with certain privileges within the Lines of Tarle. Yes, blessed is what I am.' He paused and fixed me with frightening dark eyes. 'Detail, boy. I want detailed questions.'

'What are the Lines of Tarle?'

'Oh heavens...very well then...the Lines of Tarle describe a narrow fissure hereabouts that runs roughly from this bridge, through the Skirl valley and up the hill to a tomb known as Sennak's Mound. You probably know of it.' I nodded, thinking that he had described exactly the map Iggy had in his pocket and the one I had seen in the Long Gallery.

'Within those lines, which are often no further apart than a hundred paces, exists a special state, conditions of which keep the dead from utter extinction and the living from the dead, if the potency is used to its best advantage. You are standing in one of the miracles of the universe, boyo, and don't forget it. There are only a few spots like this.' Iggy nodded, as though something had been confirmed to him. 'And this is the best, as far as I know.'

I couldn't think of any other questions, though I knew that there was much more to learn. The old man drummed his staff on the stone impatiently and looked around.

'Was there anything else?' he asked with a look of boredom.

'Yes, yes...yes there was,' I said, frantically remembering the codes and dates in the book I had found beneath the bird. 'Do the lines work all the time...I mean are there some times when they work better than others?'

'At last, a half-intelligent question, the emphasis being on the word *half*. As it happens the Lines of Tarle are subject to certain cyclical patterns. The physical laws concerning the recursive strength of this – how shall I put it? – motion are very complex. Suffice to say that the power within the lines grows and ebbs over a period of a hundred years.'

'And they're very strong now, aren't they? That's why she's come to the house?'

The old man's eyes impaled me with a particularly fierce look. After what seemed like several minutes he said, '*She*?'

'Yes, Alba Hockmuth.'

'Yesss. Alba Hockmuth. Where is she now? My information is not as up to date as I would like it.'

'She is at the house a lot of the time, but I couldn't say exactly where she is now. Is that why she's here – because it is such an important time?'

He nodded. 'The vixen comes to renew her claim once more and to consolidate her power. Mind you, she's not the only one who has turned up out of the blue, is she? I mean, you've come and dear Flopsy with his big-eared hat,' he crooked a dirty finger in Iggy's direction, 'has materialised from nowhere at a moment of interesting historical piquancy. Quite a party will be had, I'm sure.'

He considered us both. 'I wonder if you're up to the job.'

'Up to what job?'

'Of saving your sorry bones. I wonder if you can

pull it off. I will be interested to see.' He tapped the stick twice.

'How hard is it going to be?' I asked.

'Oh, very hard! Very hard indeed. To match her powers, her level of filthy, conniving, black-hearted cruelty...well, you're going to have to be very, very astute. She has already got your measure and I can tell you she has tricked and deceived and made fools of many shrewder people than you.'

I absorbed this, only half-noticing the bitterness of his expression. 'Do you know where the wishing well is?' I asked. 'We know someone who is in trouble and might be in a wishing well.

'Then he evidently wasn't wishing well enough, was he?' He smiled at his joke. 'Who told you?'

'It was a *she* not a *he.'* I looked at Iggy. 'A ghost told us – a message was written in the dust.'

'A woman or a girl, huh? So, you've been contacted by ghosts – well, watch your step is my advice to you. Ghosts come and go, but always for a reason. And sometimes they mislead just for the fun of it. They're partial to deception.'

'My friend says it was a *good* ghost.'

He considered Iggy loftily. 'Yes, I believe your friend might know a good ghost when he saw one. He is cleverer than he lets on. I admire a man who keeps his own counsel. But silence conceals cunning. Are you sure you can trust him?'

'Yes,' I said. 'I think so. Can you tell me where the wishing well is?'

He started tapping his stick to a rhythm. *'Up above the house of Skirl, where the waters run from sight, into caves black as night, this they call the Wishing Well. There you'll find your pretty girl, up above the house of Skirl.'* He paused at the end of the rhyme. 'I just made that up. Rather good, don't you think?'

I lifted my shoulders and said it was OK but that I was concerned about the woman. She was a friend of mine and I didn't feel that he should be making jokes about her.

'Her name?' he demanded.

'Bella – Bella Brown.'

He stifled a cry of anguish. 'Damn her! It did not occur to me that you were talking of Bella...' His voice trailed off. The noise of the river seemed to rise and for several minutes the old man was lost in torment and he was muttering to himself, a prayer or incantation or curse: it was difficult to tell. Then, under his breath, I heard him say. 'I feared as much. I knew it! I shall have her back. Get her back is what I'll do. Yes.'

I wanted to ask how he knew Bella but his expression was so terrifying that I though it best to keep quiet. His head whipped round and he focused on the wisp of smoke rising from a log as the flames guttered. 'I have things to do. I cannot stay here beyond the life of that fire,' he said quietly. 'You have one more question.'

At this, Iggy came out of his trance with a start.

'How much times?' he asked.

'Speak English, man! Time is *singular*...very singular.' He grinned bleakly at his little aside. 'You have as much *time* as the painting allows. You must find out when it was painted. A hundred years from that date – or is it two hundred years? – I do not recall, and the clock stops ticking... Puff, puff! The remaining chairs fall over and that's curtains and jolly old good night to you two.'

He was already making his way back across the bridge, tapping his stick as he went. 'Good bye. I don't suppose I'll be seeing you again.'

I called after him. 'If you can travel through time, you must know what's going to happen to us.'

He turned slowly and looked at me from beneath the rim of his hat in a way that made me take a step or two towards Iggy. 'Impertinent boy! Understand that this time *you* live in now is the furthest I go. The destruction, the laying waste of beauty that will follow are too much for me. I stray no further than your *present* hour. D'yer understand? It's not in my interests. I must have regard to my equilibrium – my *peace of mind*. As it is, I find myself unsettled by this meeting.'

He continued across the bridge. I looked over to the stone. Iggy's sovereigns had vanished, although the man had never been anywhere near them. The rest of the grimy little coins were still there. When my eyes returned to the bridge he had vanished also, but I could still hear the tapping of his stick in the grey half-light.

'Thank you,' I called in the direction of the noise. 'Thank you for helping us, sir.'

Chapter Six

Hell Fire, No Notion

'We know where Bella is now,' I said as we tramped back to Skirl. 'We have to go and find her.'

Iggy shook his head sadly. 'Brother Kim, how long has Bella Brown been missing?'

'About two and a half weeks,' I replied.

He stopped and lifted his shoulders hopelessly. 'That's no good. She must be dead.'

'How do you know? We must go and find her.'

He nodded gravely.

'Who was that on the bridge? Was it really the same man in the painting?'

'The Old Man of Tarle, a very important man. We will see him again.'

'"*I picks 'em up and puts them down in another time.*" That's what he said. Do you think he can really do that?'

'Yes, Brother Kim.'

'I'm glad he didn't do it to us.'

Iggy thought about this. 'But we would be living in other time, Brother Kim. No puff, puff.' I saw his point. If we travelled back in time, there was no danger from the falling chairs in the painting.

'Are you sure he's right? I mean, why would anyone living in the past want to predict my death when they didn't even know a person called Kim Greenwood would be born? Why does he think those two chairs are us?'

'Because we are brothers, distant brothers, but still brothers.'

I was beginning to understand. If Iggy really was a lost member of the Drago family, then he and I might indeed be the last of the line of the Dragos of Skirl. The Colonel's sons died in the war. My mother was dead and Alba Hockmuth was such a distant relation of the Colonel's that it didn't count. Then a terrible thought occurred to me. My mother was a Drago. Was she one of the fallen chairs? Had she died because of the painting? I stopped in my tracks. The wind tore at us. I could feel tears welling in my eyes. Iggy seemed to know what I was thinking. He put his hands on my shoulders and bent right down and looked up into my face. 'She was a wonderful mother,' I said. 'The best in the world, the kindest, sweetest person anyone could meet. It isn't fair.'

'Brother Kim, I know this. I feel your sadness.'

For a time, we sat on a log in the shelter of a great yew tree and watched the dusk gather in the woods below us. Iggy still had a piece of cheese and some of his own chocolate, which we shared, and then we fell to talking about the school I had been forced to leave. Perhaps after seeing the message written in the dust and our trip to the bridge I needed to think about something normal. Not that school was normal. I told Iggy about the rules, like wearing your jacket buttoned up and not being allowed to walk on the grass unless you were a senior. His eyes popped with disbelief.

'I was always in trouble,' I told him. 'They kept me in class for insolence – just like Quake does.'

'Insolence? What is?'

'Cheek,' I replied, but he still looked blank. Then I remembered the words used in a report by the headmaster – '"Defiance and a tendency to slyness."'

He grinned at this. 'Slyness is good. Sly Brother Kim.'

'I think they were pleased when I had to leave after Mother died. They didn't like my jokes.'

Iggy looked interested so I told him about the time I tied some string to my teacher's chair and pulled it as he sat down. It didn't seem very funny to me now, but Iggy was bent over double with laughter. It was the strangest laugh I have ever heard, a kind of high-pitched wheeze that made his eyes water. Eventually, after slapping his knees several times, he said, 'Brother Kim is the master of the fallen chair.'

It was funny and I laughed with him.

'There is something important going on here, isn't there?' I said eventually. 'Something rare and strange that happens here every hundred years. Do you think that it's got something to do with Alba? Has she got something to do with it?'

'I know only a little, Brother Kim. I know that the Old Man and Alba are enemies and that they battle across times.'

'Gosh! How do they do that?'

'We shall see. There is much that I do not understand, Brother Kim. There is much I must learn about this woman. But first I must see her,' he said, jumping up.

We continued on our way, reaching the hill that formed one side of the valley ten minutes later. Below us we noticed several lights on in the house. This was odd, since normally there were no lights to be seen except in the Colonel's rooms and the kitchen. 'Something's going on,' I said.

We crashed down through the dead bracken, slipping in the ruts made by the cattle. When we reached the drive we found an ambulance and two police cars by the front door. The door was open. People were milling about. Jebard and Amos Sprigg were talking to a police officer, and Simon Vetch stood under the front door light, smoking nervously.

'What's happened?' I said.

'Bella Brown,' said Iggy simply. 'They find her.'

This turned out to be exactly right. After we had left, Amos had gone out looking for a lost sheep and taken all the dogs with him. Applejack and Trumpet had dived down a large opening by some rocks and then refused to come out. He had shone his torch down into the dark and spotted a handbag and some shoes. It didn't take him long to see poor Bella's frozen body huddled on a ledge of the rock just above a bubbling black underground pool.

All attention was suddenly focused on Iggy. He was led to the kitchen by a detective, and Amos and Simon were asked if they could identify him from the two sightings. Was this the same man they had seen in the Shettle and observing the house from the corner of the woodland? They couldn't be sure but they tended towards the view that the man they had seen wasn't as dark in complexion as Iggy and that he had been much taller. They were dismissed and I was called into the kitchen.

Iggy was standing between two uniformed officers. The Colonel was sitting on a chair at the end of the table, his hand placed across his forehead.

'Young man,' said the Inspector, whose name was Christy, 'you have spent most of the day with this gentleman. Has he been acting suspiciously in any way?'

'No,' I replied. 'Not at all.'

'Has he told you anything about his background?'

'Yes, what he told you all before.'

Christy drew a deep breath. 'Take a seat, lad, there's no need to stand.' I sat down on the bench along the table. 'What were you doing down by the old bridge?' he continued. 'That's a long way to go on a cold afternoon.'

I looked over to Iggy, who had removed his attention to a rail on the ceiling that had once been used to hang meat. 'It's prehistoric,' I replied, 'I thought it would be interesting for him to see something so old.'

He took a few paces nearer Iggy. 'Mrs Camm

mentioned that you were asking about a wishing well this morning and when she said she didn't know of one, you went off to the Tarle Steps. Were you aware that the place where Miss Brown was found used to be called a wishing well?' He cast a critical eye around the ancient equipment in the kitchen. 'What gave you the idea that there was a wishing well nearby?'

'I don't know,' I replied. 'I think I must have heard someone talking about it on the farm and thought it would be interesting to find it.'

'Did this gentlemen suggest that you go up there?'

'No, he'd never heard of a wishing well. I had to explain what it was to him. I still don't think he understands.'

Alice appeared in the doorway with a stricken expression. Jebard was behind her.

'But that's quite a coincidence, isn't it? One moment you're talking about wishing wells, then within an hour or two Miss Brown is found dead in a wishing well. What do you have to say about that?'

'Nothing. I don't know what to say.'

'We believe that Miss Brown died when she fell or was pushed into that cave. Have you been up there?'

'No, I told you I didn't know where it was, and Iggy doesn't either.'

'This is a very serious matter,' he said, his eyes sweeping the room. 'I'm afraid we can't leave it at that. This gentleman will accompany us to the police station for further questioning. The results of the postmortem examination tomorrow will decide what path this investigation is set to take.'

The Colonel removed his hand from his forehead and leant back in his chair. He looked exhausted. 'Inspector,' he said, 'I can vouch that neither young Kim nor Mr Ma-tuu Clava knew that this place was called a wishing well. Even old Jebard probably didn't know. He looked over to Jebard, who nodded. 'And you see it has already been established that Mr Ma-tuu Clava only arrived in the country five days ago. Your Sergeant told me himself that he disembarked from the Blue Star Line on Tuesday.'

Iggy bobbed up and down enthusiastically.

'His ticket has been checked,' continued the Colonel. 'The immigration control at the port in question remember Mr Ma-tuu Clava – which is hardly surprising – and he was noticed by various officials making his way here by train and bus. Today is the 22nd of December. Miss Brown disappeared on the 5th of December, wearing the exact same clothes that she was found in this afternoon. At the time Mrs Camm described to your officers what she was wearing when she last saw her. It is therefore reasonable to conclude that she died on the day she went missing, some twelve days before his ship docked. It's simply not possible that Mr Ma-tuu Clava had anything to do with her demise.'

The Inspector looked impatient. 'Yes, Colonel, but...'

'But nothing, Inspector!' snapped the Colonel. 'You are not even sure a crime has been committed. This poor woman may have slipped and fallen into that dreadful place by herself.' I looked at Iggy: we both knew that wasn't true. 'And yet,' continued the Colonel, 'you immediately assume foul play and make the only foreigner on the horizon a suspect. Until you've established one way or the other what happened to Bella Brown, I suggest it's ill-advised to settle on a suspect. After all, without a crime there *cannot* be a suspect.'

The policeman did not like being told how to do his own job. 'I'm sorry sir. I must insist that he comes with us, just so that we can rule him out of our enquiries.'

The Colonel rose and supported himself by

placing his knuckles on the table. 'This man's a guest in my house,' he said, 'and I believe what he says about his background and his reason for coming.'

'Is this relevant to the case?' asked the Inspector.

'Certainly not! It's a private matter concerning this family.' Then the fight seemed to go out of the Colonel. He sagged and sat down heavily. Alice moved from the doorway to hover nearby, but he waved her away.

Sensing victory, Inspector Christy said, 'We're dealing with a possible murder inquiry here, sir. I'd be neglecting my duty if I did not take this man in.'

Suddenly I couldn't contain myself. 'But Iggy didn't do it, can't you see that, you stupid…'

'That's enough from you, young man,' said the policeman. 'He's coming with us and that's the end of the matter. Sergeant, take this man out to the vehicles and make sure there's no funny business with him. Don't look into his eyes.' He paused and turned to the Colonel. 'Last time he was taken into custody, sir, your guest seems to have amused himself by hypnotising one of my officers. Now, we'd better be going.'

Iggy cast around wildly with his eyes bulging

and his mouth slightly open. Suddenly he lunged in my direction before the sergeant and the constable could stop him, and hissed in my ear, 'Find date when picture was painted, Brother Kim.' He nodded to make sure I had understood before being seized by the police. I held onto him and when the constable prised my hands from Iggy's arm I lashed out with my boots, landing a kick on the back of the Sergeant's calf. He yelled out and raised his hand but the Colonel shouted, 'That's enough, Kim. Come here and behave yourself.'

After everyone had gone I left Jebard in the kitchen plying Alice with sweet sherry and ran to find the Colonel as he wandered through the house. He was moving very slowly, and after my outburst I was nervous of approaching him.

'What is it now? What do you want?' he said without turning round.

'I'm sorry, sir…I just know that Iggy couldn't do such a thing to Bella. Why would he? He never even met her. He didn't even know what a wishing well was.'

He stopped and looked down at me. His expression had softened. 'Quite a temper you've

105

got there, Kim. You're going to have to watch that in life. You can't go around kicking policemen. You'll end up in jail if you go on like that.' He studied me. 'You've got the Drago look and the family temper and rashness. "Hell fire, no notion," is what they used to say about the Dragos. It must have jumped a generation because your dear mother, as we all know, was a most gentle soul.' It was the first time he had mentioned her to me. He looked into my face. 'I am sure you miss her dreadfully, Kim, and we must make allowances for you. It can't be easy.' He gave me a rather awkward pat on the shoulder. 'Was there anything else? I'm afraid I'm quite drained, and I find this business of young Bella's death really very distressing.'

'Do you think she was murdered?'

'Well, the signs aren't good, I grant you, but we'll have to wait for the postmortem.'

'Can I ask you a question?'

'Persistence, that's another characteristic you seem to have inherited. Very well, ask your question.'

'Do you really think Iggy Ma-tuu Clava is a relation of ours? I mean, he hasn't got a temper and he doesn't look a bit like the Drago family.'

He considered me for a moment then shuffled

to a chair and sat down. 'I hope Jebard remembers to turn off all these lights,' he said. 'They're costing me a fortune.'

'Shall I remind him?'

'That would be good of you.' He fiddled with his pipe and thought for a few moments longer. 'To answer your question about our guest, there's no one else who could know what he does. He may be a clever fraud, but that's not my judgement. The Bible he brought with him *was* given to my great uncle Clive Endymion Drago – a wild fellow if there ever was one. There was a scandal of some sort – the details are hazy – and he was spirited out of the country. He was given plenty of money and told never to come back again. Seems he had a conversion and went into missionary work of some sort, at least that is what he said. Bought himself a boat and sailed the islands of the New Hebrides and beyond into the Pacific – who knows where he ended up. He died without the family ever being informed, though he occasionally sent letters back and some photographs of the East. They just stopped coming and the family forgot about him. So you see it's quite possible that Mr Ma-tuu Clava is the descendant of the original Clive Endymion and a cousin of yours and mine. Does that answer your question?'

'Will the police let him go?'

'Of course: they can't hold a man without charges and they don't have enough to charge him. He'll be back by tomorrow, I shouldn't wonder, Monday, at the latest. And if he isn't, I will appoint a lawyer to handle the case and get him released. But you know it takes money and time and I don't have much of either. Now I think it's time for me to leave you, dear boy.'

'The picture of the fallen chairs, do you know when it was painted?'

'What the dickens do you want to know that for?'

'It may be important.'

'I doubt that, but I couldn't tell you anyway. There are hundreds of pictures in Skirl, Kim. I can't be expected to know the date of every single one. But I expect it's on the painting somewhere.'

I realised he had no idea what the painting meant, and of course there was no point telling him what the man on the Tarle Steps had said. I barely believed it myself. In fact, the whole day seemed like a dream.

He passed a hand over his forehead; his face clouded with sadness again. 'Best be getting back to my rooms,' he said. 'You go off and have yourself something to eat with Mrs Camm.' He put his hands on his knees and pushed himself up with a groan. 'Don't forget to tell Jebard about the lights.'

He moved off into the gloom of the house, muttering about Bella Brown and unaware of the noises that had slowly started up around us, the scratching and sighing that had suddenly filled the hallway.

I hurried back to the kitchen and ate a plate of bubble and squeak. Alice was there with Jebard fanning her face and talking about the funeral that would have to be held for Bella. My mind was racing with all sorts of questions. When she paused, I asked her what had happened to the Colonel's sons. She pursed her lips and glanced doubtfully at Jebard.

'He lost them in the war. Then Mrs Drago died and he was left alone. Charles and Andrew were good boys. A few weeks before Andrew was killed – drowned at sea he was – they came on leave to Skirl. Before going back to the war at the end of the week they played a game of croquet on the top lawn, both looking so fine in their uniforms.' She paused to sniff and dab a handkerchief to her nose.

'A year later we had the news about Charles, though we never knew how he died. The Colonel's never recovered. I mean to say, the bad luck that runs in this family. There's no telling where it'll end.'

Chapter Seven

The Troubled Spirit of the Great Auk

That night I dreamed of Alba Hockmuth. She was standing in my room with her arms folded, examining me with a look of contempt. In my dream she was much taller than her six foot. She was wearing a black Elizabethan dress with lace cuffs and a crisp white ruff. There were many rings on her hands, and from her ears there hung the strangest of ornaments. I looked closer, and saw that each earring consisted of a golden pendant on the end of which hung a tiny man wriggling like a fish on a hook. She put a hand up to her right ear to stop one of them moving – which she did by pinching his body until he yelled out. I woke. The light was on, but I saw nothing. A few seconds passed before I again heard a voice. Was it in my head – part of the same dream? But the voice didn't belong to Alba, or anyone I knew. It was the most hollow, reedy voice that I ever heard in my life, and it was definitely in the room with me, because there was a slight echo as it spoke the following ditty. 'Do not trust the stranger,' it rasped. 'The stranger means you ill. Do not trust the stranger, he means to put you in the well. Batter your head the stranger will, and put you down the well. Do not trust the stranger. He'll put you in the well.'

It stopped. A silence fell in the room and in the house around me. I didn't move for several minutes, praying the thing would go away. Without warning, a model aeroplane, which had been sitting on a shelf, took off, moved to the centre of the room, hovered and then dropped to the floor with a crash. Bits of plastic sprayed across the room. 'Do not trust the stranger,' the voice said in a whisper, 'he'll put you in the well.' I buried my head in the pillows but I didn't sleep until first light and then only for an hour or so.

It was Sunday morning, two days before Christmas. Still shaky from the disturbances in the night, I got dressed. In my terror, I had come to the conclusion that the ghosts in the house were warning me against Iggy because he represented a threat to someone's plans. That was the only possible explanation because nothing could shake my trust in my new friend even though I had known him only a few days.

I went to find Alice, but she had also slept in late. The dogs raised their heads drowsily as I entered the kitchen. They weren't keen to go out into the cold so I let them stay by the range and made myself some bread and jam, remembering what Iggy had said about there being good ghosts and not so good ghosts. Perhaps there was some kind of struggle going on among the ghosts of Skirl. But why was the Colonel ignorant of their presence and why did Jebard and Alice seem only vaguely aware that the house was teeming with spirits?

Having felt so desperately alone during the night, I couldn't imagine things getting much worse, and in a way that lifted my spirits. I knew I had to save us from the curse and that would be my only purpose. My eyes came to rest on the four bottles of sloe gin standing on the shelf in front of the small window. Jebard had made the drink with bitter blue-black berries he found on the hillside, and having removed the berries and carefully sieved the gin over and over, he was left with liquid of the brightest pinky-red that I had ever seen. The morning light shone through the bottles like stained glass in a church, and at that moment I didn't think there was anything more beautiful in the world, and for some reason a confidence surged through me. What more could possibly happen to me? So what if there were bad dreams and evil whispers in my room? What could they do to me, a boy who had lost his mother? I would go by myself and look at the painting again, but I decided to make my way to the Long Gallery first and remove the little book I had found before Iggy's arrival and give it to him when he returned. And there were other things I needed to look at too, things that could not be so easily removed from the Long Gallery.

I hurried through the morning light of the upper floors on the East wing and arrived in the Long Gallery with my breath showing in the cold air. I went to the cabinet where I knew the old photograph albums were kept, pulled out the bottom drawer and removed the bundles of letters, which were tied together with pink ribbon, then three of the oldest photograph albums. Most of the photos were of Skirl and the Drago family sitting formally in the garden, the men dressed in blazers and boaters, the women in long dresses and carrying parasols.

There were some larger pictures of the house taken from the front with the servants lined up in their uniforms. One showed the men of the Drago family with a mass of dead birds, others the Drago children in pony traps or planted uneasily on a gloomy looking Shetland pony.

I thought that one of the family must have had a passion for photography, not just for family snapshots but for recording everything that happened on the estate, such as the arrival of the first harvester or a steam tractor led by a man with great side whiskers who was waving a flag. There were scores of studies of the people who lived on the estate, expressionless men and women standing outside their cottages in their Sunday best, young workers proudly holding the bridles of their plough horses, carters and grooms also with their horses, gardeners and gamekeepers standing to attention with the rakes, forks and spades in the light of a long-dead summer.

Somewhere in these albums I remembered seeing a man with a flowing moustache, standing on the forward deck of a small sailing boat, but before finding him my attention was drawn to a detail in a series of big family photographs taken in 1860 and 1861. There were eight or nine separate prints and in each one the figure of a tall woman was blurred. Every time the shutter came down this woman must have moved her head or waved a hand in front of her face. It struck me as odd that not once had the photographer managed to capture her. I looked at the bottom of each picture. In each of the captions her name had been scratched out. I made a note to show Iggy and moved on through the album.

Eventually I found what I was looking for and read the caption: 'Clive Endymion Drago 1882 – Fanafuti.' This must be Iggy's great grandfather – his father before four. On the facing page was a folded plan for the same boat. Printed in a very neat hand were the words: MISSIONARY YACHT FOR E.C.F. DRAGO ESQUIRE, designed and transported to the Far East in the year of Our Lord 1865 – DIXON KEMP, GLASGOW. The photograph must have been taken and sent back to Skirl as proof of Endymion's good works among the peoples of the Pacific island chains, though I thought he looked far too happy and mischievous to be a missionary. Just behind the mast of the boat sat a woman wearing a patterned sarong. She had a flat, brown face and looked away from the camera. Might she have been Iggy's great grandmother?

I needed much more than this to begin a

family tree, which I thought would be the way to work out the members of the Drago family who had died early because of the curse of the fallen chairs. I already had two names, Andrew and Charles. I began to read the letters, noting down any other likely names in the pocket diary my mother had given me the previous Christmas.

I had been there no more than ten minutes when suddenly a voice broke the stillness. 'What are you doing here again?' it said.

I spun round. No one was there.

I asked, 'What are you doing in here again?' I got up slowly, my eyes searching every part of the Long Gallery.

'Over here,' said the voice with irritation. 'I cannot very well come to you, can I? I'm stuck to this stand.' To my astonishment, it was coming from the bird at the end of the gallery. Its beak was moving and its wings were slowly rising and falling.

'I am the last of the great auks – the only one in the entire world, condemned to live in this dry, dusty room.' The bird stopped and seemed to sniff. 'Don't mind me, I'm just one of nature's victims. Carry on with whatever you're doing, though it would be nice if *occasionally* someone would pay attention to me. And you! You never look at me without that smirk on your face.'

The bird's tone was so woeful and unthreatening that I didn't feel frightened, though I was so amazed I couldn't think how to respond. I approached the chest where it stood. 'Are you really talking?' I said. 'You're a bird, and a dead bird at that.'

'An extinct bird, actually,' said the bird, eyeing me wistfully. 'Have you any idea what it's like to be the only one of your species left on this earth?'

'I imagine it's very lonely,' I said, wondering if I was really having this conversation.

'Precisely. There's no one to share your memories, no one who has known that freedom.' The bird stopped speaking suddenly and I thought I saw a tear in its eye. 'No cod for supper tonight, no more sprats and mackerel teeming on the spring tide, no more belly surfing in the white waters of the autumn storms, or scrambling on to a rocky outcrop with a gullet full of herring. It's all gone. Man came to our breeding colonies and killed every living bird, crushing our eggs underfoot, clubbing our chicks to death. Millions were killed for the fun of it. *For the fun of it!*'

'I'm sorry,' I said. 'I would never kill a bird. I love watching them fly.'

'Flying's not everything, you know. The great auks followed their fish from the Grand Banks to the Florida Keys, swimming as fast as any dolphin. You don't need wings to fly when you have two superior flippers. It's as silly as asking a dolphin to take to the air.'

'Dolphins *do* take to the air,' I said, 'they leap out of the water. Anyway, if you had had proper wings, you might have escaped the hunters who came to your colonies.'

'That's beside the point,' the bird said, raising its wings and holding them out to show me that they weren't that small. 'We were killed in a frenzy of blood lust. That's not our fault. The warped nature of man is to blame.'

I attempted to apologise again and asked if the bird would mind if I went back to what I was doing.

'See! You won't even hear the sins of your kind.'

The great auk shut its eyes and lowered its head. It wasn't beautiful, but now I was looking at it properly, its size and black and white markings were very striking, especially the patch of white feathers by its beak.

'I'm sorry,' I said. 'You see, I shouldn't be here. I don't want to get caught. I need to get on with what I was doing.'

'I won't tell,' said the bird, opening its eyes slowly. 'But in return you must listen to my story. Do I have your agreement?'

'Well…'

'And I will help you to find what you're looking for,' it added quickly. 'I've been in this room for over a century and I know what's what and what's where and who put it there.'

'Then I will listen,' I said, wondering at myself for striking a bargain with a stuffed bird. What was it the Old Man of Tarle had said about the lines of Tarle keeping the living from the dead and the dead from extinction? Perhaps nothing was allowed to die in the house.

'I will begin,' said the bird, fixing its cross-eyed gaze on a point on the floor and lowering its wings. 'One winter there was a very great storm in the ocean and the few great auks that remained were forced to strike out for land to save their lives. There was one bird among us who was famous as a specialist diver. His name in the old tongues of the North Atlantic means Dauntless Squid Hunter. He struggled to a place named St Kilda, an island where the cruellest and most stupid of men once lived. The islanders seized him from his perch above the roaring breakers and took him to one of their stinking houses where they accused the poor creature of being a witch and causing the storm. He was put on trial in front of a judge and jury. Imagine that – a bird on trial. Of course he had no chance, because any man defending him would be suspected of witchcraft. Dauntless Squid Hunter was sentenced to death by stoning. Every man, woman and child hurled a boulder at Dauntless Squid Hunter and very soon he was a bloody mass of feathers and bones. He was the last great auk to visit that wicked place.'

'That's a terrible story,' I said. 'Did you know the bird personally?'

'Yes, I *told* you it was my story. He was my mate, my other half, my second skin, my beloved companion of the deep.' The bird sniffed again. 'I was caught too and stuffed, and here I am today, the last of the great auks, with nothing but the memories of our seafaring history.' It raised one flipper and pointed it downwards. 'And you know what annoys me most? It's those humiliating words on that notice. *"He of little wings."* For a start I am a *she* and, well…we covered the point about wings and flippers earlier.'

'That's easily sorted out,' I said, using my pencil stub to cross out the words with several thick lines.

'Thank you! A human with a heart!'

'Now will you help me? I want to get that book which is in that chest. Can I move you?'

'There's no point,' said the bird. 'The book has gone. You should have taken it while you had your chance. That quiet young woman came the day after you were here and removed it.'

'Bella? She came without me and took it!'

The bird nodded. 'And then *she* came and looked for it several hours later. And *she* flew into a rage when it wasn't there.'

'Who?'

'Miss *A.H.* – that's who.'

'That woman who was here when I was hiding – Alba Hockmuth?'

'The very same.'

Suddenly something occurred to me. 'Did you fall over on purpose so she wouldn't find me?'

'Yes,' said the bird, 'a diversionary tactic.'

'Gosh, thank you. But how did Alba know the book was there? I mean, why didn't she take it when I was in here?'

'She didn't know it was there until it was gone, if you see what I mean.'

'What's so important about the book?'

'It's got secrets and she has been looking for it – everywhere. But I guarded it and no one except you ever found it.'

My mind was in turmoil. If Bella had had the book, why wasn't it found with the rest of her possessions at the wishing well? I was sure the police would have mentioned it and asked the Colonel about it. But they had said nothing. So where was it?

'I want to find out the names of the Dragos who died early because of a curse.'

'I know the feeling,' said the bird bitterly and looked up. 'I have seen many Dragos come and go, and *mostly* I prefer them going.'

'Do you remember Clive Endymion Drago?' I asked.

'Yes, he was the best of all. He may even have been responsible for purchasing me – I am not sure. He was certainly interested in me and made drawings of me for his books. But the rest – well, they were a nasty brood. Clive Endymion's brothers, Rufus and Titus, were fiends as children and not much better as grown men. Clive Endymion went away and the house was left to Rufus who, by the way, once used me as target practice for darts. Rufus later fell out of a window. That was a good day. His son, Francis, was killed when he toppled from his horse and was dragged into a shallow stream where he drowned. Titus also drowned, and his son, Richard Drago, died...I can't remember how...anyway, in America.'

I knew. In one of the later albums there was a portrait of Richard in a little bowler hat standing beside a buffalo head. He too had a big moustache, and he held a rifle, the butt propped on a big leather belt and the barrel pointing out of the picture. With a start I realised that this must have been my direct ancestor, in fact my great grandfather, and I knew from the caption that he perished in a fire in Phoenix, Arizona.

As I had heard the night before, the Colonel's sons – therefore Rufus's great grandsons – Andrew and Charles, both met their ends in accidents during the war. Eventually I had seven names in my diary. Yet there were thirteen chairs in the picture, two of which were still standing. That left four deaths to be accounted for. I was sure they must be on Iggy's side of the family, unless one was my mother, who might have died because of the painting?

I was getting quite used to talking to the great auk. I plied her with questions about the deaths and how she had learned about them and where to look in the relevant letters from this or that relation. All the while I tried not to remind her about life on the ocean. One slip and she would be off for the next twenty minutes about the difficulties of catching Dover sole or the delights of scooping up huge quantities of herring and digesting them on a rock in the spring sunshine. When I tried to return to my subject she would say, 'Never ruffle a great auk's feathers by interrupting.'

While she talked, I tore a piece of paper from my notebook and drew out a family tree. There were many gaps but by each member of the family who had died in mysterious circumstances, I wrote FC, for Fallen Chair.

The great auk carried on for half an hour or more with me, showing occasional interest with a nod or a 'how interesting!' She was in the middle of a long story about a group of great auks that befriended a pilot whale among the icebergs off Greenland, when quite suddenly she stopped speaking and reverted to the pose of the mounted specimen. Her eyes went glassy and lifeless and her feathers, which had seemed so glossy a moment before, instantly became drab and dusty.

Then I heard the sound of feet climbing the bare boards of the wooden stairway that led up to the Long Gallery. One pair was wearing high heels. I stuffed the family tree into my trousers and dived for the albums and letters, which were still strewn around the floor. But I was too late. The door swung open and Alba Hockmuth came in, looking even more terrifyingly regal than before. And the very odd thing was that she was wearing clothes not unlike the old Elizabethan costume I had seen in my dream, though with a modern look – a tight-fitting black suit, white collar and leather gloves. Her skin was as pale as ever, her lips were blood red and she was wearing many necklaces and bracelets. Despite my terror I could not help but look up to see if there were little men wriggling on her earrings. Behind her was Quake, who carried her coat.

'What are you doing?' she asked quietly.

'N...Nothing,' I stammered.

'You've been snooping in things that don't concern you? You are not even allowed up here, are you, boy?'

'I...I...I was just looking at some photographs,' I replied.

'You were *expressly* forbidden from entering this room, were you not?'

'I was just looking at the albums. I wanted to ask permission, b...b...but Alice wasn't awake.'

'I don't care for boys who lie and sneak about

126

the place,' she said. 'You have been in here before, haven't you?'

I didn't reply but shook my head.

'You will be sent to your room for the rest of the day. Tomorrow you will come to me and explain what you meant by leaving Mr Quake's tutorial in the company of the man who is now in the custody of the police.'

'Mr Quake left the room first,' I said, 'so the lesson was over.'

She was across the room in a flash and caught me on the side of the head with a stinging blow that sent me reeling.

I looked up at her from the floor and decided that I wasn't going to get up in a hurry.

'What have you been looking for?' she said, spitting out her words. 'Who told you to come here?'

'No one. I didn't have anything else to do.'

'And what about your studies?' said Quake, who was enjoying his revenge. For the first time I thought I saw more than plain old nastiness in his eyes. Something sinister and evil lay in his expression. 'You have work to do. Have you completed the exercises I set yesterday?'

'No, I was going to do them today,' I lied.

Alba indicated to Quake that he should pick up the bundle of letters that were at her feet. Leering cruelly at me he stooped and then handed them to her with an adoring look.

'These are none of your business. Nothing in here is your business, do I make myself *perfectly* clear?' She walked a few paces round the room, with one hand on her hip and the bundle dangling by its ribbon from the forefinger of her right hand. The click of her high heels reverberated around the vault above us. She held a pose and gazed out of the mottled glass of the window, then spun round with a look that bore into me.

'What have you done with the book?'

'What book?'

'The book that was in this room and has now vanished?'

'I haven't taken the book.'

'So you know which book I am speaking of.'

'No...no, I don't. I haven't taken anything out of this room.'

'Get up! Stop cowering on the floor like that.' As soon as I had got to my feet she took a few steps towards me, dropped the letters, grabbed me by the shoulders and shook me. 'The book! What have you done with it?'

I concentrated on the things I could say that were true. 'I haven't taken a book. I haven't taken anything out of this room.'

'Where is it, then?'

'I don't know – really I don't.'

'It was here. We know that. And now it isn't. It could only be you. What have you done with it?'

I shook my head, trying very hard not to cry. Once I cried she had won.

'Stand still,' she screeched. 'STAND STILL. I won't have you snivelling in front of me. I WON'T!' Then, very quietly, she said, 'You will stand here until you tell me where the book is. You will not move, do you hear?'

'I don't know what you're talking about...I... I was just looking at the photographs of the family...the...old pictures.'

But she wasn't listening. Suddenly she seemed to have lost interest in me. She turned towards the door. 'Clear this mess up and, Mr Quake, be so good as to take the boy to his room. Perhaps you would then join me in the blue sitting room.' She marched from the room and set off down the stairs.

A gleam of anticipation lit Quake's face as I started putting the albums and letters back into the drawers of the cabinet. 'You will use the time confined to your room to complete the exercises, and I will inspect them tomorrow. You will have no food and you will talk to no one. Do you hear me, you snot-faced little tyke? You will learn the meaning of obedience.'

When I had closed the last drawer, he grabbed my ear and twisted it. This was too much for me and I lashed out with my fists at his legs but failed to hit him.

'Right, you'll pay for that,' he said through clenched teeth, and he cuffed me across the back of the head twice.

As I was hauled out of the room, I did not look around but I was sure the great auk had seen everything.

Chapter Eight

An Ominous Sky

Nothing moved in my bedroom for the next fifteen hours. At first I was grateful, but then I become so bored that part of me wished a ghost would come and liven things up. The house also seemed unusually quiet; practically the only sounds I heard during the entire time were Alice's footsteps when she came at six to deliver a little soup and bread on the orders of Alba, who had relented about the food. Quake was there to check that I got the very minimum, but as she handed me the tray she winked and looked down. Later I found a slice of ham under the napkin that covered the tray, and also some squares of chocolate.

At ten the next morning Quake came to collect me. He scowled when he opened the door, grabbed my collar and marched me to the blue sitting room where Alba was waiting at her desk. Her fingertips were pressed together so the veins stood out on the backs of her hands.

'Bring him over here,' she said, without looking in our direction. She was very still and she reminded me of the crocodiles I had once seen on the banks of the Zambesi. Her head turned slowly towards to me. A reptile blink followed. 'The Colonel has taken a turn for the worse,' she said without a trace of sympathy. 'The strain of looking after you is no doubt responsible for that. He has been confined to his bed, though I am led to believe that this will do little to ease his condition: it is a matter of age rather than illness. I am therefore taking sole charge of the house and you. Mr Quake is moving to Skirl and he will supervise your days. You will learn to work, not just at your studies but to contribute to the smooth running of this household. Apart from myself, Mr Quake is the only authority in your life. Jebard and Mrs Camm will have no part in your day, except when Jebard is required to find you work around the house. Is that understood? You are answerable only to Mr Quake and myself.'

'But...'

She rose, moved round the table and folded her

arms. 'You will not question what I decide is best for you. Remember you are a guest in this house. You are the object of charity and I expect you to understand that from now on. You *will* do what I say. Mr Quake has arranged a programme that will begin today.'

'But it's Christmas Eve,' I said, looking down at the carpet.

'Do not interrupt me,' she said. Out of the corner of my eye I saw her hand twitch, but then resume its place in the crook of her elbow. 'Now…I want to know what you were doing up in the Long Gallery.'

'I told you,' I said, wishing I had thought up a good excuse. 'I was bored. I wasn't doing anything wrong.'

'Why were you prying in that particular cabinet?'

'I was looking at the old photo albums to see if I could find Iggy's ancestors, that was all.'

'Iggy?' she said.

'The man under arrest,' offered Quake.

'That savage! He has no relations here. He is an impostor.'

'The Colonel believes him,' I mumbled.

Again the hand twitched. 'The Colonel is an old man given to fancies and sentiment.' Her eyes moved to the window. I followed them. A huge number of rooks twisted out of the trees on the other side of the Skirl River. 'What else were you doing?'

Quake had moved to stand behind me. 'You have written names in this book,' he said flourishing the notebook I had left behind in the Long Gallery. I was grateful that he hadn't found the family tree I had begun to make. 'This is your scrawl, is it not? I would know it anywhere.'

'What were you doing with those names?' Alba demanded.

'Just felt like it.' I said. 'I wanted to know who all my forebears were.'

'No! No! No!' she shouted, banging the desk with a clenched fist. 'I will not be lied to. What are you doing with these names in your book? And this? What were you doing with this diagram?'

I had completely forgotten that on the evening Iggy was taken away I had drawn out a grid of sixty-four squares like one of the tables in the book. I had filled it with my name and other people's names and played around jumbling the letters.

'I was making up a puzzle. That's all.'

Without warning a blow came from Quake, sending me crashing forward. 'You will tell Miss

134

Hockmuth what you were doing. Make no mistake, you will suffer if you don't.'

I was close to tears, but something began to resist. 'You can't hit me like that. If you do it again I'll tell the Colonel...I'll...'

This earned me a stinging slap on the cheek from Quake.

'That square,' said Alba when I looked up with my cheek burning. 'What interest do you have in it? What are you doing with it?'

'I was playing – that was all.'

'We heard voices,' said Quake. 'You were talking with someone else up there. Who is in on this with you?'

'No one,' I replied. 'I was by myself.'

They exchanged looks. 'We saw no one else,' said Quake, 'but they could easily have left by the door at the other end of the Long Gallery, or effected a disappearance by other means.' At this Alba shook her head. It was as if Quake was going too far. This made me wonder whether they knew that Skirl was teeming with ghosts which murmured all night and wrote things in the dust and caused model aeroplanes to fly and crash. I knew there was something going on between them – some secret that they thought I might have discovered.

'There was no one there with me,' I repeated. 'Alice wasn't even awake when I went up there, and I haven't seen Tom Jebard. Who else could it have been?'

The logic of this didn't seem to interest them. Alba had removed herself to the window. 'See to it that the boy is occupied,' she said, 'and has *nothing* to eat until this evening. Jebard has work for him to do. We will continue this discussion when he has had a chance to reflect on his position.' She turned. 'I can make life very, very hard for you if I don't receive your full co-operation.'

I was locked in a small room next door and left with a pile of exercises, together with a warning that I would not be allowed out until I had finished them. Occasionally I heard voices on the other side of the door and once I crept over to place my ear against the keyhole. Alba was saying, 'There's nothing he can do. Just keep him occupied until the time comes.'

Then Quake said. 'But what if the girl told him…What if he tells the others?' He then said something about an accident but I didn't catch the whole sentence.

Alba must have turned in my direction because I heard her clearly. 'No, it must happen as it has been ordained for both of them.' Her voice was so near that I rushed back to the desk. It was then that I noticed there were words written on my exercise book. 'Be my friend – Silverfish.' The handwriting was scratchy and I knew that even though I was tired and hungry I couldn't have written those words without knowing it. Who or what was Silverfish?

Moments later the door was unlocked and Quake stormed in and took hold of me. 'I will check your work later. You had better have done it properly or you'll be doing it again.'

I was taken to Jebard, who regretfully gave me a broom and a pan and led me to the old stable yard where I was told to sweep and pick out the dead weeds until the clock struck one. After that there was another job for me in the farm – shovelling cattle slurry across the yard into the edge of a field. It was cold, messy work, made harder because so much of the top layer was frozen and I had to break it down with the shovel. Amos Sprigg and Simon Vetch gave me sheepish looks. Simon slipped me half his lunchtime sandwich, but hurried away because he knew Quake was never far off.

It was near four o'clock when my eye caught a glint of light reflected in the windows of one the farm buildings. I looked to the west and saw that the sun had set, leaving a thin band of mother-of-pearl blue along the top of the moorland. As I watched, the clouds over the valley became a battlefield of browns, reds and different shades of ochre, and then for one magnificent moment the sky directly above Skirl swelled purple and bloody like the plume of a volcano lit from below by molten lava. I had never seen anything like it, not even in Africa, and I was sure that such terrible beauty did not bode well. I wondered if Mrs Camm had seen it too, and instinctively looked back to the house. What was that in the windows? In about a dozen different places the glass seemed to be filled with seething forms. I immediately put this down to the strange condition of the sky, although it was odd how so many of those reflections seem to resemble faces and hands clawing at the last of the light. I shuddered. The colours disappeared from the clouds, night fell and a heartless chill settled in the valley.

About ten minutes later I was called in by Jebard who told me to clean up and go to the blue sitting room again.

Alba was seated in an armchair. Quake stood behind her with a glass in his hand. I was still very hungry and the warmth of the roaring log fire made me drowsy after so long in the cold. My fingers began to tingle and I could feel my nose running. Alba started on me again in that high penetrating voice, which I knew from overhearing her in the last few months would rise and rise until she was screeching and the words poured from her in a vicious, scalding torrent. Her rage was one of the most frightening things about her and I had heard from Alice that it made grown men like Amos and Simon cower.

'What were you doing with those squares?' she asked. 'And the names in your notebook – why did you need them?'

I mumbled something about the picture but didn't go any further.

'Speak up, boy,' shouted Quake. 'What are you saying about a picture?'

'The fallen chairs...I...I was trying to...'

She gave Quake a meaningful look. 'What are you talking about?'

'The picture with the fallen chairs – I wanted to know if Iggy and I were next. I was working out who had been killed.'

'Whose idea was this? That savage who killed the maid? Or was it her? Did she talk to you? Did that interfering little madam tell you about

139

the picture? Did she? And what about the book?'
She leaned forward and peered into my face then
grabbed my arm and dug her nails in. 'Look at me
when I am talking to you.'

'Nobody told me,' I said, glancing upwards into
her eyes and briefly wondering at the evil depths
of the expression in them.

'You're telling me you dreamed this up by
yourself?'

'No…I don't know.'

'Who mentioned the picture? You will stand
there until I have an answer.'

'I can't for much longer,' I replied. 'I'm very
tired.' I staggered a little but neither of them made
a move to catch me. Then something strange
happened. I was aware of myself speaking, but the
words in my mind didn't come out. I had intended
to say that I would tell them everything I knew as
long as I could sit down in the kitchen and have
some food. But what I actually said was, 'You put
Bella in the wishing well.' Not, '*Who* put Bella in
the wishing well?' as the message had appeared
in the dust, but '*you*'.

Alba shot me a disgusted look. 'What did you
say? What do you mean by that?'

'It just came out,' I stammered 'I…I…I don't
even know what I meant by it.'

'I see,' said Alba, pressing the tops of her fingers together, then examining a stone in one of her rings. 'Perhaps you're trying to divert the blame for the death away from your friend? Is that your plan?'

I shook my head as her voice began to rise and the veins on her neck stood out. I looked away. The room was beginning to spin. Then I was aware of the floor rising up to meet me, and my nose filling with the dust of the carpet.

Chapter Nine

Christmas Eve Proper

The next thing I knew, there was a man in a brown overcoat peering down at me. It was Dr Champkin.

'The lad fainted, that's all,' he said. 'He's got very low blood sugar for the type of work you say he's been doing in the cold.' He sniffed and straightened. 'It's nothing a cup of sweet tea won't mend. But you should be careful in the future. A boy like that with so little fat on his bones won't take being worked like a pit pony.'

Alice had placed some biscuits at my side and now held a cup to my lips. It was then that I realised that I was not in the blue sitting room, but in the kitchen. Alba and Quake were nowhere to be seen: instead, kindly faces surrounded me – the Colonel, Jebard and another man, who looked exactly like Dr Champkin. For a moment

I thought I was seeing double for the two men were almost identical, right down to their red noses and rosy patches on their cheeks.

Dr Champkin smiled. 'This is my twin brother, Felix, the lawyer of the family. Quite fortuitously he was bringing Mr Ma-tuu Clava out to Skirl, and I came along for the ride, partly, I confess, to see that those pills I sent out to the Colonel were working. I'm glad to say that all's well in that department, isn't it, sir?' The Colonel grunted to indicate that he was fine.

Iggy appeared from behind him and crouched beside my chair. 'How is Brother Kim?'

'I'm feeling better now, thank you. I don't know what happened...I was... The police let you go?'

'Yes,' he replied.

'Where was I when they found me?' I asked.

'On the landing of the main stairs,' replied Alice.

Did Quake and Alba leave me there, or had I staggered from the blue sitting room and collapsed again? Had I imagined those words that I uttered about Bella Brown? I just didn't know.

'Tom brought you down here,' Alice continued. 'He found you by the old clock. Gave him quite a turn, you did. Mrs Hockmuth said she had told you to come down to the kitchen and you must have passed out before you got there.'

Both Champkins beamed down at me.

'And they let Iggy go? They don't suspect him any longer?'

'Of course,' said Felix Champkin. 'They had no reason to hold him against his will. Mr Ma-tuu Clava is now the client of Champkin and Partners and from now on he will be protected from such unfair treatment. They were wrong to arrest him.'

'Quite so,' said the Colonel. He still looked a bit drawn but his eyes were much more alive. 'The postmortem proved that the poor girl died some time before our friend here entered the country. But they still don't know how she died.'

I wondered if I should tell them about the conversation I overheard, but then I was distracted by the memory of the words that had been written on my exercise book by a spectral hand. How could I explain that? What did it mean? And who was Silverfish?

'Now it is Christmas Eve,' the Colonel continued. 'I believe we have reason enough to celebrate this fact, to say nothing of the return of our guest, Mr Ma-tuu Clava and the recovery of young Kim. It's time to bring some life back into the old house. Mrs Camm, is it conceivably within your power to prepare a dinner for us all, and of course yourself, Mr Jebard and the men who work on the farm?' She began to protest. 'Good, good, well done,' he said, giving her a pat on the shoulder. 'I knew I could rely on you.' He turned to Dr Champkin. 'You will both stay for dinner? Good, good. Jebard, we'll need to bring wine up from the cellar, and please tell Mrs Hockmuth and Mr Quake that I shall expect them in the dining room at eight-thirty sharp.'

With that he beckoned to the Champkin brothers and led them from the room.

There was much I urgently needed to tell Iggy – my failure to find out anything more about the Master of the Fallen Chairs, the encounter with the great auk, Alba Hockmuth's return to Skirl and her close interest in what I had been doing in the Long Gallery and the words that had been written on my exercise book, as well as those that had popped into my exhausted mind. Feeling better, my mind swam with so many possibilities and questions that I barely knew where to begin. But we weren't allowed a moment to ourselves. Jebard put us to work, laying the long mahogany table, polishing glasses and placing new candles in brackets along the wall, while he hurried about the dining room, decanting wine and shining the silver, which had been brought from the safe. Everything had to be done quickly, and Jebard moved with unusual speed, checking everything that we did, inevitably finding it wanting, then saying it would have to do. Amos Sprigg appeared with a Christmas tree, which had been cut down in the dark and was still damp, and wedged its trunk with bricks in an old copper bucket. Though an expert in Christmas pudding, Iggy had never, it seemed, heard of a Christmas tree. To his evident mystification, we were asked to decorate it with bows made from red ribbon and a few pieces of tinsel, which had seen better days. I tried to snatch a word with him, but he shook his head and then told me he had to find a place to sleep that night. He went off and asked Mrs Camm, leaving me to arrange the holly along a sideboard. As he left, I noticed the distant and also rather furtive look in his eyes, which I had seen when we were in front of the Master of the Fallen Chairs.

He returned an hour or so later wearing a mustard yellow tunic, a striped skirt of dark greens and pinks and a huge smile. Soon the guests began to arrive: Amos with his wife, Sarah, Simon Vetch and his mother and a woodsman known as Softly Perkins who had a broken neck and held his head bent forward, so that he looked benevolently from beneath his brow. In the valley he was known simply as Softly. He came carrying a violin case and wearing a limp bow tie, which he kept on straightening. Then the Colonel entered in a smoking jacket. Behind him walked the Champkin brothers, each with a drink in their hand. They were laughing and much redder in the face than before.

The atmosphere seemed a little awkward because none of the people from the valley had ever sat down for supper at the big house with the Colonel. The Colonel put an arm round Softly's shoulder and gestured to the table. 'What a spread, eh, Mr Perkins? Skirl hasn't seen it's like since before the war. And may I say that it is very good to have you all here.' Softly nodded and was guided to a seat.

The glasses and silver sparkled in the candlelight and arranged along the centre of the table was cold chicken and ham, baked potatoes, sausages and pies, freshly baked bread and cheese and mince pies. In the grate at the centre of the room a fire roared. The dogs sneaked in to lie down in front of it. Having some idea of the feast, which lay just out of their reach, their eyes never left the edge of the table.

The Colonel clinked his glass with a fork and the room fell silent. 'Where's Alba?' he asked, turning round. 'Did you tell Mrs Hockmuth that we were dining, Jebard?'

Jebard nodded. 'Yes, sir.'

'Well, it's near nine o'clock now, let us not wait for her any longer.'

Just as the conversation had resumed, the door was opened by Quake, who made a great show of standing aside to let Alba pass into the room, as though she was royalty. She took a few paces then paused and nodded to the Colonel. 'So glad to see you are recovered, dear Cousin. 'You had us all *quite* concerned.' she said, her face registering not the slightest concern.

'That's as may be,' he replied cheerily, 'but I'm doing very well now, thank you, and so is young Kim. Really, Alba, you must remember he's a Drago and a member of this household. You worked him too hard. It was wrong, and there will be no more of that over Christmas – or at any other time.' She couldn't have mistaken the criticism.

Everyone's eyes had gone to her. Her black hair was pinned up with jewelled hairpins that glinted as her head moved. She wore a long, black velvet dress that was fitted tightly at the waist and rose to a high collar where it was edged with dark turquoise silk. The dress was fastened at the front and at the sleeves with pearl buttons. Under one arm she carried a small black evening handbag and in her right hand a red fan fixed to a tortoiseshell handle.

She held herself so straight that she seemed to be by far the tallest person in the room. But it was her skin that was so startling in its unearthly whiteness. Her eyes and lips were made up with such care it was as if an artist had painted them on a piece of canvas. She moved slowly to the end of the table, hardly turning her head, but nevertheless taking everything in and making her disdain felt.

'Come along, Alba, hurry up,' said the Colonel. 'We'd like to start.'

Alba sat down at the far end next to one of the Champkin brothers and nodded formally to him. Quake, who was equally spruced up for the occasion with a special handkerchief, tie and waistcoat, took the chair to her left and exchanged smiles with both Champkins. I longed to tell the brothers how, only a few hours before, Alba and Quake had been bullying me.

Grace was said in Latin by the Colonel, then he raised his glass to the table. 'You all bring much warmth and happiness to Skirl. I welcome each one of you to this old room where my family has dined for hundreds of years.' He checked himself as a sad memory flooded his face for a second. 'I...I...I want to take this opportunity to wish you all a very Happy Christmas and to thank Alice Camm who, with Mrs Vetch and Sarah, has performed a miracle in the kitchen this evening. Please raise your glasses to Mrs Camm, Sarah and Mrs Vetch,' he said, putting his glass to his lips. Iggy grinned and gave Alice one of his bows, but did not pick up the glass of dark red wine in front of him.

'It's odd,' said the Colonel, still addressing the table, 'how the Drago family is suddenly renewed after so many tragedies. Last winter I was pleased to welcome my distant cousin Mrs Hockmuth to Skirl. Alba, as you know, has spent most of her life in Austria, but she now takes a keen interest in the running of the old place, and I am grateful to her for the time and energy she gives us.'

Alba's face remained impassive but she jerked the fan just beneath her chin. Quake shook his head in agreement, and wiped his lip with the tip of his finger.

'Then along came young Kim – as if to underline a fact that I had all but forgotten – that the Dragos have a future! He is a Greenwood by name, but there is much of the Dragos in him.

'Then out of the blue came Mr Ma-tuu Clava.' He paused. 'Or Iggy, as young Kim likes to call him.' He took a sip of wine. 'I firmly believe that Mr Ma-tuu Clava is a member of the Drago family. Indeed, I am certain of it. In the year 1863 my ancestor Clive Endymion Drago left this house and renounced all claim to his inheritance. We know quite a bit of what happened to him because Clive Endymion was a scrupulous, if an infrequent, correspondent. Letters arrived at Skirl and eventually a small boat was ordered and built to carry him on missionary work through the Southern seas. It's really quite a story, and as I read his letters I can tell you I found myself warming to the black sheep of the family. He was a good deal better than most of them, and certainly a kinder, nicer, more interesting fellow than my own grandfather Rufus.'

Alba had begun to fan her face more vigorously and was looking about the room with boredom. The Colonel smiled at her. 'I will not be long, Alba, but since you have not met Mr Ma-tuu Clava, I did want to show you that he is indeed the person he says he is.'

'Dear Cousin,' said Alba regretfully. 'You cannot

expect me to believe this person shares the same blood as you or I. Having been informed of all the relevant details, I feel it's clear that the man's an impostor. He has no proof for the claims he makes.'

The Colonel shook his head and withdrew an envelope from his pocket and laid it on the table. 'I think I may have the proof that you desire. This is a letter written by Clive in 1867. It's one of the last that reached Skirl. In it he announces that he has married a good woman of native birth and that the union has produced two children. I read this letter for the first time last night. It is part of a bundle which was passed to me by my father many years ago.' He drew a deep breath and looked around the table. 'I am sorry to labour you all with this before the festivities but I want to put everyone's mind at rest with this little test for Mr Ma-tuu Clava.' He glanced at Iggy, who wore his most open and simple expression. 'Iggy – may I call you that? – Clive Endymion Drago had at least two children. I wonder if you could give us the names of those children and of his wife.'

All eyes were turned to Iggy. Except for the crackling of the fire the room was utterly silent. It seemed to have grown darker around the edges and the pictures on the walls had become mere shadows. It was as if the very being of the house, together with things that lurked in its most obscure recesses, were straining to hear his reply.

Suddenly he stood up, beaming and clapped his hands. 'His missus was called Lam te-Shalla – which means in English, born from a seashell, his son was called Nim Ma-tuu Clava and his girl called Aita Ma-tee Clava. My grandfather is this man, Nim Ma-tuu Clava, and he has a son called…'

'Exactly,' said the Colonel, cutting him short triumphantly. 'All those names are here in the letter. He couldn't know them unless he was the descendant of Clive. This letter has remained sealed in a box until I opened it last night, and the chances of him discovering the names independently are very slight indeed.'

'But not impossible,' Alba interjected.

The Colonel turned to face her by shifting his whole body. 'Alba, he asks for nothing. He came here with his own funds and has told the police that he plans to stay in this country no more than a matter of weeks. He makes no claim on me, or this house, you understand. No claim whatsoever. So, in the spirit of Christmas I suggest we welcome him here with all our hearts. And that's an end to the matter. Now, I ask you all to raise your glasses to Iggy Ma-tuu Clava, a long-lost son of this house.'

Iggy, who was still standing, took a bow, then broke into a song of his own language which was sung in a high voice and included the various forebears, most of whom seemed to be either called Ma-tuu or Ma-tee Clava. It was accompanied by many dramatic gestures and once or twice he put his hands to his ears and made his eyes pop. Most of his audience was startled at first but then seemed to enjoy it. Alba and Quake stared frostily down the table, their eyes fixed on a point somewhere to the left of Iggy.

When it was over he sat down and raised one hand to indicate that there was more to come and began to feel in his tunic, eventually spilling a handful of small round containers on to the table.

'What's that you have there?' asked the Colonel.

'Presents for brothers,' Iggy replied, beaming.

Each box was woven out of very thin strips of bamboo and varnished so that the greenish gold colour shone in the candlelight. Having examined the contents by squinting under each lid, he began to distribute them. Alice and Jebard opened their boxes to find a gold sovereign each and Alice exclaimed several times that this was 'Christmas

Eve proper'. The Champkin brothers received tiny scrolls of parchment painted with butterflies and birds. Amos Sprigg and Simon Vetch were awarded three fishing hooks, which Iggy insisted would catch any fish in any sea or river, no matter how wary or cunning the fish might be.

The Colonel lifted the lid on a box to find a miniature of a woman in Victorian dress. Iggy popped out of his chair and rushed round to him. 'This is mother of Clava.'

The Colonel looked amazed. 'My goodness, you're right. This is Lily Drago, my great great great grandmother and Endymion's mother. I would know her anywhere. Her portrait hangs outside my rooms and Endymion must have carried this until his death. There, Alba! What more proof to do you need?' Then, turning to Iggy, he said, 'Why the Dickens didn't you show this to me before?'

'This is my Christmas surprise for you, Brother Drago.'

In each box there was a present that delighted: Mrs Vetch and Sarah Sprigg oohed at their brooches made from seashells. Softly was overwhelmed by a tiny folding knife and looked up from beneath his brow with a crooked smile.

By now Iggy had come to stand behind my

chair. He put his hand on my shoulder. 'Brother Kim, you must open my present for you.' I prised open the lid of a box to see a pendant with a small metal lyre, formed out of two Ss facing each other. Five rigid metal prongs were fixed between them. I made to pluck one but Iggy quickly put his hand over the instrument. 'You will need this special music later,' he said, putting it on the chain and placing it around my neck.

Only two boxes remained unopened. They lay in front of Alba and Quake. 'Come along, Alba,' said the Colonel, 'don't spoil the fun. Open your present. Mr Quake, I see yours is untouched also.'

Alba was the first to move. She held the box at a distance and flipped the top off so it flew a few feet away from her. There was a small glass pot inside with a dull yellow top. She glanced coldly at Iggy, her first direct acknowledgement of him, unscrewed the top and looked at the contents with distaste, then laid the pot aside.

'It's nothing but a grey putty,' said Quake scornfully.

Dr Champkin held the pot to his nose. 'Some kind of balm,' he reported to the table. 'Very sweet to the nose! My word, I've never come across anything like it.' He sniffed again. 'Remarkable. There are layers to this smell.

Almond essence! Sweet Gale! Honey! Something like turmeric or ginger, dew on the grass and flowers in abundance. Some kind of resin is lurking in the background. Oh yes, yes, yes, and I can smell coconut and – my goodness me – the sea as well.' He looked down the table to Iggy. 'What on earth is it, Mr Ma-tuu Clava?'

'Everything on earth,' replied Iggy. 'Present for most fine lady.'

Dr Champkin passed the pot along the table for others to sample, and in each case it produced expressions of wonder. No two guests could agree on the ingredients, not even the Champkin brothers, who were at one on everything. 'I don't smell the sea, Rudi,' said Felix Champkin to his brother, 'but freshly turned soil in the garden, the embers of a bonfire at dusk just as the dew is about to settle, fresh leaves in the spring, hay, cider, mint and lavender, yes, most definitely lavender.'

Everyone summoned a distinct experience. The Colonel was taken back to his time in Egypt and the smell of the souk, the matting on his bedroom floor, newly ironed linen, the smell of leather rising from a hot saddle.

When it was my turn, my nostrils were filled with the flowers along the verandah at home, the peculiarly sweet smell of the cattle in the sun and the dead leaves of the eucalyptus trees being burned by James, the gardener – smells that I didn't even know that I had remembered.

The pot eventually made its way back to Alba and was placed in front of her by Dr Champkin. Rather than showing the terrifying cold anger that we all knew she was capable of, she seemed a little flustered. 'You open yours,' she told Quake.

Quake gingerly prised the top off his little box. When he saw what was inside he drew back and dropped it.

'It's a huge stag beetle,' cried Simon Vetch with amusement.

The creature had rolled onto his back on the tablecloth. It was dark blue and slightly larger than a matchbox.

'That's one for the collection,' cried the Colonel, enjoying Quake's discomfort. 'I'll have it, if you don't want it, Quake. Come on, Alba, tell us what you smell.'

She picked up the box and sniffed several times quickly. 'Nothing,' she said. 'I smell absolutely nothing.'

Everyone was so taken up with Quake and the beetle they didn't pay attention to what she was saying.

'Why can't she smell anything?' I whispered.

Iggy didn't reply. 'Watch, Brother Kim.'

Suddenly the beetle began to move. It righted itself and then, as though it was acting under orders, moved to face Quake, reared on its back legs and directed a squirt of liquid in Quake's direction. A much more powerful shot followed and caught him on the chin and left a sticky trail on his waistcoat. Quake cried out in horror and jumped up wiping his face furiously with a napkin. The table was in uproar.

'Most amusing beetle,' said Iggy with delight.

Eventually things quietened down. The beetle was captured and replaced in the box by Simon Vetch, and Quake returned to his chair, having been assured that the beetle was not poisonous.

'What's in Alba's box?' I asked. 'How can so many smells be fitted into one pot?'

'The spice of life,' he replied. 'All the smells of the world.'

'But why can't she smell anything?'

'That is most interesting question, Brother Kim,' he said, giving me a light smile that was designed to conceal the importance of what he was discussing from the other end of the table. Alba Hockmuth may not have been looking in our direction, yet I knew there was not a moment when she was not watching Iggy.

Chapter Ten

Into the Night

Everyone ate their fill and talked and laughed more than any of them could remember. Softly played a sweet violin and Jebard, after much persuasion and one or two glasses of sloe gin, stood up and sang country airs remembered from his youth in a surprisingly fine voice that made eyes water around the table.

Soon after this, Alba's patience gave out. She rose, complaining of being exhausted, and walked regally from the room, head held high, with Quake stalking after her. Not long afterwards the Colonel's energy suddenly waned, so he got up and thanked everyone for one of the best nights of his life. He shook us all by the hand and ushered the party from the front door into the bitterly cold night, then went off to bed.

'There's a storm coming,' said Jebard when we

were alone. 'Snow's on its way, and wind too, and they speak of it staying.' He did not leave for his own cottage immediately, but instead led us to our rooms at the back of the house with a hurricane light. 'A grand evening, warn't it?' he said on the way. 'Good for the old house. Good for us all to have a bit of fun. Now, don't you go spoiling things by getting into mischief.'

When we reached our rooms, he handed me the lamp and a box of matches. 'That's in case the electric goes down.' He looked at us hard, murmured something and sat down heavily on a chest outside my room. 'You're to stay in your rooms till morning. Do you hear?' He searched our faces for signs of compliance. His eyes were kindly but in deadly earnest. Iggy nodded but Jebard wasn't convinced. 'I mean what I says. Something's afoot. It always gets bad at this time of the year. But this year…well it's worse. You may hear noises, but don't pay them any attention. You leave them be and they'll leave you be.'

'Who's *they*?' I asked innocently.

'You know very well what I'm talking about, Kim Greenwood, and so does your friend here. So don't pretend otherwise.'

'Has this got something to do with the old house and the Lines of Tarle?'

162

'I don't know about any Lines of Tarle. Maybe the old house comes into it but that don't need to concern you. You're in the modern part of Skirl. Leave the old house to its own devices tonight. Don't you go messing with Stinking Billy, Old Havoc or any of the others because you'll come off the worse, I warn you.'

'Who are *they*?'

'You'd try the patience of a saint with your questions, Kim. Take a leaf out of Mr MacTulava's book. He don't go asking questions, do he? But just so as you know, they're the names given to the spirits that are seen at this time of year.'

'Does the Colonel know about them?'

'Course not. He don't need to bother hisself with these things. My father told me about them and before that his father told him, and nothing's changed since them days. Have I got your word on this?'

'We won't go in the old part of the house tonight,' I said, thinking that it would be easy to navigate a route to the room where the picture hung by going round the bits of the old house that I knew of.

'Right,' said Jebard, heaving himself to his feet. 'I'll bid you a happy Christmas for tomorrow and be off to my own bed.'

With this he shuffled off into to the dark. I called after him. 'Does the name Silverfish mean anything to you?'

He mumbled something to himself then said, 'Never heard of anyone of that name. Good night to you both and remember what I said to you.'

We went into our bedrooms and closed our doors, but no sooner had the sound of Jebard's footsteps disappeared from the corridor than Iggy was with me, dressed in his hat, boots and one of his collection of overcoats. He held a long stick, which he said he'd found earlier. I put on my warmest clothes, for I knew the house would be freezing, and out of habit slung my bag over my shoulder.

'What do you need that for?' I said, pointing to Iggy's stick.

'You will see. Come, we don't have much time.'

'I want to know what's on your map.' I said. 'Why won't you let me see it?'

He looked shiftily at me. 'Which maps?'

'I'm not going anywhere until you show me,' I said. 'I have a right to see it.'

Then he smiled. 'There are two maps.'

This was news to me.

'I show them to you now.' He felt in his clothes and pulled out the Bible then spread two pieces of paper on my little table. 'First map has Lines of Tarle with house inside, Old Man of Tarle and little hill called Sennaks's Mound and maybe this is wishing well,' he said, pointing to some crude drawing near the top left hand corner.

I agreed. 'Clive must have copied it from the book I wanted to show you. Only it's gone. There were interesting squares of letters in it too. I thought they might be codes.'

He nodded.

'Do you know what these symbols mean?'

He lifted his shoulders and frowned with puzzlement. I began to study the second map, which was also crudely drawn, but gave a detailed plan of the house. I couldn't remember seeing this one in the book and wondered whether Clive had made it for his own reference. 'Look!' I said. 'It shows where the old house stood and where the picture of the Master of the Fallen Chairs is.'

'And other picture. We go now to see other picture.'

He checked the little instrument around my neck. 'Make music if there is danger,' he said.

'Is this magic like the smelling pot you gave Alba?'

'Small magic only,' Iggy said.

'What about the big magic you were going to

borrow from the Old Man of Tarle? Why didn't you ask him?'

'He gave us information. To investigator like me that is big magic.'

'Oh, I thought you were going to ask for some serious magical powers.'

'Come, Brother Kim, no more talk.'

I thought we were going straight to the picture of the fallen chairs, but Iggy led me off to the centre of the house near the courtyard. We ended up in one of the first-floor passages that were filled with pictures and dusty tapestries, but not much else, and came to a T-shaped dead end. Either side of us was a run of three stone steps, which led down into a kind of large alcove, around which were hung more portraits. I had never been here before. It was damp and very cold and there was a mustiness in the air. Iggy consulted the map and chose the steps on our left. Then he took the lamp from me and prepared to fix the handle in the cleft at the top of his stick. He peered up at the walls then found what he was looking for and hoisted the lamp above.

'This other picture,' he said.

Above us was a beautiful frame of carved wood flecked with gold, and within that frame was a woman in Elizabethan dress with a high ruff that hid all of her neck. Between the thumb and forefinger of her left hand she held a key and in her right hand she clasped a white fan, which rested against the jewelled bodice of her dress. Iggy brought the light closer to the painting and we saw how fine and rich her clothes were. Pearls and precious stones were sewn into the sleeves of the dress, and beneath the ruff was a gold necklace from which hung three rings. The woman was young – no more than eighteen, I guessed – but we knew instantly who she was. The incredible whiteness of her skin, the flared nostrils, the set of her mouth and the prominent eyebrows belonged to Alba Hockmuth. The same steady gaze that we had seen at the other end of the table only a few of hours before now looked down upon us, though in the portrait it was less obviously superior, and there was none of the threat that I was used to seeing in her expression.

Her head was turned slightly so that you could only see one of her well-shaped ears, but from that ear hung the tiny gold figure of a man. It was much smaller than the one I had seen in my dream yet I could just make out the same struggling movement in his arms frozen for all time.

'This painting is well over 300 years old. How can she still be alive? Is she a ghost?' As I asked the questions I knew it couldn't be as simple as that. I myself had felt her breath when she was screaming at me in the blue drawing room. She was as alive as me, or Iggy.

Iggy lowered the lamp to a panel on the bottom of the frame and I stood on tiptoes to read it. '*Countess Ahrinnia Hecht,*' I read out loud. '*Mistress of Skirl, wife of Sir Henry Drago. Believed to have been born in Hungary to the Margrave of Hartzberg and Princess Erzesebet of Bohemia in the year of our Lord 1544.*' I looked up at the picture again. 'I don't understand. Are they the same person? Can Alba Hockmuth be the same person as Countess Ahrinnia Hecht?'

He nodded.

'But how can that be?'

'I am thinking this woman...she comes here from older time and then goes back to older time.'

'Is that what ghosts are? Do they travel forward in time like that?'

'No,' he replied, shaking his head slowly. 'She is not ghost. She comes from other time. She is living.'

'But she couldn't smell the magic in your pot.'

'This is true because beautiful lady has heart full of worms.'

'Worms!'

'Yes,' he said with a look that implied I was being stupid.

'Does she come over the Tarle Steps?'

He shook his head. 'I not know, Brother Kim.'

He put the lamp even closer to the picture and stood on tiptoes.

'Ah-ha! Here is secret writing. Fetch chair.'

I dragged a large oak chair over to the picture and Iggy mounted it.

'Hold light, Brother Kim.'

He began to trace a faint inscription along the bottom of the painting, which had been disguised by an intricate pattern of golden threads in her dress. Because the old script was difficult for Iggy to read I got up beside him and we worked it out together.

'It's a poem,' I said and began to read.

Uncage her beauty from the bars of death!
Give this fairness forever life and breath
Unslave her radiance from earth's distress
Make this woman for all time Time's mistress
And with this painted secret I do impart
No small measure, but my traveller's heart.

The verse was dated 1562. I looked at Iggy. 'You know what this means?' I said, 'She's been alive for over 400 years! Imagine that.'

This interested Iggy less than the idea that someone had loved her so passionately that they might have given her certain secrets that would preserve her beauty. He repeated the line, 'Give this fairness forever life and breath,' as though he were trying to drum the unfamiliar construction into his head.

'Maybe I know someone who can help us,' I said. 'The great auk in the Long Gallery.'

'Auk? What is great auk?'

'A bird, a funny looking bird that talks. I forgot to tell you about her.' I lowered my voice just as Bella had done when she talked to me. 'Follow me,' I whispered.

We tore through the house, with the shadows from the hurricane lamp pursuing us along the walls. On the way up the stairs to the Long Gallery I paused to glance through a tall window. The snow lay an inch or two thick on all of the stonework outside. I could just make out the greyish glow of a snowy landscape although the snow was now falling fast...

We tumbled into the Long Gallery and rushed to the chest where the old bird stood. 'We've come to ask you some questions,' I said, putting the light down on the floor. 'Will you help us?'

Nothing happened. The bird did not move a

muscle. Its feathers remained limp, its eyes the dull glass of a museum exhibit. 'Will you help us?' I begged. 'I know you can hear us.'

'This bird does not talk,' said Iggy.

'Perhaps if we turn away and go over to those cabinets, she might begin to talk,' I said. 'Besides, there are things over there that you should see.'

I pulled out the albums and showed him the photographs of Clive Endymion Drago and the women who bore him children. Just when we were most absorbed, the bird came to life.

'What are you doing in here again?' The voice was croaky and had none of the lustre of before. 'Why are you bothering me again?'

I ran back to the chest, dragging Iggy with me.

'I wanted to ask you about Ahrinnia Hecht. Is she the same person as Alba Hockmuth?'

'And who is this?' asked the bird, turning her huge, mournful eyes on Iggy.

He glanced at the notice then bowed extravagantly. 'Oh great bird, it is honour to meet you. Igthy Ma-tuu Clava, Lord of Ro-Torva presents compliments to magnificent bird of Northern seas.'

The bird seemed satisfied by this and looked at me as though I could take a lesson or two in manners from Iggy. I explained Iggy and Clive's line of the family in the South Seas, how he had come to the house and how I was helping him find out about the picture. The bird looked bored but when I mentioned that Iggy came from a group of islands in the Pacific where supplies of fish were plentiful, its curiosity picked up.

'Is Alba the same person as Ahrinnia Hecht?'

'Shush,' said the bird. 'Of course she is. But keep your voice down.'

'Is she a ghost?'

'No. There are many shades of existence between the quick and the dead.'

'Why she here?' asked Iggy.

'She comes in winter, in a different disguise for each new generation and with a different story, too, so that she can move freely among the people who live in the house at any time she chooses. That is the story I have gathered over many years of listening and watching. People speak freely in front of me because they do not know I can hear.'

'Why didn't you tell me this before?' I asked.

'You didn't ask.' The bird raised its beak and looked the other way. 'In my position, I must use my discretion, and that includes not answering questions that I have not been asked. That is my policy.'

'What about the book – the book with all the

diagrams that was in your chest? Who took it?'

'The young maid, of course. The gentle one. She came one night and she moved me and took the book. She knew what she was looking for. I concluded that you had told her about it.'

'Yes, I did, but I didn't know she would take it without me being here,' I said, wishing I had had the sense to remove it. All we needed to know was in that book. After all it was from its pages that Iggy's maps had been copied. I asked Iggy why Clive hadn't taken the book with him to the Southern Seas and he replied that Clive probably left it at Skirl because he wanted someone to find it.

'What's going on here?' I asked the bird. 'Why are there so many spirits? What are they doing?'

'How would I know?'

'Because you're a ghost,' I said, and instantly realised that it would hurt the bird's feelings.

'I am not a ghost! I do not haunt anything except my own body! If I am a ghost, you are a ghost. I remain here to bear witness to the fate of my species – the noble great auk. That is my purpose. That is my mission!' She paused. 'I will tell you what I have picked up over the years, as long as you undertake to tell the world the story of the great auk. Do you promise?'

I nodded.

'And your friend, he must tell my story too.'

'I will tell Iggy the story and then I am sure he will.'

'Very well...hundreds of year ago, a young woman came as a child bride to Skirl.'

'Ahrinnia Hecht,' I said.

'Don't interrupt,' said the bird. 'Her name was indeed Ahrinnia Hecht. She came all the way from a place where there is no sea with her own title and her own magic. She was young and at first she pined for her homeland, but then she began to love Skirl because of its special powers. Skirl is not just an old house you know, but a place of great importance. She bore Sir Henry Drago three fine sons and they grew up and married. When Sir Henry died there was a great falling out between the sons, for each laid claim to the estate. Two of the brothers fought and one was run through by the other's sword here in this very room. I believe he died not far from where you were standing, over there by the cabinet where there is a stain on the floor. Then the remaining two brothers fought a duel: both were wounded and died within days. You see! You see! The mother had pitted her sons against each other

174

so she could remain Mistress of Skirl. The only thing she cared about was this house, and so it remains. She comes through the centuries to watch over this place and make sure that everything is as she wants it. That is the story of Ahrinnia Hecht or Alba Hockmuth....' She stopped and looked at us. 'And now we have reached the time of *Renewal*. Though this does not concern me.'

'Renewal? What's that?'

'I am not sure. I have only been here for one time of Renewal. All hell broke loose. It is the time when there is maximum...er...agitation. It happens every hundred years when the powers of this place are at their height.'

Iggy coughed politely. 'Honourable bird, who is woman's lover? Who wrote this poem on old painting of her?'

To my astonishment, he repeated the poem word perfect –

Uncage her beauty from the bars of death!
Give this fairness forever life and breath
Unslave her radiance from earth's distress
Make this woman for all time Time's mistress
And with this painted secret I do impart
No small measure, but my traveller's heart

'Who is traveller?'

The bird raised its wings. 'This is all before my time. I can't tell you.'

Iggy changed the subject. 'Do ghosts serve this woman?'

'Yes, there are ancient spirits here that have become the essence of themselves through the powers of this place and they attend to her every need and command...that is what I have heard, at least. Naturally I have nothing to do with that.'

'So she's not dead?' I said.

'No, she lives for a few weeks in the present each year, much more during Renewal, but returns to the past so that she does not become old. The rest of them...are dead.'

'And you are neither,' I said. 'Neither dead nor alive?'

'If you want to know what I am, I will tell you. I am *nailed* to this old board and I would very much like to be un-nailed. Would you be so kind as to un-nail me, after all that I have done for you?'

'Honourable bird shall be un-nailed,' said Iggy and he began to tug with his gloved hands at the nails. But not until he used the blunt side of a penknife did he manage to lever them out.

The bird raised her huge webbed feet one by one. 'It's evidently going to take some time for the circulation to return,' she sniffed, but she did look happier. We thanked her for her help and, assuring her that we would never forget the extinction of the great auk, and never lose an opportunity to tell people about it, we left and went from the Long Gallery into the great hushed gloom of Skirl.

Chapter Eleven

Old Havoc

The blizzard seemed to intensify as the night wore on, probing the house and finding all the gaps under the doors and every cracked windowpane. Powdery snow swirled in eddies in the corridors and in some places little drifts had formed on the stone floors.

As we made our way to the picture of the fallen chairs I asked Iggy why the Colonel didn't know Alba from the old portrait of Ahrinnia Hecht.

'Confounded mystery,' Iggy replied, then he said that he thought the picture might be able to change, or that the Colonel was simply an unobservant man. He mentioned that the same symbol appeared by both paintings on the map and that this might mean that they had 'big magic', or that they were at least both important.

'What is big magic? Have you ever seen any big magic?'

'Yes, I am detective of big magic. This is my speciality.'

'I thought you were a specialist in murder – "the foul play mostly", is what you said.'

'That is profession. Big magic is hobby.'

After a few more paces, I asked, 'Was your father before three – Clive Endymion Drago – trying to escape the curse of the painting when he went away?'

'I believe it,' he replied. 'He knew about these things. Remember the Bible where he write clues. He came to my island but then one day he was eaten by big fish. Very big fish.'

'A shark?'

'Yes, a shark.'

I stopped in my tracks. 'The gargoyle in the picture of the fallen chairs – that ugly sculpture of a fish on the roof in the painting: there's something in its mouth. The head's tilted backwards as though it's swallowing something.'

'I know, Brother Kim, I saw fish before.'

'Why didn't you say?'

'Ghost came to make writing on the floor.'

He led me to a pair of oak library steps, which stood in the room where Quake taught me.

We folded them and lugged them through the house to set up right in front of the painting. At the top of the steps was a kind of platform used for books, which I was able to sit on so that my legs dangled over the side. Iggy climbed up behind me and swept the room with the lantern. There was nothing there and not a trace of the writing that had appeared.

He turned the light on the picture. The first thing I noticed was that it had been painted on a thick wooden panel, not on canvas, as I had assumed. From the ground, it still looked clumsy but when I got really close – within a few inches – it seemed much bigger and better painted. I felt myself being drawn into its world and the longer I looked, the more real things appeared. There was damp on the stonework of the building, wind in the trees, and the waters of the river sparkled. I noticed many new details that I hadn't been able to see from below. For instance, there seemed to be figures lurking in the shadows of doorways and in the windows there were reflections of people inside the house who were watching the disasters going on all around. I glanced up at the big carved fish on the roof and saw a single bare leg sticking out of its mouth, and nudged Iggy. Way up behind the house in some woods there was a man falling into a fire. Near him was another man, no bigger than my finger, tumbling from an apple tree. These might have been taken for a joke, but being a few inches away we could see their terrified grimaces.

Iggy murmured something. I turned to him to ask him what the matter was. He told me that his grandfather had died in a mysterious fire out in the jungle and that his uncle, Man Li-tuu Clava, had been killed when a high wind blew him from a coconut tree and impaled him on some fishing harpoons stacked beneath the tree.

Then there was a drowning by the bridge and the evidence of someone falling from a window, which we had seen before. Five deaths, three of which were in Iggy's family. There was much else waiting for us: a man being crushed by falling brickwork in a distant part of the walled garden, another individual seemingly being swallowed by the earth in a little grove of trees off to the left. And there was evidence of Francis Drago's drowning, which the great auk had mentioned. A pair of riding boots was caught in a thicket and behind this we saw a riderless horse contentedly grazing in the meadow.

Eventually we counted eleven deaths to match the eleven toppled chairs, but there was no clue as to how the Master of the Fallen Chairs intended us to die. Iggy thought that maybe there weren't any clues to find. Maybe the painting changed once a death had occurred but did not predict the manner of the death beforehand.

I raised myself on the platform, holding onto his shoulder, and discovered a stone set into the brickwork of the house over the front door. I knew this didn't exist in real life. Moving the lantern to the surface of the painting, I was able to read the words, 'Death to the *Dragomen*.'

'Dragomen!' I exclaimed. 'That must mean that only *men* die because of this painting.' Iggy nodded. He knew that I was thinking of my mother's death.

'Does this mean the Colonel will be killed?' I asked.

He wrinkled his brow and thought. 'No need. His sons die. He is old and he will die soon. So picture does not need to kill him. There is no chair for him.'

The next discovery came beneath the carved stone. It was a date written in Roman numerals: 'XXV.XII.MDCCCLXII.' – 25th December 1862. The picture had been completed exactly 100 years before – on Christmas Day, 1862. Then I noticed the clock on the bell tower above the coach house in the courtyard. The real one had stopped working years ago but in the painting the hands both touched twelve. Twelve o'clock, Christmas Day. Was that the time we had to beat? But which twelve o'clock? Midday, or midnight? Iggy considered this for a moment then pointed to the moon in the sky. He thought it was midnight, but he wasn't certain. Either way, we had exactly twelve or twenty-four hours to stop those chairs falling. At that very moment, we heard a distant chiming of clocks round the house, each in turn signalling that Christmas Eve had turned to Christmas Day.

I crouched down to sit on the platform again.

'Happy Christmas, Brother Kim,' Iggy said. I was so close to him I could see the flecks in his eyes and the tiny freckles that swarmed either side of his nose. He was smiling but I could see the worry in his eyes.

'What are we going to do?' I asked.

'Old Man of Tarle. I am thinking that the Watchman he see us now as before.' He stopped. 'Others see us now too.' His hand drifted to the left side of the house in the painting to a room with large windows. It took me a few moments before I realised that he was pointing to the very room that we were in at that moment. And

184

behind the carefully painted windows things seemed to be stirring – odd shapes that you couldn't put a name to. I shuddered. Iggy placed a hand on my shoulder.

'What's the matter?' I asked.

'Not turn your head, Brother Kim. *Not!*' His hand gripped me. But another force was turning my head and when I saw the figure on the far side of the room, I nearly fell clean off the steps.

Standing silently in a pool of light on the far side of the room was a boy. His knees were bruised, his arms were scratched and his cheeks were dirty and streaked with tears. It was unmistakably me, though he was not dressed as I was in a coat, scarf and sweater, but in a shirt and shorts.

'It not you, Brother Kim! This Old Havoc. He pretends he is you. Turn away!'

'Why? How?' I stammered, unable to look at the wretched image of myself. Then all the sadness of my life that I'd done so much to try to forget hit me like a punch in my stomach, and overwhelmed me.

'This big magic, Brother Kim. Old Havoc play his tricks. He tries to frighten us.'

Seconds passed. Then the image of me crumpled to his knees in despair and seemed to utter a silent scream before disappearing. All that was left in the room was a faint disturbance around us – a crackling noise and the thin, distorted voices, which I remembered sometimes broke into the programmes on Jebard's radio in the kitchen.

'Old Havoc doesn't want us looking at the picture,' said Iggy.

'How…how…do you know it was Old Havoc?' I stammered.

'Father before three,' he said without offering further explanation. 'Look at picture.'

'But there's nothing more for us to see,' I said. 'It's useless. We only have a few hours. There's nothing we can do'.

'Brother Kim, we will stop these chairs falling,' he said, patting me on the back and rubbing my shoulder. I shifted on the platform and moved the lantern closer to the painting.

'Look, look,' I exclaimed after a few moments. 'The Old Man of Tarle has moved away from the fire. He used to be standing right by it, but now he's come down to the edge of the frame.' That wasn't the only thing that had changed while we weren't looking. The ravens had moved to a spot near the Old Man of Tarle; the white hare had streaked away from the hunting dogs and seemed to be heading across the hills to the place where one of the victims had fallen into a hole in the earth. This was much larger now, and in the newly made hollow I noticed there was water – deep black water bubbling from the ground – and I thought of the wishing well where Bella Brown had been found.

'What's it all mean?' I asked.

Iggy gave me baffled look, then returned to the figure of the Old Man of Tarle and the ravens. He raised his finger. 'We will go to the bridge now and visit Old Man.'

'It's snowing. It may be difficult.'

He stroked his chin. 'Old Man has many questions to answer. Like who painted this picture and who loved bad lady.' He pointed to the inscription, '"QUI MAGISTRUM SELLARUM DELAP-SARUM MAGISTRAVERIT SUPERERIT UT REM REFERAT." Same writing as poem.'

Of course it was. 'So whoever painted this is likely to have done the portrait of Alba.'

'But they are hundreds of years apart.'

Iggy gave a rapid nod. 'Brother Kim is certainly very clever. We go to bridge now.'

He was right. It was the only thing to do. But no sooner had we climbed down from the steps than we became aware of another presence. I clutched Iggy's arm.

A young girl of about my age in a grey and white dress was standing stock still in the middle of the room. She smiled at us meekly. She seemed familiar to me, though I couldn't think why. Slowly she raised her arm to point to the door we had come through. She nodded her head encouragingly and made a sweeping gesture with her other hand, as if to shoo us out of the room.

'What shall we do?' I whispered.

'Wait,' Iggy replied.

When we didn't show any signs of leaving, the ghost became agitated. She kept on looking over her shoulder and drawing the hair from her face anxiously. Then we realised that she was not alone. There were others, not as distinct as she was, but we could see they were dressed in rags and were terribly thin. Most of them were women, but there were one or two children and some exceptionally haggard looking men, who seemed much weaker than the rest – mere outlines, drawn by some ethereal chalk in the night. The effort of showing themselves to us seemed to cost them dear. They flickered as we looked upon them and none would engage our eyes. They were aware of our presence, that much was clear, but it seemed they could not look on us, or rather into our eyes. When they did, we could see it caused them immense pain. The grimaces of the child ghosts were heartbreaking to behold and their glances made me wonder if they were yearning for the unthinking luxury of our flesh and blood.

'What do they want?' I hissed. Then I shouted out to them: 'Tell us what you want!'

The girl just kept on pointing to the door and now the others joined in, reaching towards us and gesturing with frantic motions towards the door.

Iggy took my hand. 'Maybe they try to help us, Brother Kim. They are good ghosts.'

I was sure they were trying to warn us of some impending danger and nodded.

We were just about to leave the room when the double doors at the far end crashed open and a light shone through. To my astonishment, Trumpet and Applejack, the two terriers that never usually strayed far from the kitchen, shot into the room and ran towards the line of ghosts without the slightest fear, and started worrying and snapping at them. The wisps of beings were thrown into a panic and darted hither and thither in flurries of phosphorescence that quickly decayed into the dark.

Through the doors came Jebard, grey-faced and sleepy, holding a lantern that brought a strange glow to the room, much brighter than the light given off by ours. I was relieved to see him, though I knew he'd have something to say about us disobeying his instructions. And he'd certainly want to know what we had been doing in the room with the library steps. The expression in his face didn't alter and he said nothing, but beckoned urgently towards us.

Without thinking, I rushed towards him. Iggy hesitated then followed.

That was our big mistake.

Chapter Twelve

Slipcandle

The moment we were through the double doors they shut behind us with an almighty bang. Jebard was nowhere to be seen and Applejack and Trumpet had evaporated like the spirits they'd just been chasing. I called out, wondering why the dogs hadn't scampered into the light to welcome us. But there was no movement of any sort. I turned to Iggy with a question on my lips but his expression answered it: whatever had summoned us was not Tom Jebard.

We were alone in a room, which was odd because I knew from my rambles round the house that on the other side of these particular double doors lay a long dark passageway. Iggy took a few paces and looked around. I moved with him, being careful not to stray from the pool of light. I had the sense of being in a forest at night, a forest that stretched for miles and miles and contained unimaginable horrors.

'That wasn't Jebard, was it?' I said.

'Old Havoc.' He replied. 'He copies you. He copies Mister Jebard and dogs. He is a very powerful ghost with many tricks. Big magic is here.'

I shuddered. 'Where are we?'

'Ghost of a house.'

I took this in, 'You mean the old house, the house that used to stand here.'

Iggy nodded slowly. 'We are in the place that lives beside us.'

'What people call the other side,' I said. 'We have to go back. We've got to get through the doors and go back into that room.'

'No, we cannot, Brother Kim.'

I looked around. We had taken only a few paces but there was no sign of the doors; just a long stretch of bare stone wall.

A weird thought occurred to me. 'Does it mean we're dead?' I heard the panic rising in my voice again.

He shook his head and moved his hand to my cheek so I could feel the warmth of his skin. 'You not dead, Brother Kim. And Igthy Ma-tuu Clava alive and ticking.'

'It's alive and *kicking*,' I said. 'Not ticking!'

He shrugged and started humming and tapping his foot.

Then, a minute or two later, we saw a very faint glimmer of light. As it approached I noticed a strange smell rising up around us. Suddenly we were fighting for our breath. It was like nothing else I had ever smelled in my life. Like sticky air, the stench slipped around us and enveloped our bodies, invading our hair, touching our faces and coating us with the smell of death. I covered my face with my scarf but nothing could stop it and within a few seconds both of us had fallen to our knees with our eyes streaming and our lungs gasping for air.

'Play the music,' Iggy croaked. 'Make music with harp.'

I fumbled for the harp and began to pluck the prongs furiously.

'Put in front of mouth,' shouted Iggy and then clamped his hands over his face.

I held it up and struck the instrument again so that a tinny twanging sounded in the hollow of my mouth. It was all I could do to stop myself from vomiting, yet I managed to continue for I knew our lives depended on it. In my panic, I noticed that however randomly I plucked the prongs, the notes fell from my mouth and took off by themselves to become music, and instead of fading they grew louder and louder. The ball of light came to a halt and began to tremble. Vapours were still seeping from its interior and stealing across the floor like a heavy gas, but the smell had lessened and we were able to scramble to our feet and fight for our breath.

The thing seemed to be pondering its next move, and while doing so the light pulsed and an audible growl of frustration came from its centre. Then, quite suddenly the light was no more, and we were confronted by a man dressed in a long velvet jacket of pale green, and breeches. He was bending over with his bottom facing us.

'It must be Stinking Billy,' I shouted.

'A ghost that talks through his rear end,' said Iggy.

A face turned to peek a look at us, evidently certain that we couldn't see it. The skin was a dusty white and he seemed to be wearing rouge and lipstick. He held on to a grey wig with one hand while the other reached to part his coat tails over a very round velvet bottom.

'Stinking Billy is fart ghost,' said Iggy, approaching the smelly phantom. 'Fart ghost is very small magic.' With this he jumped forward and raised his hands before bringing them down to his face and pulling his mouth wide open with his fingers. His eyes popped and stared and from the deepest part of his being came a high-pitched yell. At the same time he stamped his feet down one in front of the other, slowly edging towards Stinking Billy until he was within a few feet. Then he lowered his arms and grimaced. Suddenly the ghost realised that he had become visible to us and tried to hide his face. Without thinking, I ran towards him shrieking and aimed a kick at his bottom. Instead of passing through him, my boot encountered a spongy mass, as though I had hit a tuft of sphagnum moss. By his expression, I knew Stinking Billy had felt the blow too and he let out a howl of pain, then he reeled sideways before sending one more evil smell in our direction. It was far worse than before and my eyes were stinging yet we could see he was beaten because he was beginning to fade. Soon there was nothing but a smudge of light in the air.

'This Lord of Stink is one-trick pony,' Iggy said, turning round to me with a triumphant look on his face. 'See! We alive and *kicking*.'

I managed a smile, wiped the tears from my eyes and cleared my throat. 'Let's look for a way out,' I said. 'There's not much oil left in the lamp.'

We set off in the direction that we'd come from but soon realised that we had lost our bearings. It was as if the Skirl I knew no longer existed. We heard none of the familiar sounds like the wind blowing or the clocks chiming, just our footsteps echoing around us. We trudged along dark narrow corridors for what seemed like hours, occasionally turning into rooms on the way. These were all deserted and mostly bare. But one or two panelled chambers, some of which were not much bigger than a closet, had a few pieces of furniture. I thought of them as monks' cells because they each had a little reading desk and in one we found a quill laid down by a pot of dried ink.

We were beginning to despair. Even Iggy looked downcast. But then I saw an arch that I recognised because on either side of it there were empty niches. In the newer house these had been bricked up and plastered over, but the outlines of the stone poked through the wall so you could see where the arch had been. I explained to Iggy that we were on the eastern flank of Skirl, not far from the courtyard and stable block. Maybe there was a way back here. But of course there was no sign of the newer building. The arch just led through to another passageway, which had long vanished in the modern house.

'It's useless,' I said after feeling the stone, hoping that I could somehow push myself into the parallel world of the living. 'We're trapped here forever.'

'Still have time, Brother Kim. That's why they led us here. They are thinking we know secrets of picture.'

'But we don't,' I whispered.

Iggy looked down at me. He mouthed some words, making no sound at all. He was telling me that they didn't know that. Then he cocked his head to the emptiness. 'Something is here,' he whispered. 'It watches now.'

'Who?'

'Maybe Missus Alba. I can feel something big here. Big magic.'

There was a rushing sound all around us; lights were streaking past us and before I knew what had happened, the oil ran out in our lamp, and the flame guttered. I clutched at Iggy's arm but felt him being wrenched away from me, and then for a split second I saw what had grabbed hold of him because it illuminated itself with a furious glow – a scrawny creature with sinuous legs and arms and bulging muscles. Then an impish face flashed in the gloom – a horrible exultant face with reddish skin that was blistered and peeling. It had seized hold of Iggy's other arm and with each tug was sending an electric shock that shot through Iggy and into me, which made it very difficult for me to keep hold of him. There was the sound of a whip cracking in the air and sparks were flying about. I lifted the harp to my mouth, but because we were being hurled around so violently by the creature I couldn't keep it there long enough to make a sound. I dropped it and held on for dear life to Iggy's coat. But I wasn't strong enough and after a few more tugs Iggy slipped from my grasp and was gone.

The terrible noise died and I was left in silence and darkness. I cast around in the gloom calling out Iggy's name, but no answer came. I don't know how long I remained there, wishing we had stayed in our rooms that night and left the painting until morning. I couldn't stop thinking about the thing that had snatched Iggy, its dreadful face and the savage power in its arms. I saw his helpless expression and I knew that none of his tiny bits of magic or pulling of faces would work with a demon like that. There was a glimmer of hope left in my terrified brain. If we had been tricked into coming from our world to the other side and the ghosts had moved from their domain to ours, it must be possible for me to go back again. I began walking.

Soon I became aware of a scuffling beside me. Then a silky little voice came out of the gloom.

'Be my friend,' it whispered. 'Please, be my friend.'

I was shocked at first, but then I tried to reply in my most normal voice. 'Go away, whatever you are. I'm going back to where I belong, and there's nothing that will stop me.'

'And, where do you belong?' asked the voice with amusement.

'In the world of the living,' I snapped. 'Now, get away from me, whatever you are.'

'T'ain't so bad to be my friend, I can show you things.' It was then that I remembered the words that had appeared in my exercise book when I wasn't looking – 'Be my friend – Silverfish.'

'Have you been writing messages to me?' I asked. 'Was it you who wrote that thing in the dust about Bella Brown? Are you called Silverfish? Where are you?'

'Be my friend and I will show myself.' I saw nothing, but whatever had joined me was very close.

'I already have a friend,' I said. 'But he was taken away by one of your kind.'

'Firebrat took him and I am *not* of his kind. Firebrat is an ancient, evil spirit.'

'He looked like a devil straight from hell.'

'But I'm not from hell. My name is Silverfish. Be my friend, Boy.'

'And mine's Kim. So don't call me *Boy*.'

'Be my friend, *Boy*,' said the voice mischievously and then darted round me singing something.

'Get away,' I shouted.

'There ain't no need to shout. It's rude to shout. Silverfish is kind and loving. Come, take my little paw and be the friend of Silverfish. I wish you no harm.'

'I can't see your hand and I don't want to be your friend. Where did the thing you call Firebrat take Iggy?'

''Tis a secret. I only tell secrets to friends.'

'You wouldn't tell me anyway,' I said bitterly. 'You're all the same. You lie and trick and cheat because you're locked up in this dreadful place and you envy the living.'

There was silence for a good five minutes and I assumed I had offended the creature. But then I heard it singing a little way off and the next moment it was at my side again.

'If I oblige thee, Boy, will you be my friend?'

'Oh, all right then,' I said, softening my tone. 'I'll be your friend.' Maybe this thing really meant no harm.

'Good, sweet Boy,' said the voice. Then, just like that, the thing came out of the blackness and formed itself into a girl of about my age – the same girl as we had seen in front of the picture of the fallen chairs. She was quite a pretty girl, as far as I could make out, though she seemed to have trouble keeping her shape for the first few seconds. Eventually she settled down and looked at me shyly. She was about my size and wore a long grey dress with a white collar and cuffs. Her hair was dark and reached down to her shoulders. But what was most striking about her was the flush of her skin and her eyes, which burned so brightly.

Now I recognised her properly. She was the twelve-year-old I had seen in the picture on the day when I had used a ball of string to keep track of my route through the house.

'You picked up my string and...'

'Just my little joke, Boy.' She clasped her hands in front of her and swayed.

'Are you going to trick me again?' I asked, now feeling a bit easier about talking to her. 'Are you going to turn into something else, like Stinking Billy, and torment me?'

'Stinking Billy, you shouldn't mind him. He's just an old smell.' Then she gazed at me with a kind of wonder and shook her head sadly. 'Boy, you be my first friend for hundreds of years. I am so lonesome in this place that sometimes I lose my reason. But now I have you, *Boy*.' She giggled and put her hand up to her mouth, then reached to touch my face. A delighted smile spread across her features and to my amazement I felt something.

'How long have you been dead?'

'I don't rightly know. When you come to this place, you forget things. I forgot almost everything because they tell you, "*Knowst not what thou ist nor what thou didst.*" Sometimes I try to remember, but I find it very hard and my head does hurt so.'

'You make it sound like a prison,' I said.

''Tis a prison, you are right in that, Boy, and I am in it with all the others and they don't know why or how they came to be here either.' She stopped and looked at me shyly. 'I spied you in the house. I been watching you.'

'I know that,' I said. 'Do you know who killed Bella Brown?'

She nodded gravely.

'Tell me.'

'You will learn soon enough,' she said.

'You understand that they are trying to kill me and my friend, Iggy. Will you help us find our way back?'

'I watch you play by yourself and I says to

202

myself, that boy will be my friend. That boy needs a friend too.'

'And now I am your friend,' I replied with a weak smile. 'Silverfish, that's a pretty name. Who gave it to you?'

She shrugged and wrung her hands awkwardly. 'I don't know how I came by it.'

'Can you help me find Iggy? Can you help us escape?'

'But then I'll lose my friend.'

'But Silverfish, I don't want to die. You don't want me to die as young as you did and be trapped in this place away from all the things I love?'

She put her finger to her lips. 'Ssh…don't talk. Earwig is coming.'

'Who's Earwig?'

'Earwig is a spy. He creeps and he listens and he tells *her* stories.'

'Her?' I said. 'Is it that woman in the portrait – Alba Hockmuth – Ahrinnia Hecht?'

She nodded and put her finger to her lips.

'Is Firebrat *her* slave?'

'And Stinking Billy,' she hissed. 'And Earwig and the Ravens and Lyncher and many, many others.'

'Lyncher – who's that?'

'You'll see.'

'But you are not her slave. Why's that?'

'I have no business with that woman and she has no business with me because I led my life well. I went to Church and I says my prayers and I was kind to everyone I met along my way. And I loved life, Boy. I loved it so. I weren't a bad person like the others.'

I was beginning to understand. Alba Hockmuth was only interested in the evil spirits that she could use for her own purposes. The others, like Silverfish, were of no interest to her.

'Then let's go where Earwig can't hear us.'

She put her hand out towards me and began singing about a young woman who fell in love during the hay-time. The song went on and on. I couldn't make out all the words because Silverfish kept on bursting into giggles when she reached the saucier lines. She looked at me with such pleasure as she sang that I could not help but like her and wondered what it would have been like to explore the valley with such a spirited girl.

'I wish we could meet in the hay-time, Boy. I thought that when I first set eyes on you a hundred years ago.'

'You must mean someone else,' I said. 'I am only thirteen. I wasn't alive one hundred years ago.'

'Yes, you was. I saw you clear as day. I thought I'd like to run with thee in the fields at that very moment. Oh I do remember how the fields used to be in summer and the larking we had in the warmth of the sun. Oh, it was fine in them days.'

The girl must be slightly mad, I thought, and dropped the subject. 'When are we going to go to a place where I can speak without Earwig overhearing us?' I asked.

'Why, Boy! We're here.'

'But I didn't move,' I protested. 'I didn't move an inch.'

'I took you on my arm while I sings. Didn't you notice?' She winked at me. Maybe this was my chance to break through to the other side and run from the house. If Silverfish could scrawl messages in the real world, then she must be able to show me how to get back. But then I thought of Iggy – I knew I couldn't go without him. I had to hope that Silverfish really did want to be my friend and was not planning to trick me.

'I have to find my friend Iggy,' I said. 'Do you know where Firebrat took him?'

'He rides in the night with him and hides him in the place where nothing comes and nothing goes and there is always darkness.'

'There must be some way of getting him out.'

She put her finger to her lips and considered this. 'Maybe there is, Boy. But now we must watch them play. They only plays Slipcandle on this night.'

'Slipcandle – what's that?'

She pointed to the end of the passage. I saw several figures emerging. They were greeting each other, but they made no noise.

They were all dressed from different periods in history. One wore tights, another was in breeches and a large hat. A third was in a big ballooning white shirt and had a red sash around his waist. Several were in white tie, as though they had just come from a grand dinner. And some, I noticed, were in army uniform.

'Can they see us?' I whispered.

She nodded, but seemed too absorbed in what was about to happen to answer.

Each man held a pewter plate with a lighted candle on it, which he shielded with one hand. The man wearing the large hat swept it off and laid the plate on the floor. He glanced along the passage with a keen eye and pushed the plate very gently into the dark. It slid along on the polished wood floor nicely and came to rest about twelve feet from him with the candle still alight.

'Ah! That's a good'un,' said Silverfish, clapping her hands noiselessly.

'What're they doing?'

'It's a kind of race to the end of the passage. Each player takes his turn and he keeps going as long as the candle stays alight, but it takes an artful hand to keep that little flame alive. If it goes out he leaves the game.'

Soon there were nearly a dozen candles at different points on the floor. If I hadn't been so nervous and frightened of what was going to become of me, I would have marvelled at the strangeness and beauty of the game as the phantoms glided up and down the passage, looking so real and solid, bending down to judge the draughts and the bumps and the most polished parts of the floor. When one took his go, the others stood back so as not to be accused of causing a movement that would snuff out the candle. But the light died easily when the plate went too fast or hit a bump and the flame was shaken from the wick. And when this happened the player took up his plate, straightened and bowed to the others and began to recede into the dark, bidding goodbye before finally disappearing.

Eventually there were just two players left.

They were both young and wearing army uniform. As I looked upon them with Silverfish at my side, their faces seemed oddly familiar to me. They kept on glancing in our direction, but I couldn't work out whether they were watching me or just acknowledging Silverfish. 'Who are they?' I asked.

'Why, surely you know your own kin,' she replied with a wicked little grin.

Then the penny dropped. It was Andrew and Charles, the Colonel's sons. Their photographs were all over Skirl and they looked just as they did now, cheerful and handsome and full of high spirits.

'And the others, who were they?' I asked.

She smiled. 'Also your kin.'

Then I understood why she had brought me to watch the strange game of Slipcandle. These were all the victims of the painting of the fallen chairs! I recognised the man in the big white shirt and sash as the spirit of Iggy's great grandfather, Clive Endymion, drawn back to the house which he'd fled to escape the curse of the painting. Something told me that the men had left the game in the exact order in which they'd died. Perhaps there was no chance or skill to Slipcandle. Perhaps the order of play was predetermined. Just as each chair falling over in the picture represented a death, so the guttering candles of each player repeated it. Slipcandle was a re-enactment of the curse.

And then another thing occurred to me. 'They all died on Christmas Day, didn't they? That's one of the secrets of the painting. And the other secret is...' I thought furiously. I knew there was something I was missing, and it concerned Iggy's great grandfather. Surely his spirit would not have chosen to return to the very house that he had fled? Somehow he had been forced back to Skirl. Why? Did the curse only work if all the spirits of the victims were imprisoned in Skirl's nether world? That had to be the right solution because there was only one person who stood to gain from keeping the rightful heirs to Skirl locked up, even though they were ghosts, and that was Alba Hockmuth. I blurted all this out to Silverfish. 'And that's why she's kidnapped us, isn't it? She's got to make sure that we die by the end of the day. The curse of the painting doesn't work unless all of us die and all of us are held captive here by her.'

'You are a canny fellow!' said Silverfish.

'Why don't you tell me everything?' I said urgently. 'If you're my friend, why do you wait for me to work it out? Are you part of the plan?

Are you going to turn into something else, a devil like Firebrat?'

A look of hurt flooded her face. 'I cannot tell you everything,' she said. 'I am not allowed to…'

'Then why are you here with me?'

'I like you, Boy. You are good and kind, and I wish you well.'

'Then help me,' I said. 'Please help us. We have so little time.'

My mind had been so full of worry that I hadn't noticed that the game had stopped and that the two remaining figures – Andrew and Charles – were approaching us with their hands shielding the candles. One offered me his.

'They want you to play,' said Silverfish.

'No, I can't!' Then, much louder, I said, 'I won't, I won't do it.'

They both nodded to me. A secret look passed from the dead to the living, from one generation of Dragomen to the next, a warning that not even Silverfish picked up.

The brothers returned to their places in the corridor, lowered their candles to the floor and proceeded to complete the game. But there was a change in the way they played now. Instead of seeing how far they could push the plates along the floor, they moved them just an inch or two at a time. It made me wonder if they were stringing out the play to stay in each other's company for as long as possible, but eventually a draught nipped at both their flames and the passage was returned to darkness.

All I could see was Silverfish.

Chapter Thirteen

Interview with Earwig

Time was the only thing that mattered now. But time might not be the same in this place. Maybe it moved more quickly here. Or was it more slowly? There was no way of telling.

'What ails thee?' asked Silverfish, searching my puzzled face.

'I was thinking about time.' I didn't explain further because I still wasn't sure that I trusted her entirely. If Old Havoc had tricked us by pretending to be Jebard and the dogs, he could certainly use Silverfish to delay me and thwart our attempts to escape back into the real world and try to save our lives. Over the months the other inhabitants of Skirl had observed my lonely life and I reasoned that it was quite possible that Old Havoc had made me a companion that I would trust because she too claimed to be lonely. Yes, I might even have to accept that Silverfish was Old Havoc in another guise. I would put her to the test.

'Where is Iggy? Take me to him. Only then will you prove your worth as my friend.'

'Silverfish *is* your friend! I likes you.'

'Prove it.'

She offered me her hand again. 'It will not be easy. No one from your world has ever seen these things.'

Before very long we were in a different place, a kind of underworld that appeared to exist deep beneath the old and new buildings of Skirl. It was as though we were going deep down into the ocean. Things flickered in the darkness like the fish that make their own light to hunt with. Some of these creatures pulsed with energy and I saw their complete human forms as we passed; others glimmered very faintly. On the way, Silverfish explained the difference between the vigorous spirits like herself, which were known as *vitals*, and the very ancient and decayed ones, which were called *squibs*. You had to be careful not to bump into *squibs*, or step on them. Even though they were weak they were still capable of giving you a nasty sting if angered. We met many *vitals*. The first was a big fellow with a sheepskin tied round his shoulders, who placed himself in our way. 'Seen my dog, 'ave you?' he bellowed. 'Seen my dog? Where you put my dog?'

'You ain't got no dog,' came a cry from the dark. 'You ain't got no dog coz your dog's gone. Your dog's gone. Your dog's gone. Your dog's dead.'

He took no notice and wandered off shouting the same question. 'Seen my dog? Anyone seen my dog?'

A washerwoman carrying a basket came up with a toothless scowl and swore at us. Silverfish called her an 'old ratbag' and told her to go away. We saw men toiling at imagined tasks, children crying for mothers who had died centuries before, old women sitting staring blankly ahead of them, gentry dressed in fine clothes strolling aimlessly, tradesmen hawking their goods, blacksmiths, grooms, shepherds and a parson with two altar boys.

'Why are there so many of them here?'

'Because they are trapped like me.'

'Trapped by the Lines of Tarle. Is that what you're saying? Is that what you mean?'

'That's what they say about all those who die near Skirl,' she said.

Eventually we were joined by another being, which did not show itself immediately but kept pace beside us with a rolling motion. When it started squeaking, Silverfish reprimanded it, 'Go away, Earwig, we don't want to speak to you.'

At this, a rotund gambolling creature materialised. His body was short, with long arms and spindly legs. He had no neck to speak of, but a large head that was sunk into his shoulders. 'Isn't life grand?' he chirruped by way of an opener. 'Now lassie, tell us what you're about and who this fine gentleman might be. Give us the news. Give us the gossip – the goss, the SP, the word on the street. You can tell me.' This all came out very fast and as he spoke his little eyes twinkled with pleasure but also with devilment.

'Be off with you,' she said. Silverfish tried to ignore him and hurried on, bearing me on her arm. But Earwig wasn't going to be shaken off so easily.

'No doubt you have permission for this *violation*, for that is what I'd call it. If I am not mistaken, he is a *live one*. I spotted the booby myself not a few nights ago on the other side. Have you come over permanently, laddie, or are you just passing through?'

'Passing through,' I said.

'Don't speak to him.' Silverfish said to me. 'No good will come of talking to this lowlife.'

'Ah, if only I was a lowlife. If only. Passing

216

through, are you, laddie? Now that is what I call *news* fit for the telling. News! How I love to spread it. It's the spice of life, the pearl of days, the coin glinting in the sand, the egg that nestles in the straw, a mushroom in a dewy meadow. Ah news! That's what it's all about.' He rushed round and blocked Silverfish's path. 'Hold on there, lassie. I've got a question for you. Have you got permission to bring him here? Have the relevant authorities been informed of the situation vis-à-vis this scurvy toe-rag from the other side?' He gurgled a laugh and gave me another wink.

I took a step forward to confront him. 'You should look at yourself before you start calling people scurvy toe-rags,' I said to him. 'Now, leave us alone. I have important business here, and I warn you I have enough magic around my neck to reduce you to a thimble of dust.'

'I will take that as a *no* to my question.' He made as though he was licking a pencil and writing something in a notepad, though he possessed neither. 'I'm sure the authorities will be most interested to hear about you, Silverfish, and your little sweetheart from the other side, especially after his shameful treatment of Lord Billy, Duke of Stink.' He turned to me. 'The way I hear it, someone gave him a fine old drubbing.

Have you any comment to make on that? Come along, laddie, answer the question! We need a comment from you.'

'I don't have anything to say,' I said.

'Then you admit it. You admit everything.'

'I don't admit anything.'

'Then why don't you just say so, laddie?'

'I did! I just said *I don't admit anything.* There's nothing to admit.'

He sighed heavily. 'Years of experience have taught me denial is as good as admission. A "no" is really a "yes". The facts speak for themselves – that's what I always say.'

'Go!' commanded Silverfish. 'Otherwise he'll do for you, Earwig.'

'A toe-rag like this – not on your Nelly, he won't do for the remarkable Earwig.'

'You know a thing or two?' I ventured, looking at Earwig hard.

'I should say so,' he replied, polishing the tops of his dirty fingernails on the end of a ragged tie.

'Then you know that the only news around here is that we – that is to say I and my friend the great sorcerer Iggy Ma-tuu Clava – have cracked the code of the painting. A person as well-informed as you must understand the importance of that.'

'I have some idea,' said Earwig, a very sly look entering his eyes.

I could see that he was concentrating doubly hard so as to remember every word that I said. But he also kept a smile on his face as though he was just passing the time of day. 'It's well known that I can keep a secret. I'm silent as the grave, if you see what I mean. Trusted by high and low alike for my discretion. Go on.' He rubbed his hands and moved a little closer.

'There's nothing more to say, except that you'd better keep on the right side of me because I know things that you wouldn't dream of. I have information about *you*, Earwig. Things that are important for the future of a *vital* like you. You understand?'

There was something so contemptible about the gossip of the underworld that all my courage returned. I could feel Silverfish looking at me doubtfully, but I just gazed into Earwig's cowardly soul knowing there was nothing for it but to take a risk. I kept staring deeper and deeper until signs of doubt began to show behind the malice in his expression. 'You see, I am making lists of those who help me and those who don't. Which is it going to be for you? The good list, or the bad list?'

'The good list, of course,' said Earwig quickly.

'I always lend a hand. Famous for it, aren't I?' he said, darting a look at Silverfish.

'Well...' she began.

'There, you see! Put me on the good list. Sign me up at once and tell me all.'

'It's very simple,' I said, at last letting my gaze drop. 'I know how to destroy the Countess Ahrinnia Hecht and end her rule in this place. You see, she's not one of you, but she is one of my kind and I know wherein lies the source of her power.' That phrase, meaningless though it was, seemed to strike home with Earwig. He leaned forward.

'How?'

'That I cannot tell you, but let me just say that when we were tricked into following Old Havoc, we were letting ourselves be led through those doors because we wanted to bring our own power – our own special magic – into this place. It was Old Havoc who was tricked, not us. And now we are here, we plan to use it.'

'Phew,' exhaled Earwig, barely able to contain himself. 'That *is* news, laddie! I've been saying for ages that Havoc's a spent force. Trouble is they won't listen.'

'Well, they should have listened to your wise insight, Earwig. You heard what we did to

Stinking Billy. That was just a sample of our power. Nothing showy mind you, because we didn't want to tip off the authorities that something big is about to happen. But you don't want to end up like him, no bigger than a smudge of light, no more important than the spirit of a…of a slug.'

'Perish the thought,' said Earwig. 'What can I do to help?'

'Wait for the word of command, and then you must rise up. A *vital* like you, bursting with energy and ingenuity, must have a lot of influence down here.'

'Contacts, that is what I have, laddie,' he replied eagerly.

'Then you must expel her. And we will finish her off with our magic in the outside world.'

This was too much for Silverfish, who had been looking anxious for several minutes. 'Pray, hold your tongue, Boy. You don't know what you're saying.'

'Oh, but I do, Silverfish. I do. Now, let us go and deal with Firebrat and whip him with the lashes of eternity.'

'What're they?' asked Earwig, fetching a grubby forefinger and thumb to his ear lobe, and yanking it slightly. 'The eternal lashes – what are they?'

'Eternal pain,' I replied confidently. 'No creature dead or alive has survived it without going mad.'

'Firebrat's already mad,' said Earwig. 'Mad as can be. He can't get any madder. I mean, you've seen him.'

'Even Firebrat will succumb,' I said, and just to add more weight, I held the harp in front of my mouth and plucked it as hard as I could. The noise took off like before and both Earwig and Silverfish shuddered and shrank from me. Silverfish went so weak I thought she was going to dissolve into the night. Then, after a minute or two, the vibration stopped and they crept back to me. 'What is that?' cried Silverfish.

'Hell's teeth!' exclaimed Earwig, shivering all over. 'What did you go and do that for?'

'That's just a taste of what I can do. Take me to Firebrat, Silverfish. Are you coming?' I asked Earwig.

'Eh, no, laddie. I have pressing business elsewhere, but when I hear the word I will bring all the greatest and bravest spirits to your side. Just one thing, when will that be?'

'Before the day is out. Before Christmas is done.'

'By the end of the day!' said Earwig, shifting his

corpulent frame a few paces away. 'What news is this! A revolt, an uprising! I can't wait to…eh…to help. Do you have a code word? We must have a code word of the most secret kind. What is it?'

'Don't tell anyone,' I whispered. 'It's Kilimanjaro.'

'Kilimanjaro! Wey, hey! Isn't life grand?' he said and vanished.

Chapter Fourteen

Firebrat's Place

'Why did you say all that to Earwig?' asked Silverfish when he had scuttled away. 'He will tell everyone.'

'I know,' I replied, but I wasn't going to explain what my plan was because I had decided that I could trust nothing and no one, so I changed the subject. 'Take me to where Iggy is. I have very little time, Silverfish.'

'It's not a pretty sight down there,' she said, with a worried expression.

'Down where?'

'In the dungeons of Skirl.'

'Dungeons! There aren't any dungeons in Skirl.'

'To be sure there are. They call them the "lock-ups" and that's where Firebrat stays, down there.'

'What is Firebrat?' I asked. 'Where did he come from?'

'From the old times. Some say he's been here thousands of years and he's the slave of the ruler of this place.'

'What about you? How old are you?'

'I don't know,' she said, wrinkling her brow.

She took my hand again and we moved off. I had no impression of going anywhere, but I did notice the air becoming warmer. And then I began to see some of my surroundings, like when mist clears from a mountaintop and you suddenly spot the trees and rocks that have been there all along. We came to an opening above a pit. All around us were stone walls that were sweating damp, and above us were several greasy black beams supporting a roof that I could not see. There were chains, pulleys and wheels fastened to the beams, and meat-hooks like those that hung from the ceiling in Alice's kitchen, but much larger.

'Look,' whispered Silverfish. 'Firebrat is there.'

'Where?'

'By the wheel.'

I looked down. The creature that had torn Iggy from my grasp was resting on a stone slab. His legs and arms were twitching with regular convulsions and the head that had given me such a fright lolled forward so the pointed chin touched his chest. He was too monstrous ever to have been human, but Silverfish whispered that Firebrat had indeed once been like everyone else. His wickedness in life had been distilled into the essence of evil over many centuries in the limbo of Skirl. 'But he's not as powerful as Old Havoc,' she said. 'He's the only one that can change shape.'

'Where's Iggy?' I said, peering about.

'He's got him down there in one of the lock-ups.'

'Take me.'

She started shaking her head. 'No, Boy. I've never been down there. You take yourself. I'll stay here and watch.'

She pointed to a flight of stone steps that I hadn't noticed before. I hooked the lantern into the crook of my elbow and put the harp to my mouth, ready to strike the prongs if Firebrat stirred, then I started down the steps. Once his head rose and swivelled, his eyes did not open and I guessed that he was scenting the air in his sleep. I stayed rooted to the spot for a minute or two, hardly daring to breathe. When I got down to his level, I looked across the floor and saw piles of dust, which were glowing. I realised they were *squibs* – the burnt out spirits which Silverfish had told me could still deliver a powerful shock.

I wondered if they were the remains of Firebrat's victims, or whether he had left them littered around the place like mines, so he would know if anyone was approaching?

The light was not good but I was close enough to see the dreadful blisters and boils that covered his scalp. In other places his skin was peeling away like bark from a tree, and every point of his flesh seemed to burn and pulse with heat that came from inside him. I looked at his face. The eyes were set wide apart and one was lower than the other. The nose was tiny but with large nostrils that flared in time with the shudders and twitches that coursed through his body. But it was his mouth that held my attention. It was opened in a grimace of pain. Terrifying though he was, the torment in Firebrat's being was easy to see.

I glanced up at Silverfish, who had come a little way down the steps. She was pointing to something, but I didn't understand what. I looked again and saw a wooden door with strips of iron bolted to its panels. The door was standing ajar but I couldn't see inside.

I began to pick my way through the *squibs*, which sensed my presence and were shifting towards me, exactly like flat fish creeping along the seabed. Each time one got too close I held the harp down to it and it scuttled away. Again I peered through the door but could see nothing. Where was he? Half of me wanted to call out to him or shout up to Silverfish, but when I darted a look to the top of the steps I saw she had vanished. At that exact moment I became aware of a nasty pulsing in my right foot and realised that one of the *squibs* had crept up behind me and attached itself to my boot. A second or two elapsed and then I felt the pain shoot up my leg. I yelled out and kicked the *squib* away. The next moment Firebrat was in front of me, his sinewy arms writhing in the air, sending tiny forks of electricity into the dark above him.

'You cannot touch me, Firebrat!' I shouted.

He shook his head and leered at me. I noticed foam had gathered and dried at the corners of his mouth. 'Pray, why?' His voice sounded like a shovel being scraped across stone.

'You cannot touch beings from the real world. It's against the laws of this place.'

'Laws! No Laws HERE, except Laws what Firebrat MAKES. Anyway...Firebrat already touch your friend... NOTHING happened to Firebrat.' He screeched a laugh and kicked aside the *squibs* that had gathered around us. Then he hopped right up to me and fixed me with one terrifying bloodshot eye. He was not much taller than me and later I would remember the loathing that seethed deep in his expression. He laid a hand on my shoulder, a hand that scalded my skin through three layers of clothing. I flinched. 'Come child...Firebrat...has GAMES to play. Yes, GAMES!' The other hand was flung up to the ceiling with one finger pointing at the chains and pulleys. I glimpsed a torturer's armoury hanging there – spiked objects, blackened saws, blades of every size and shape, and implements to flay and pierce. 'Games what make child HURT. Games what Firebrat invents for Pleasure. Games what Firebrat tries on LIVING FLESH! Flesh like yours. FIREBRAT wants REAL LIVE FLESH for experiment. He waits for a long time to get his hands on REAL FLESH!'

He grasped hold of my coat collar and, with incredible force, hauled me towards some chains that hung down from the rafters. I shouted for Iggy but no answer came. Before I knew what was happening he had fastened the chains round my arms and hauled me up so that my legs dangled a few feet from the ground.

He hurried over to a chest. There was a clattering and chinking as he rummaged and tossed things aside. Then he reappeared in front of me, brandishing a flail – a spiked iron ball attached by a short chain to a stick – and some knives that appeared red in the glow coming from his body. 'Which game does child want Firebrat to PLAY FIRST? Shall we do the STRIPPING of the skin with this?' He held up a knife, a devilish instrument as thin as a skewer. 'Or does the BOY want this toy what Firebrat has been saving for SPECIAL occasion?' He took a step and swung the spiked ball at a board, which cracked and sent a shower of splinters into the air. 'Gives many good bruises and breaks bones. Or, does Boy prefer burning hot pokers and boiling water? Everything is here for Firebrat's delectation.' He cackled a laugh and eyed me with anticipation. 'And we have time BOY. We have a hundred years of GAMES in front of us. And I HURTS you MUCH.'

'If you touch me you will spoil the curse of the painting,' I said. The Master of the Fallen Chairs does not predict that I will die at the hands of a hellish monkey like you.'

He sniffed and looked around. 'WHAT YOU TALKING ABOUT?' Then he got really close to me so that I could smell the sulphur on his breath. 'Firebrat has blessing of great Lady,' he whispered.

231

'Firebrat does what he wants down here with great Lady's permission. FIREBRAT love great Lady and she love FIREBRAT. She LOVE Firebrat more than any other SPIRIT except LYNCHER.'

'Bully for you,' I said. 'Your breath stinks.'

'FIREBRAT not stink! FIREBRAT is BEAUTIFUL and great lady LOVES him.'

'Iggy!' I yelled. 'Where are you? Help me!'

'No good shouting for FAT friend: he sleeping for hundreds of YEARS.' He swung on the chains. I looked up and caught sight of nameless horrors hanging in the gloom above me, shapes that once might have been men, but who had long ago been hoisted to the rafters on Firebrat's pulleys, to rot and die. With all my might I pulled at the chain and managed to snatch the little harp hanging round my neck and place it between my teeth. I pushed it into position with my tongue, then somehow reached up with my index finger to pluck the prongs. Firebrat cocked his head with interest then yanked the chain so that my hand fell from my mouth. 'Boy STOP doing that NOW!'

But a single note had escaped my mouth and was reverberating around Firebrat's chamber of horrors. As before, it didn't have any effect on him but I wasn't going to give up now. I swung on the chains, lifting my legs back and forth to gain momentum. For a moment Firebrat didn't seem to know what to do. Then on the forward thrust, I put my boots together and managed to hit him on the head. It sent him sprawling but he instantly sprang up and took a swing at me with the spiked ball. It missed me but I knew he would connect with the second shot. I turned and twisted on the chains to make it more difficult for him, all the time shouting for Iggy and Silverfish.

Then I caught sight of Iggy. He was standing in the doorway of the cell looking bleary-eyed. I screamed out, 'Iggy! Help me!' He shook his head and tried to pass through the door but something stopped him. An invisible barrier was holding him prisoner. He took a few steps back, then lunged at the doorway, thrusting his arms through, then one of his legs. There was a sucking noise followed by a whoosh. He was free and making towards Firebrat.

Firebrat rounded on him with the flail, his features spread in a terrible grimace of pleasure. Iggy stopped, put up his hand, smiled and pulled something out of a pocket. He waved his hands, as though doing a conjuring trick, then held something up in front of Firebrat's face. From where I was, it looked like a disc but I couldn't see it properly. Firebrat dropped the flail and began to feel his head, touching and prodding the pustules on his bald pate, fingering the flaking skin, tugging his ears and nose as if trying to wrench them back into place. He leapt towards Iggy, seized the object from his grasp and gazed at it with total absorption for a few seconds, then, throwing his head back, let out a howl of agony. Iggy ran to a spot below me and tugged the chains so that some pulleys high above worked and lowered me to the ground. In a second he had the knots around my arms loosened and I was able to drop my arms and rub the circulation back into my hands. He grabbed me and together we staggered towards the steps. The heat poured from Firebrat's body, electric shocks forked from his extremities and curses poured from his mouth. After several more blood-curdling howls, Firebrat sank moaning to the ground. 'What has become of me? Where is me? What is this? WHAT IS FIREBRAT?' His hands opened in despair and the disc dropped and rolled towards us, wobbling before falling over with a dull ring on the stone at Iggy's feet. He picked it up and returned it to his coat, but not before I saw that the disc was nothing but a mirror.

It was then that I realised Iggy knew that Firebrat had no idea what he looked like, no idea of the changes wrought over many centuries as the evil in his soul had taken over and made him into a monster. Somewhere in Firebrat's being was a man who could still be shocked by the transformation that had taken place.

We raced up the steps with Firebrat's agony ringing in our ears, but Silverfish was nowhere to be seen. I called out for her.

'She's gone,' I said. 'Her name was Silverfish. She was helping me, but now she's gone. Without her we won't ever get out of here.'

Iggy looked around. He didn't seem to be in the slightest bit bothered by what had happened. 'How did you know he had never seen himself?' I asked.

'Old trick,' he said, smiling. 'A bad spirit does not like to see his face.'

I didn't dare to think what we would have done if the mirror hadn't worked its ordinary magic on that terrible creature.

'What are we going to do?' I asked.

He didn't answer but just grinned at me. 'Brother Kim has done well to bring Igthy Ma-tuu Clava out of this place.'

'His name was Firebrat,' I said, anxious to tell him all I had learned from Silverfish as well as my experience of watching Slipcandle.

'Firebrat,' he mused. 'A good name for a devil with own heating.' Then he told me that every phantom, ghost, spirit and spectre had a weakness. The trick was to play on the tiny grains of humanity left in these creatures, for their weakness in life would also be their weakness in death.

Chapter Fifteen

The Sessions of Christmastide

We found ourselves back in one of the cavernous corridors of the old house, and without any sense of where we were, we set off to find our way out. We must have walked for an age through one deserted thoroughfare after another. By now I was exhausted, and hungry too. Iggy had no food with him and told me the best way to deal with hunger was not to think about it, which didn't help one bit. But I knew there was nothing for it but to keep trudging and not give up. We came across no other spirits in those long hours. But we noticed that it was lighter than before – there was an increasing number of disturbances in the air around us. Something was definitely following us.

Several times I called out to Silverfish but no reply came. 'Maybe it's Earwig keeping tabs on us,' I whispered. 'He's a low kind of creature only interested in news and gossip. I told him we had a plan to deal with Alba and the code word was Kilimanjaro.'

Iggy's eyes widened. 'Why? Why you tell him this?'

'Because I wanted...' But before I could get the sentence out, a deep jowly voice sounded behind us. 'You are summoned. You're required, now! This minute! Come!'

We looked around and there on a stone bench, which we had failed to notice, was a large man with a double chin.

'Where? Who wants us?' I asked.

'That's not your business,' he said, examining a clipboard.

He looked up in our direction. 'Chop Chop! Fall in line. Follow me.'

'How can we follow you when you're sitting down?' I said.

The man rose. He was huge, with a distraught, bad-tempered expression and his face was bumpy with warts. He was carrying a very large staff, with a silver knob on the end and he wore a reddish brown coat with a riding cape and breeches, which rose over an enormous stomach to halfway up his chest. Everything about him was fat: his double chin wobbled when he spoke and he had huge plump fingers, blubbery ears and a bulbous red nose. A hand occasionally darted to his face, as though he was popping food into his open mouth.

I glanced at Iggy, who was taking in our new companion with an astonished look. 'Your name?' he said rather formally.

'Is Semaj Trow' asked the man, puffing himself up and checking a watch at the end of a gold chain. '*The* Clerk of the Sessions and secretary to the Committee of Renewal.'

'What Sessions?' I asked.

'The Sessions of Christmastide, nincompoop.' He passed a hand over his face.

'I've never heard of them.'

He studied me with contempt. 'No, I don't suppose you have.'

'We don't want to go with you. We don't belong here.'

'That's as may be,' said Semaj Trow. He pulled a spotted handkerchief from his pocket, mopped his forehead and flourished it in a vague sort of way around his nose. 'I am charged with conveying you by any means to the Sessions. We will go now. You have no choice.'

Before we knew it, we were standing in a very

large banqueting hall with several long tables running from one end to the other. At the far end there was a large seat, which looked as though it was carved from rock. 'Remain here,' said Semaj Trow before moving off towards the other end of the hall.

'What happens now?' I asked Iggy.

Iggy lifted his shoulders. 'Missus Alba comes.'

I looked up to the huge ceiling above us and saw that each beam ended in a wooden figure, carved so it seemed to support the weight of the roof on its shoulders. My gaze moved to the chandeliers now lit by hundreds upon hundreds of candles then, out of the corner of my eye, I noticed that the carved figures were shifting and buckling under their burden. But it wasn't only the roof that was supported by wooden slaves. All the tables were held up by things, which crouched in the shadows. Did nothing die in Skirl's second world? Not even wood?

I turned to Iggy. 'How do we get out?'

'I have idea, Brother Kim. When I play trick you go to Old Man of Tarle. Old Man takes you back in time.'

'What about you? I can't go by myself.'

'Of course,' he said with finality. Iggy had a way of answering things but not answering them.

I wasn't going to put up with it this time. 'We both have to go. I can't go back in time without you. You will die.'

But it was no use. Iggy's attention had darted elsewhere: something was happening in the hall. Fires were being lit by unseen hands in the great fireplace, and the tables were being laid with glasses and plates, which miraculously took shape out of thin air. Semaj Trow looked up and down and then banged his silver knob on a door at the side. It opened and hundreds and hundreds of spirits filed in procession into the hall. Some were mere shadows, shimmers in the air such as you see above a candle, without any distinct bodily form; others appeared as solid and as human as Semaj Trow, or Silverfish. And then there were the *squibs*, the creeping remnants, which came in flurries of glowing dust. I saw all the phantoms of the night – the washerwoman, the man looking for his dog, the lost children, the ghosts who had for that brief moment with Silverfish crammed our way like a street scene from old London. These were followed by hideous malformations, things that had been contorted by their own wickedness into creatures that were mostly unrecognisable as having any seed of humanity. They limped, crawled, shuffled and dragged themselves through the milling crowd to find their places at the end of tables where they appeared to supervise the crowd. One moved very slowly on its stomach, grubbing its way on tiny stumps, making a noise like a pig.

Two black-hooded monkish figures followed and stood at either end of a smaller table, which ran across the hall just beneath some steps leading to the stone seat. The monks were careful to conceal their features in their cowls.

Even after all the terrors of the night, I still managed to find a new fear and that was the chilling idea of Iggy and me joining their number in eternity, shuffling into the hall for the Sessions, whatever they were. I shuddered at the sight of so many bleak, wicked and lost souls and wondered why there weren't more like Silverfish. Come to think of it, where was she? I scanned the multitude, avoiding eye contact with any of them and certain she wasn't there. Perhaps I had guessed right – the sweet young girl was just an illusion who had now returned to some more hideous form. After all, she had led me down into Firebrat's dungeon when she knew the dangers that lurked there.

We watched as Semaj Trow patrolled the far end of the hall, occasionally using his stick to prod a spirit out of the way. Satisfied that everything was in order, he thumped on the floor and called for silence, which was odd since the only thing that could be heard were the *squibs* occasionally discharging voltage into the air. Then behind us another door opened. The first figure to emerge was Earwig, who bustled down the aisle between the tables wearing a happy grin. As he passed us he whispered, 'I see you've found your friend, laddie. Funny looking fellow, isn't he? Ah, isn't life grand?'

There was a pause – a mood of expectation seemed to be bubbling in the hall. We waited, uncomfortably aware of being inspected by hundreds of pairs of lifeless eyes. 'I hate this,' I murmured. 'Please, let's do something, Iggy.'

'Wait, Brother Kim,' he said out of the corner of his mouth.

After what seemed an age the phantoms that I had seen playing Slipcandle came through the door that Earwig had used. The party was led by the Colonel's two sons, Andrew and Charles. When Clive Drago came with his flowing moustache and billowing shirt I nudged Iggy. He looked puzzled for a second then nodded and smiled to his father before three. He passed without showing the slightest interest in Iggy and the listless procession moved on to the table where the monks stood. Instead of there being eleven men, I counted twenty-two. I remembered what the great auk had told us about Alba's first victims. So determined was she to keep control of the house that she had actually arranged the deaths of her own sons. Was that why a few of the ghosts were dressed in doublet and hose? Were they the very same men who had hacked each other to death over the succession at Skirl? And perhaps the others were also victims in the long history of curses and scheming? I realised then that the curse of the Master of the Fallen Chairs must be just one of a number of devices she had used to control Skirl for hundreds of years.

It all seemed so clear now. The Colonel, Iggy and me were the last in the line of the Dragomen. It didn't matter who the Master of the Fallen Chairs was. There were just two chairs left and once they fell, everything would be Alba's. She didn't have to worry about the Colonel's death because he was so old and frail that she could wait for nature to take its course.

I thought back to the portrait of Alba. It had been painted exactly 400 years before and dedicated to her with that strange inscription at a time when the strength of the Lines of Tarle were at their height, just as they were now – in 1962. Everything had been timed by her to resolve in her favour on this Christmas Day. In a matter of hours she would have complete dominion over the living and the dead of Skirl. But why? What was so important about Skirl when she had already been given eternal life? Surely that was enough for anyone. What did she want with this multitude of spirits trapped in the lines of Tarle? There was only one person who could answer and that was the old man on the bridge. He knew much more than he had let on to us. Of that much I was certain.

I looked up at Iggy and knew he must have had the same thoughts. There was a new commotion at the far end of the hall. Suddenly Alba Hockmuth, otherwise known as Countess Ahrinnia Hecht of Bohemia, appeared dressed in very nearly the same clothes as she was wearing in the portrait. The jewels in her hair and those sewn into her dress sparkled like ice crystals, and her skin shone as never before – like paper lit from behind. She surveyed the crowd before her with a look of regal contempt. Her eyes missed nothing and her lips were slightly parted with a private enjoyment of her power.

Semaj Trow bowed stiffly and drummed his staff. 'The Sessions are now open, madam. The time of Renewal is upon us.'

She nodded and looked out across the crowd of faces. 'The year has passed,' Alba said very slowly. 'And again the earth is cloaked in night and all living things are held fast by ice and snow, silenced by the charm of shadows, watched by the moon alone. The worlds of the living and the dead are one. It is *our* time and I come to you in the sacred darkness of winter to pay homage to your world and await your favours and obeisance.' She gave a fractional tip of the head and sat down.

'We will hear reports now.'

At this, Earwig appeared on the dais and bowed deeply. 'I have much news, my lady. Many items of interest, not the least of which is the foul and devilish plot against you.' He turned a gaze of vicious glee towards us. 'Those two are planning a rebellion. A revolution! They say they are going to *do* for you.' He pointed at Iggy. 'The one over there is the great sorcerer from the East, and he has come to kill you. They say that they allowed Havoc to trick them so that they could gain access.' He looked nervously up to Alba for her reaction. 'I grant that they look like a couple of boobies but believe me they are more artful

246

and more cunning than they seem, particularly the funny one from the East.'

There was a murmur around the hall, yet the ghosts at the top table remained staring ahead of them...except Clive, whose eyes had strayed in our direction. He was looking at Iggy with the vague interest that the two young men in uniform had shown me. There was something in Iggy – a manner or look – that this dead soul recognised.

'And they have a code word,' continued Earwig excitedly. 'It is Kilimanjaro. That is the plot! I beg your grace to remember me in your favours. For it is I, Earwig, superb great gatherer of news, friend of royalty and all important people, who brings you this information at this Christmastide when all the Dragomen will finally be yours and you shall have absolute power in this, your domain.'

Despite Earwig's many bows and ingratiating manner, Alba seemed unimpressed. He crept closer and attempted a confidential tone. 'They plan to destroy you, My Lady! They are bent on it. They have allies – the one that is called Silverfish is in the plot too. It was she who led the boy to Firebrat's quarters, which is specifically against the rules. She broke the law on telling as well for she told the scurvy lad all our secrets.

All *your* secrets, I should say. I have it on the best…er…the best authority.'

There was a pause before Alba gave Semaj Trow a signal. 'Bring the prisoners forward,' he called out. At this a very thin man in a leather mask pushed his way from the shadows carrying two lengths of rope. A murmur grew in the crowd of ghosts until they were chanting, 'Lyncher! Lyncher! There'll be a lynching tonight.'

Two formless creatures sprang from under the tables so fast that we didn't have time to see them and dragged us to a spot above where the monks were. Lyncher followed us with his ropes. I knew what they planned and furiously wondered if there were any clues about hanging in the painting. But then I noticed three beautiful carpets laid along the top of the steps. The colours were dazzling and the design so intricate that I couldn't take my eyes from them.

Very slowly, Alba turned her head to look at us. Her eyes were as black as I had ever seen them: they radiated triumphant cruelty. How I despised her pitiless beauty, and it was that hatred which suddenly overcame my fear of what Lyncher might be about to do with those ropes, each of which ended in a fat hangman's knot. 'You can't do anything to us here,' I shouted. 'So let us go.'

She considered this for a moment. Then a cold, wry smile flickered at her mouth. 'What a foolish young man you are,' she said, turning her head to the gathering. 'In this place I do precisely what I want, and always have done.'

'No you can't,' I retorted. 'Because you can't kill the living in the land of the dead.' This was the theory that had kept me going all night. Even though I wasn't very sure of my ground, the logic of what I had said seemed right. I looked round nervously and my eyes came to rest on the figure of Bella Brown, exactly as I remembered her before she disappeared. As in life, her eyes were meekly trained on the floor and her hands twisted in the folds of her skirt. 'We know that you have to kill people outside, like you killed Bella, like you murdered your own sons and all the other rightful heirs to this house.' I pointed to the men around the table. 'You can't change a thing. Our destiny is already set down in the painting of the fallen chairs.'

'Is that what you think?' said Alba looking into the distance.

'It is what we *know*,' said Iggy, as usual coming to life rather late in a conversation.

'You know nothing,' she said.

'We know things,' I said. 'We were sent.'

249

Alba let out a sarcastic laugh. 'Who sent you, Kim Greenwood? Your mother? Your drunken father? Who sent you?'

I began to say something but could only stammer. Iggy came to my rescue. 'By fate we are sent,' he said.

He turned to the hall. 'Brother Kim and Igthy Ma-tuu Clava are sent by fate ¯– to come to his place and fight battle with lady, who is no more than we are – an ordinary human being who breathes for short time on earth.' He looked down sadly at Clive Drago's motionless and expressionless ghost then took out the Bible. 'This is my father before three and this is his book. I come to do battle with this woman.'

It was clear he was beginning to gain an audience among the ghosts. And the heads of some of the more recognisably human spirits, which we hadn't seen before, turned with interest. There was an audible shuffling and fizzing in the air. Semaj Trow banged his stick and shouted, 'Order! Order!' The hooded monks revolved menacingly, and Earwig moved a pace or two away from Alba.

'Brother Kim is right,' said Iggy calmly. 'She cannot kill us in this place. She makes foul play only in the world of the living. That is why she kill poor girl who found her secret – or part of secret. And she make others die with her own hand and by curses laid many years ago, but she cannot kill here. And she know that.'

Alba rose from the stone seat. 'Your time is up. You have no more *time*!' she yelled, spitting out the words. 'Time is of the essence and you have *none* of it, as you will find out.' She waved to Semaj Trow, who seemed to draw back a curtain right in front of us. We both knew immediately that we were being shown our world, because we saw the kitchen, as we knew it. Something on the range was steaming. Alice was sitting at the table with her head in one hand. Tom Jebard had just come in from outside. Snow was on his boots and the dogs had left wet footprints all over the floor. Amos Sprigg and Simon Vetch were by the range warming their hands. Softly was also there, his hair and shoulders flecked with snow. Everyone except Alice was wearing heavy overcoats and carrying a stick. Alice looked up to hear something Jebard said. Softly nodded. She shook her head and let her gaze drop to the table. They all seemed worried.

'They've been looking for you,' said Alba. 'They've searched high and low all through Christmas Day.' She laughed. 'I myself offered to

251

help. But as night came, you understand that I had other business to attend to.'

All through Christmas Day! What did she mean by that? I could see it was dark outside the kitchen window. Was Alba saying that Christmas Day was nearly over? My eyes darted to the hands of the clock on the kitchen wall. It was past seven o'clock. That meant we had been trapped for nearly sixteen hours. There were only five hours before midnight when the clocks would begin chiming around the house. Just five hours to get to the Bridge of Tarle. Five hours to save our lives.

She read my mind. 'Time passes so quickly when you're enjoying yourself. All those hours flashing past – just like that!' She laughed again and snapped her fingers. Semaj Trow made as though to draw the curtain back and the images of the kitchen faded.

'You must let us go,' I shouted.

'Oh, I *will* let you go, but not just yet. When I do, it won't be very long before the chairs fall over and you return to take your place down there in front of me where I keep an eye on all the sons of Skirl. All *my* sons for you all – even the savage one – owe your life first to me. You are all of my bloodline. You are my family! What delights

I have in store for you. As for the savage, I reserve special treatment for him at the hands of Firebrat.'

A gurgle of pleasure came from somewhere and then the grating voice, 'See! See! LADY LOVES Firebrat. She LOVES him!'

Iggy smiled and folded his arms to let her know that he wasn't in the least intimidated. 'How many of you hear that?' he asked. 'Now she agree she cannot kill us in this place. She must let Igthy and Brother Kim go to make sure we die.' He paused and looked round to make sure he had the hall's attention. 'But why she want everyone dead while she lives for hundreds and hundreds of years? Igthy will tell you – because she wants power in afterlife *and* in world of the living.'

'Stop him,' screamed Alba. 'Bind him! Scourge him!' Lyncher moved forward ready to throw ropes round our necks. 'Where's Havoc?' Alba screamed. 'I demand he shows himself.'

Semaj Trow cast around as if to look for him and then lifted his shoulders helplessly. 'Ma'am – he will be along, I am sure.'

Firebrat, scenting action, slipped to the front of the crowd with two unsavoury characters – a dog-like creature and an emaciated being with greasy, brown limbs that were gnarled like the roots of an ancient tree. But then other spirits seemed to form up in front of him and block his way. I could see an intense fluttering of the air in front of Firebrat, who suddenly seemed to be forced back onto his haunches, and remained smouldering at the bottom of the steps.

'Havoc,' she cried again. 'Where are you?'

Nothing showed itself. Iggy shrugged and continued. 'This fine lady, she flies between world of living and place of the dead. And not only this – she move like devil from present times to past. That is her *secret*. This why she does not change with time.'

A fidgeting of lights attracted my attention at the far end of the steps. I thought it must be a *squib* though it was moving with much more purpose than a *squib*. The lights gathered in a mound near Alba's seat at the corner of one of the three carpets and then randomly began to form themselves into the figure of a man, so that part of an arm appeared hanging in the air before the legs were in place. It took no more than a few seconds for the head to appear and finally the face.

And then we were looking at Quake!

He was standing in that way of his, with that pleased-with-himself look on his face, one hand behind his back, the other nipping at his handkerchief. 'Where's your homework, boy?' he demanded. I told you to have it done by this morning.' My stomach tightened with an automatic dread, yet I already knew this wasn't the real Quake. Too often I'd smelled his breath, reeking of tobacco and sherry, and felt the pain of his hand on the back of my head or across my ear. Quake was no ghost. Quake was an ordinary human bully. This was a copy of Quake – one of Old Havoc's little jokes.

For some reason my eyes followed Iggy's, which had come to rest on the figure of Bella Brown. She was looking very agitated and pointing towards the image of Quake with a shaking hand. She was mouthing the word *murderer*. We both knew exactly what that meant and so did the other ghosts. They knew Quake had murdered her because Silverfish had tried to tell us with the writing in the dust and it had popped into my mind to ask the question of Quake just before I fainted. Who put Bella in the wishing well? They knew who it was. It was Quake, acting on the orders of Alba Hockmuth.

I turned to Alba and shouted, 'Murderers!' Then, without thinking, I flung my lantern, but she raised her hand and the lantern froze in mid-air. She snapped her fingers at the figure of

Quake and the thing began to change again. At first I couldn't absorb what was going on, or rather my brain refused to accept what it was seeing. I recognised the dress first, the dress with a pattern of white daisies that my mother used to wear on special occasions. Now she was standing in front of me, smiling and arms held out to greet me. Iggy touched me on the shoulder. 'This not your mother, Brother Kim. This photograph in Brother Kim's bedroom. Remember? He makes your mother in black and white like photo – not colour. This ghost is a pudding head.'

I stared for a few moments more, then shot Alba a look of hatred. 'I'm glad you saw my mother,' I shouted, 'because if you live for a hundred centuries, you can never hope to be as beautiful as she was. You're an old hag and you should have died years ago.'

'Brave words from a boy who faces certain death by the noose tonight,' she said.

I glanced back at the image of my mother, which was now disintegrating. Old Havoc's hologram was fading for lack of material. He could easily impersonate me and Jebard, even the dogs, because he'd observed us in the house over a long period of time, but the precious little black and white snapshot of my mother didn't have nearly enough for him to make a convincing copy of her. Alba snapped her fingers impatiently and the image disappeared completely.

'I am not interested in your pranks tonight, Havoc,' she snapped.

The experience of seeing my mother left me with a feeling of total emptiness. I honestly didn't care what Lyncher would do to us. Iggy looked at me and seeing my expression, gave me a wink, then he advanced purposefully to the place where Havoc had been, turned and drew a bag from his sleeve to sprinkle something on the ground. Folding his arms, he stood back. A blue light appeared, rose from the ground and hovered in the air like a magnificent pale sapphire, which then grew like crystals in a glass into the unmistakable shape of a Christmas tree. He clapped his hands and shouted. 'Mishiwaw! Mishiwaw! Mishiwaw!'

His eyes bulged and with each Mishiwaw he threw his splayed hands into the air. Suddenly the tree was alive, quivering with thousands upon thousands of tiny butterflies that had opened their wings on his command.

At first the inhabitants of Skirl's netherworld gawped with incomprehension, but then gradually a strange kind of warmth spread across their tired faces. To my astonishment some of the dead were managing a faint smile, and even Firebrat and Earwig seemed to have lost themselves in the dazzle of Iggy's Christmas tree. They pressed forward to marvel at it. Iggy acknowledged his audience with a quick bow and returned to his place beside me. 'Ready, Brother Kim?' he gripped my hand.

With all the fuss I didn't notice that Bella Brown's ghost had used the opportunity to sidle up to us. She began speaking in an urgent whisper while looking the other way. 'You will find all you need in my room. There's a little red notebook and a letter. That will prove he put me in the well.' She stopped and glanced about anxiously. 'It's in my room beneath the top drawer of the chest of drawers.'

'But what about the book? Where's the book with all the secrets of Skirl in it? Where did you put it?'

'Quake has it. He's got it and he won't give it to her because he wants her power.'

That certainly made sense to me. Quake, an ordinary sly mortal, coveted Alba's position and concealed his ambition with an oily devotion to her.

Bella gave me a final longing look and said,

'I want rescuing. Tell him to do it. He knows how.'

'Who? Who can rescue you?' I hissed. But she had slipped away into the ethereal churn of spirits.

Suddenly, there was a crack of lightning. Alba was standing and pointing at Iggy's tree, which was covered, not with butterflies gently opening and folding their wings, but a coating of slime.

'You dare,' she said, rising to her full height, 'to challenge Countess Ahrinnia Hecht of Bohemia, the Eternal Mistress of Skirl, with these *party tricks*!' She sat down again. 'I will show you party tricks.'

Out of the corner of my eye I saw Earwig rubbing his hands, but the other ghosts didn't seem too happy about the loss of the butterfly tree from which gobbets of slime were now dripping to the floor. 'This our moment, Brother Kim,' whispered Iggy, looking around.

Chapter Sixteen

Kilimanjaro

He delved in his pocket, then with one hand cupped over the other informed the Eternal Mistress of Skirl that he had a real Christmas present for her. 'But present needs name before I gives him to you. I will call him Kilimanjaro,' he said, with another theatrical wink.

'That's the code word!' shouted Earwig, bustling around Alba's throne. 'That's the word of command. I told you. You heard it first from me. See! I told you they were plotting a rebellion and none of you would listen to me.' But then he hesitated, suddenly aware of a change in the mood around him. 'Maybe,' he said, 'it isn't such a bad idea. Yes, a rebellion could be just what we need.'

He glanced around to gauge the reaction to this, but the truth was that no one was listening to Earwig.

Iggy moved with his usual speed and placed something small and furry into Alba's lap. She froze and screamed and then shot up. A mouse dropped from her seat and scuttled away, but it didn't seem unduly bothered by the commotion and stopped about ten feet from Alba and sat down to contemplate its next move.

'Seize that mouse,' shouted Alba. 'Kill it. Destroy it. Squash that mouse!'

Kilimanjaro had other ideas. Having scented the air, he set off again, unconcerned about the mass of spirits a few yards away. He even came within a whisker's distance of Firebrat without bothering about the snarling features that were lowered to his level. None of the ghosts seemed to know how to catch a mouse and most stood about watching with mild interest. Only Semaj Trow and Earwig, who had suddenly proclaimed his expertise in mouse hunting, were pursuing Kilimanjaro with any kind of purpose. But neither was quick enough for him as he darted first in one direction then the other in his quest to find a way back to the place where the surroundings and smells were familiar.

That was the brilliance of Iggy's plan. When and where he had caught the mouse I could not imagine, but clearly something had told him that we might need a guide to lead us to the world of the living and that the uncomplicated instincts of a mouse who knew his way about Skirl would be the surest means.

Suddenly Kilimanjaro turned and shot back in the direction of Alba, at which point the Eternal Mistress of Skirl jumped up on her seat shrieking. This did her very little good with the cowed masses of the underworld. One or two of the Dragomen in front of us actually began to smile, while the hooded monks started to look restlessly around them as the centuries-old authority of Skirl's dark region began to slip away.

Iggy watched the mouse intently as it darted about. His eyes followed every twist and turn. Suddenly he shouted, 'Brother Kim, follow Mister Kilimanjaro. Go Now!'

I didn't need any further encouragement. Kilimanjaro was about to disappear into the shadows behind Alba's seat. I fell to my hands and knees and scuttled after it as fast as I could, with Alba's screams ringing in my ears and certain knowledge that Lyncher would not be far behind. But I didn't look back.

I just kept going with my crab scuttle, hoping that Iggy was following. Once or twice I lost sight of the mouse, but then I caught a glimpse of a darting shape in the gloom and shouted back to Iggy that I'd found the way.

The instant the cold air hit my face I knew I'd reached the other side. A sliver of moonlight was coming through the frosted windows and in front of me I could see Kilimanjaro stop and brush his whiskers with his front paws. He stood on his hind legs and looked up and down the passageway. His nose was twitching and I guessed he was taking in the familiar smells of the house to get his bearings. Then he dropped to all fours and scurried out of the patch of moonlight.

Where was Iggy? Had he been caught before he could escape? Or had he decided to stay behind? Why would he do that? He knew we had only a little time to reach the Bridge of Tarle.

I got to my feet and set off in the direction of Bella's room, my mind already beginning to doubt the extraordinary things I had seen. But if I found her notebook I would know for sure that I hadn't been dreaming it all, and somehow I needed that proof. I ran low and fast, darting through the patches of moonlight, all the while fearing that Old Havoc or Lyncher would break through from the other side and seize me. When I got to the room I didn't turn on the lights but felt my way to the chest of drawers. Bella had said the notebook was hidden beneath one of the drawers. I pulled them out and straightaway found it under a piece of lining paper in the space at the back of the chest.

Without another look, I dashed from Bella's room and ran to the kitchen where there were lights on and I could hear the sound of Christmas carols on the radio. Alice was asleep in front of the range. I hesitated in the doorway and stared at the clock. How could it be just past nine? Where had the hours gone? And where was everyone?

I looked at the rise and fall of Alice's chest. She was a heavy sleeper and I reckoned I could creep over to the sideboard and take a hunk of cheese and some bread without her waking and get on my way to the bridge.

Just as I reached the sideboard I became aware of a strange sound coming from the radio. At first it seemed like interference, but then I remembered the strangulated whispers and squeaks that come from the speaker before, and now I heard a familiar voice. I had no doubt that it was speaking to me, clearly as a ringing glass, through the snug warmth of the kitchen. 'Boy, can you hear me? Boy! It's me – Silverfish! Say something.' My hand froze over the cheddar. 'Go to the bridge,' she continued. 'I'll meet you on the riverbank, where your little craft lies.'

The raft! Of course! That would be the only way to get to the bridge in the snow. But then I wondered if this was a trick. I took the cheese and bread and put it in my bag. As I hacked a piece of ham from the joint left over from Christmas Eve, I said, 'How do I know it's you speaking and not one of the others?'

'You don't. You will have to trust me,' she said.

She was right. I had no choice.

'Where's Iggy?' I hissed.

'He will find you. Now! You must go now!'

I turned, put the notebook on the table and made for the door but in my haste, I knocked one of the chairs into the table. Alice woke with a start and in a split second she was hugging me and crying out.

'What've you been doing all this time? We were worried sick. Where've you been?' She held me at arm's length and searched my eyes. I shook my head. I couldn't explain. Not in a hundred years.

'And Mr Iggy, Where's he got to? Where have you both been for all this time?'

'He's...in the house,' I mumbled, 'but...'

Just then the back door opened and a man's voice sounded in the passageway. The dogs shot into the kitchen first and made for the range, where they shook themselves and Black started to gnaw at the lumps of ice stuck to the fur behind his legs, then Tom Jebard, Amos Sprigg and Simon Vetch came in, all wrapped up against the cold. They were carrying sticks and were covered in snow. They patted me on the back roughly and shook me and told me how glad they were that I hadn't been found curled up dead in a snowdrift.

Yes, I was pleased to see them but inwardly I was wondering how on earth I was going to escape and find my way to the bridge. Then there was another noise in the passageway and Quake came in wearing a kind of cape and a deerstalker. Instinctively, I backed away from him, fearing that he was Old Havoc, but his breath showed in the cold of the passageway and the end of his nose was purple and dripping. All I could think of was the ghost of Bella Brown raising an arm and mouthing the word 'murderer'.

'Go,' I said to myself. 'Go, or otherwise you'll be here all night explaining to them.'

Quake wiped his nose and stared at me angrily. 'You've been a most selfish young man to cause so much trouble. Inconsiderate, I would call it. You should be sent to your room without supper.'

Suddenly a booming voice came from the passageway. 'There will be no punishment in my house without my say so. D'yer hear?'

The Colonel entered the kitchen and aimed a look of disgust at Quake. 'What a frightful little tick you are, Quake.'

'He's not just a tick,' I said. 'He's a murderer too. He killed Bella. He pushed her down the well so she wouldn't be found. He stole her book – the book which tells about the secrets of the house.'

'What are you saying, Kim?' asked the Colonel.

'Bella was on to their secret. She knew about Alba and Alba had to stop her. So she got Quake to kill her.'

'Knew what about Alba?' said the Colonel. 'Knew what about Alba? What are you saying?'

'That Alba…is…I can't explain… In Bella's room I found a notebook and a letter.'

'Show them to me,' said the Colonel.

I glanced around desperately. How could I get away?

'What do they say, Kim?' demanded the Colonel. 'Come along, tell us.'

There was nothing else for it. I read out the note in which Quake begged Bella for her own good to meet him at seven o'clock one morning. He told her he had things to reveal to her about Miss Hockmuth and that it was of the utmost importance that she should tell no one of the rendezvous, least of all Miss Hockmuth.

'You did away with her,' cried Simon suddenly. 'It was you!'

Alice put her hands to her face.

'That's enough,' said the Colonel. 'We will give the letter to the proper authorities and let them draw their own conclusions. Let me have it, Kim. What else is in there?'

'She discovered a secret about Quake and Alba,' I said, keeping it as vague as possible. 'Bella was watching them, and they didn't like what she found out. It's all here, sir.'

An appalled look suddenly flooded the Colonel's face. Quake had pulled a revolver. He lunged in my direction, grabbed me and held the gun to my head.

'Stand back, or the boy gets it,' he shouted. He hooked his arm round my chest and started to drag me backwards in the direction of the door. I felt the cold metal of the revolver beneath my ear.

'Now, put the gun down,' the Colonel said quietly. 'You're in enough trouble as it is. You want the boy's death on your conscience?'

Quake seemed to hear nothing. He manhandled me up the two stone steps into the passageway. 'If you follow I will kill him,' he shouted before hauling me off into the dark of the house.

But Quake had not allowed for the dogs who

had pursued us. Applejack was the first to attack, taking hold of Quake's ankle as though it was the fattest rat he had ever seen. Then Black leapt from the dark at his arm. Quake let off two shots. The bullets didn't hit the dogs, nor did they scare them. Black bit Quake on the arm and then went round his back to bite him on the bottom, which made him yell out. His grip slackened and I was able to slip my head under his arm. I wriggled from his grasp then ran for my life to the front door. Two more shots rang out behind me. Praying the dogs hadn't been hurt, I tore back the bolts on the door, turned the key and stumbled down the steps into the snowy night.

Instantly, I knew I had never in my life experienced such a profound, penetrating cold, but luckily I was still wearing my coat and scarf. I adjusted my bag around my shoulders and set off. The snow was covered with a hard crust of ice, which crunched underfoot and sparkled when the moon broke from behind the clouds and flooded the countryside. There was a little breeze, which drew particles of ice from the ground and whipped them into eddies of spindrift. The ice glittered magically in the air, just like the dust in a room picked out by shafts of sunlight.

I headed straight for the riverbank. My plan was

to follow the river up to the shallow bay where the raft was tethered between two alder trees. Because of Quake's lessons and homework it had been several weeks since I had visited the spot and I was worried that the raft might have been torn from its mooring lines during the heavy rains a fortnight before.

Although the snow was deep with drifts three or four feet high, it was so hard I was able to skate across its surface without sinking in. I soon reached the black water's edge, which was rimmed with shelves of ice, and made my way upstream. The first good sign was that there was easily enough water for the raft, which now seemed to be the only sensible way of reaching the bridge. Going cross-country, as Iggy and I had done that first time, was a shorter route, but navigating the hills and woods in this weather would be impossible, especially if the moon disappeared behind the huge bank of cloud in the north.

I found the raft sitting proudly in the bay, gently tugging at its moorings. The pole I used to steer it downstream was still wedged upright in the fork of a branch in a nearby tree. My numbed fingers wrenched the icy knots apart and I pulled the raft on to the beach of slate pebbles so I could check the six oil drums, which Amos had helped me fix to a platform made from two old doors. They were still buoyant and the lashings of oiled twine were as tight as they were on the maiden voyage, when we had named the raft HMS *Spider*. Satisfied it would take my weight, I turned to look across the fields towards the house, hoping to see Iggy's familiar figure making its way towards me. But nothing moved in the bleak landscape, which was as ghostly as anything inside the house. The surge of optimism I'd felt suddenly evaporated. Even if Iggy did manage to escape, how would he know where I was? And did I really think that I could take the raft downstream, negotiate the boiling current where the waters of the Skirl River met the Tarle and then shoot the rapids that led to the bridge? And all before midnight! I sat down on the edge of the raft, feeling despair sweep over me and I thought longingly about Alice's soup.

'What are you waiting for, Boy?' It was Silverfish. She was close by, but I couldn't see her.

'Where are you?' I said.

'Why, on the *Spider* craft, fool!'

'Where's Iggy?'

'We will find your friend at the bridge.'

'I would feel easier if you showed yourself,' I said, coiling the stern rope.

'Not yet! I must keep all my strength, for it costs

272

me dear to show myself in the world of the living. There is another coming with us and you *will* see her.'

'Who?'

'The bird.'

No sooner had she uttered the word than a dark shape appeared from the shadows of a blackthorn bush and waddled towards us.

'She is going with you to the bridge.'

'What? Why?' I stammered, amazed at the sight of the great auk in the moonlight

'She will cross the bridge with you for she wants to be with her kind again and to…'

'To swim amongst the shoals of herring and mackerel,' trilled the great auk happily. 'To taste the salt in my beak, to feel the wind in my feathers, the foam of crashing waves against my eyes.'

'Yes, yes,' I said quickly, having heard all this before. 'But how do you know the Old Man of Tarle will let you cross the bridge?'

'No one could fail to be moved by my story. It's a matter of simple humanity. He will respond favourably, I am sure of it,' she said, hopping a little clumsily onto the front of the raft.

'But I think he has rules about who he lets across, and in what time to set them down in.'

'I have nothing to lose. Besides, you will need my specialist skills on this voyage of yours. There's not many creatures that can swim in this cold.'

I was too tired to argue. Too tired to consider whether the great auk was a ghost or had come to life in the strange conditions that existed between the lines of Tarle.

Silverfish's voice was at my side. 'Waste no more time, Boy. Please, lose not a minute more. You have but little time to midnight.'

I clambered on to the raft, placed the metal pole against the root of a tree and pushed with all my might until the bow swung into the current. We were spun round once then borne along under the vault of bare branches that covered more or less the whole river and in summer made it look like a dark green tunnel. The moonlight flashed through the trees, illuminating the white parts of the great auk's markings and the curvy border of ice either side of us. The bird stood at the front, waving her little wings and shouting out directions in a high, excited voice. 'Hard to port…a touch towards starboard…rocks on your port bow…heave to.' But I knew this stretch of the river well: the sunken logs, the eddies that would trap the raft and the deep black pools where the current slowed and I'd have to find the bank with my pole and shove very hard. Everything seemed to be going well. We reached the arched bridge where one of the victims of the Master of the Fallen Chairs had met his end, and slipped beneath it without difficulty, except the bird took fright at her own echo as she called out some instructions about ducking. Then we came to the flat bridge where the drive passed over the river to the house. Skirl's few lights now vanished behind dense woodland, which I knew would last until our journey ended near the Bridge of Tarle.

We were alone with the murmuring river and the moonlight and the endless silent woods. 'There was never a night like this, Boy,' whispered Silverfish with awe. 'Never so beautiful. Never so quiet. It makes you glad to be alive, don't it?'

It seemed rude to point out that she had been dead for several centuries. But then I thought that the previous twenty-four hours had made me doubt the distinctions between the living and the dead. Silverfish was alive in some way, and because it was dark, it didn't matter that I couldn't see her. She was there with me, willing the raft down to the River Tarle and then on to the ancient stone bridge, and I was glad of her company, whether she was a ghost or not.

About a hundred yards on, we met our first problem. A tree had fallen under the weight of snow and ice and was blocking most of the river. The current pushed the raft into its branches, which sprang back and lashed at my face. I struggled with the pole, but we were trapped.

Without a word, the bird picked up the bow rope in her bill, dived into the water and disappeared. Very slowly the raft began to edge away from the tangle of branches to a point where I was able to stick the pole into the riverbed and push so that we rounded the end of the tree and sped on. The great auk appeared at our side and then with a powerful thrust shot out of the water. 'Ah, the mighty Auk!' she said, dropping the rope on the deck and shaking her body. 'So strong, so sleek, so *nooooble*!'

'And so modest,' I called out from the stern. 'But thank you, dear bird, for your help.'

'Modesty has nothing to do with it. When you're the last of your species you have to boast a little. Otherwise the world forgets. The very names great auk and garefowl will be lost forever. I have a heavy responsibility to all that have gone before me. I am the last and the greatest...'

'What a bird, eh?' Silverfish murmured.

Just then, something dark passed above us, a black shape gliding silently through the air. 'What was that?' I hissed.

'Ssh, it's one of the ravens. She sends them to take you.'

I remembered the picture and the two large birds, which had moved from a wall down to the riverbank. But those were birds. 'Whatever that was, it was far too large and fast to be a bird,' I whispered.

'They ain't birds. They just be called *the ravens.* They are very ancient and dreadful spirits, some say the oldest that are known. They *fetch* people for her.'

'How do they know where we are?'

'If I knows what you were up to, she will know too. The ravens have been sent to make sure you don't reach the bridge.'

'Cripes!' said the great auk.

My eyes searched the night sky for signs of movement. 'Perhaps they've gone,' I whispered. No reply came. 'Silverfish? Where are you? Silverfish, say something.'

Only the river lapping at the sides of the oil drums disturbed the night. Silverfish seemed to have deserted me. The bird followed a few seconds later. Having looked nervously up and down, her eyes blinking rapidly in the moonlight, she dipped her head and dropped into the water.

With several streams joining the river along this stretch, the waters grew wider and deeper, and the raft had begun to pick up speed. I moved to crouch in the middle with the pole pointing upwards, for HMS *Spider* was looking after herself and there was no need for me to steer or fend off the bank.

Suddenly there was a clattering and splintering noise as something fought its way through the branches behind me. A shower of snow cascaded from the trees into the water. I ducked as the thing swooped over me and disappeared into the night, but not before I jabbed at it once with the pole. All was silent again and I began to put together an image of what I had seen in that fleeting moment. I had the impression of a vast black cloak descending on me at incredible speed, its corners flapping and threatening to engulf the whole raft. But there were limbs also in that vision, thrown in silhouette against the moonlit clouds – I could not say how many because they were moving so fast – and a head which was sleek and pointed like a bird's but which had eyes and a leering grimace that were human. I shuddered, but I had seen so much to astound and terrify me in the previous hours and I was not about to go meekly into the next world without a fight.

I gripped the pole and readied myself for the next attack. Nothing happened for a few minutes, then a terrible scream shattered the stillness, a primeval noise that chilled my blood and made my hair stand on end. I rested the pole on the deck and let it lean against my shoulder so as to free my hands to use the harp. I plucked it once in front of my mouth to see if it would work in the cold. At first there was only a dull twang, but before I tried again the noise seemed to magnify and spread of its own accord so that even the snow was shaken from the branches some distance from me. Dreadful moans came from the woods and another cry – a strangulated voice, half human, half bird, like the sound a crow sometimes makes when perched high in a tree and seems to be almost speaking to the world around it. 'Go away,' I shouted to the darkness. 'I will not give in. Go away!'

Seconds later they struck from behind and in front. Two huge shapes reared up from the water and the raft began to rock violently. I clung on with one hand and waved the pole at the creatures with the other, though it did no good and I couldn't strike the harp again because the raft was being shaken so violently. The stench of their breath filled the air and their wings beat against the water with terrifying power, sending showers splattering across the ice on the riverbank.

Just as I had given up all hope, the pole was wrenched from my hand and flew into the air above me, whereupon it levelled itself and did a little jig before laying about the ravens, moving with such speed that I only just managed to keep track of its path through the air.

By this time I guessed it must be Silverfish who had come to my rescue and I shouted out to her as the pole whistled past my face for the third or fourth time and clobbered the creature that had taken hold of the back of the raft. Then, not to be left out, the bird appeared from nowhere, streaking out of the water into the moonlight with a series of leaps. She seized one of the ravens in her beak and dragged it away from the raft. The pole kept up its work, jabbing, beating and spearing. Little by little the raft stopped rocking. The flailing limbs and wings retreated and the black shapes faded into the dark. One or two more squawks of rage rent the air before the woods fell silent again.

'Where are you?' I said to Silverfish.

The pole returned to my hands. 'Here,' she said. And she showed herself very thinly, like a wash of paint in the air. 'I am so tired I can hardly think.'

'You saved my life,' I gasped. 'They were going to tip me into the water and I would have drowned. Thank you.'

Silverfish nodded, but seemed too exhausted to say anything else.

Then the great auk popped onto the deck and shook her feathers.

'Thank you, dear bird,' I said. 'You were magnificent.'

'It is only what you would expect from a great auk. That's just a sample of what we can do.'

'You were both very brave,' I said, standing and feeling for a post at the stern, which allowed me to use the pole as a rudder in the faster current.

A little later I spotted the outline of two big elm trees, which appeared fifty yards before the place where the two rivers met. I steered the raft into the slack water of the left bank to slow our speed, with the roar of the two rivers crashing into each other in my ears. There was far more water in the Tarle than the Skirl and, although I had never reached this point before on *Spider*, I knew the current that would hit us was much stronger than the one had that carried us this far. An added complication was the boulders that stood where the waters met. No raft, however well made, could withstand the battering from the Tarle after being swept on to them. It would mean certain death in the icy torrent for me. I nudged the raft along the bank to the mouth of the Skirl and looked across the seething tide. I could see from the ripples in the moonlight that there were several different streams to the current.

'Bird,' I called out above the roar. 'Can you drag us into that calm water over there?' I pointed into the middle. 'Just below the log there's a glassy patch. Do you see? If we can cross this current in front of us we'll be all right.'

'Most certainly,' replied the great auk, who had been looking about with a professional eye. She picked up the rope again and plunged into the water.

We were at the point of no return. The raft spun round and dithered, as if not knowing which current to obey, then suddenly took off towards the centre where it was buffeted by the faster water that hit us from above and broke over the oil drums with a hollow ring. The deck became soaked, and twice I nearly slipped off trying to use the pole as a rudder.

'Take care, Boy,' said Silverfish in my ear. 'We cannot lose you now.'

Inch by inch the raft edged across the fast stream. The line slackened and tightened by turns as the great auk jerked us forward with each stroke of her little wings. At one stage I thought she had lost the struggle and I tried to hold the raft against the current by placing the pole against a group of rocks to my left. But then the bird broke to the glittering surface and brought us the last few feet into the calm water. 'Hooray!' I shouted. 'Bravo!'

Silverfish came to the side to look at the great auk. 'Some bird,' she said, truly impressed.

'It may not be as salty as we auks like,' enthused the bird, 'but it's a tonic to be diving in cold waters again and to be back in the swim of things, so to speak.' Instead of returning to the raft, she cruised alongside us as we glided through the placid waters, warbling something that only just resembled a song.

'But she can't sing!' murmured Silverfish as an afterthought.

Not ten minutes later we reached the place where the river spread into a wide pool about a hundred yards from the bridge. The water was shallow and I was worried we might become grounded in the middle so I steered for the side, beached the raft and jumped ashore. The ice just above the waterline shattered as I scrambled up the bank.

I turned back to see Silverfish's form poised over the ice. 'What are you doing? There's no time.'

'It be so pretty – do you see the ferns that grow in the ice and sparkle in the moonlight?'

'Yes,' I said impatiently, 'you were the one rushing me earlier. I think I should go.'

'Is it cold?' she said urgently. 'Do you feel the cold on your cheeks?'

'Yes,' I replied, noticing the plumes of my breath. 'It's very sharp – my cheeks are burning and I can't feel my fingers and look, there are icicles in my hair!' I shook them so they rattled.

She smiled. 'I forgot how all that feels,' she said wistfully.

I looked away. I didn't know what to say so I searched for the matches that I had been using to light the lantern. They were still safely tucked in my inside pocket, and more importantly they were dry. 'Come along,' I said.

We set off across the open ground towards the old stone. The bird waddled behind me and talked to herself about the great achievements of her species, while Silverfish slipped along at my side.

Not a living thing moved around us. The trees stood motionless. No fox, no owl disturbed the night. Only the crunch of my footsteps across the icy clearing could be heard.

We came to the middle where it was as hard and white and flat as a dinner plate, and there Silverfish started to skip and dance with her hands beckoning playfully at the moon and the scudding clouds. I watched for a few moments, but when she saw my expression she let her arms drop. We both felt awkward, yet the sight of her had made my mind race with a possibility.

I was not the only one to be watching. I caught sight of a slender shape moving quite slowly between the trees. At first I thought the shadows were playing tricks on my eyes, but then I saw a face that stared out blankly from behind some cover. I told Silverfish. 'They are here, to be sure,' she said. 'Those that come to see; those that wants to know what happens and how you fare.'

'Do they mean me harm?'

'They want you to live.'

'Are these the same spirits as in the house?'

'No, most of them stay out here in the woods.'

We reached the place where the stone was, but I had to dig with my hands in the snow to find it and read the inscription, which again struck me as odd: My name is Watchman, heir am I still watching day and night welcoming all persons that comes heir to pay with silver and cross to the other side.

Silverfish looked down. 'You know what they say about this stone? They say that a fancy gentleman took it away. Dug it out he did, and had it raised onto a cart by a couple of strong men and then they took it to his property and set it up as a curiosity. Next morning the stone was back here and the gentleman was lying by its side, dead as a dormouse. Killed he was by the guardian of the stone that lives hereabouts and left here for everyone to see with his throat cut and his eyes taken from him. They say the guardian ordered the birds to peck them out. And then the two young men that helped him, they died within the year, but not so horribly.'

Beneath the snow where we had set the first fire there was a ring of charred wood. I piled it together then asked the great auk to look for some tinder. She said she didn't know what that was, and anyway she wasn't used to fetching and carrying, and being ordered about.

'If you want to get over to the other side,' I told her, 'find me dry leaves and twigs quickly.'

'There's no need to use that tone with me,' she said, putting her head in the air and turning away.

'Well then just get on with it,' I snapped. I was tired and worried about Iggy and, despite all she had done for me, the bird did rub me up the wrong way.

I found several big branches, dragged them over to the spot, then broke them down to size by standing on them and pulling up, or hitting the larger ones against a tree trunk. The sound of the snapping wood rang through the woods like rifle shots.

Soon I was standing by a small wigwam of wood. At the base I left a hole, which I stuffed with the leaves and twigs the bird had collected and some coarse lining that had come loose inside my jacket.

'I wish I knew the time,' I said, 'I don't want to light the fire until Iggy comes.'

But the great auk and Silverfish weren't listening to me. Their attention had gone to the woods, and I could see that both were straining every sense to plumb the depths of the night.

'What is it?' I whispered.

The great auk looked at me and shook her head. Something was wrong. I knelt down and placed a few matches inside the pile so they would catch fire when I lit the tinder. Then I glanced up at Silverfish.

'She comes now,' she said. 'Light the fire and you will be saved. Light it! Quickly!'

I struck a match but the head broke off and I fumbled to open the box again. The thought flashed into my mind that even if I did manage to light the fire, I had no money and nothing of any value whatsoever to pay the Old Man of Tarle. Then I noticed that Silverfish had vanished.

'Where have you gone?'

'Light the fire, I will be close by,' she replied.

Shielding the match, I placed it between the leaves and the piece of lining. It flickered and then one or two of the strands from the lining began to glow. But by now something behind me was wrenching my attention and every part of my being was jangling with nerves. Slowly I turned my head. Alba was standing motionless in the centre of the clearing, still dressed in all her finery. Behind her stood Semaj Trow, Earwig, Firebrat and Lyncher, but they were nothing like as distinct as they had been in Skirl. There were others who were barely visible.

'A few smouldering twigs will not save you now,' said Alba in a voice as clear and sharp as the night. 'It's time for you to join my little party of Dragomen, as fate has decreed.'

'Fate decrees nothing,' I shouted back. 'Where's Iggy? What've you done with him?'

'He too will die,' she said, moving towards me. 'I will attend to him after I've dealt with you.'

So he was still alive. I wondered frantically where on earth he had got to. 'We both escaped from you and we will again. The Master of the Fallen Chairs only says what *has* happened, it does not foretell what *will* happen,' I shouted.

There was a movement beside me. Possessing no powers of invisibility, the great auk had edged closer and had now crept behind me. 'Please do something,' she said. 'She will have us both for breakfast if you don't.'

I reached for my pole and shouted, 'You're human. You were frightened of a mouse. I'll hurt you, if you come near us.' I was hoping that Silverfish would snatch the pole from me again and beat Alba over the head, but it stayed firmly lodged in my hands.

'Brave talk from one who is certainly doomed. Seize him!' she yelled. 'Seize him, *smash* him against the rocks and *sink* him in the freezing waters and there hold him until he is *drowned*. Let us be done with him!'

The hooded monks moved out from the shadows and into the open ground where their black habits began to flow outwards and unfurl into the wings of the ravens. Their cowls fell back to reveal terrifying half-bird, half-human faces. They hopped grotesquely across the snow and leapt into the air, and soon their terrifying silhouettes were moving noiselessly into the night sky. I jabbed the pole when the first one dived and then tried to hit the second as it came low, flapping just a few feet from the ground like some prehistoric monster. But I didn't manage to connect either time. My hands were too cold and the pole was too heavy for me to use it like a sword. 'Silverfish,' I cried. 'We need you now! Help us!'

No answer came. The ravens soared higher and higher. Any second, they would turn to earth and swoop down upon us with ferocious speed. We were all but dead. But as their wings folded into an arrow shape, something caused them to stall and then plummet to the ground screeching.

'Look!' said the great auk excitedly. 'Look up there. Look!'

'What?'

'Look, you idiot,' she said, waving her wings excitedly.

'I can't see anything.' But no sooner had I said

it than I saw a wisp reaching high up above the trees. 'What is it?'

'It's the spirits from the wood. They've made a barrier that nothing can pass through. They are defying *her*.'

There was no time to lose. Without looking to see Alba's reaction I turned to the fire, knelt down and started to blow. The leaves burst into flames, but when my breath ran out the flames died back and the fire returned to smouldering. 'Flap your wings,' I shouted to the great auk. 'And I'll keep blowing.'

Her wings may have been very small but they could beat as fast as a hummingbird's and very soon the draught was fanning the flames beautifully.

Just then a very unexpected sound reached my ears – the familiar chugging of the Massey Ferguson tractor that was used on the farm. I'd know its engine anywhere. I jumped up and saw two lights forking through the woods as the 'Fergie' made its way along the track that we'd come down the first time.

'Oh cripes,' said the bird. 'Now I'm done for. They'll take me back to the house and fix me to that stand with double nails!'

'No they won't,' I said. 'You're coming with me.

291

You, Silverfish and Iggy are all going to cross the bridge.'

At the first sound of the tractor, Alba's army of spirits began to melt into the shadows, leaving her in the middle of the clearing. She raised her hand. 'I will have you as my own soon,' she called out. 'You will be chained in the afterlife as my servant forever. Don't think you can escape. It is impossible!'

She held her hand out until the tractor's headlights broke into the clearing and swept the ground, then she vanished. I put my hands up against the lights and tried to see who was driving. It was only when the tractor had turned and pulled up that I recognised Softly Perkins, the woodsman. Sitting on the mudguard of one of the huge rear wheels was Iggy, beaming and gesticulating in the moonlight. He was wearing his hat and various pieces of cloth wrapped round him, and he looked more outlandish than I had ever seen him.

He jumped down and rushed over to me. 'Brother Kim,' he shouted at the top of his voice. 'Look at Fergie. Is it not the most beautiful machine that ever exists?' Then he clasped me by the shoulders. 'And you are best and bravest of all brothers. But why you bring bird?'

The great auk had now reverted to her stuffed bird pose. Her feathers no longer wore the sheen of moonlight but were drab and lifeless, her wings hung morbidly, her eyes were glassy and unseeing. There was nothing that looked more dead than the great auk when she affected to be a museum exhibit. 'Come along,' I said to her. 'They're not going to do anything to you.'

'It's the other man,' she mumbled out of the corner of her beak. 'We are not acquainted.'

Softly had climbed down and was walking towards us.

'If he drove Iggy here on the tractor,' I said, 'there's nothing for you to worry about. He's a friend.'

'Very good friend,' said Iggy. 'Very, very good friend. He finds me in the snow and he scoops me up and brings me all the way on the beautiful Fergie.'

'Hello,' I said to Softly.

'Hey-up,' he replied. 'So, you're going to cross the bridge?'

'How do you know that?'

'Your friend's been telling me. Anyways you couldn't live in these here woods for as long as I have without knowing a thing or two about what goes on. When I was a young'un, I was told to keep away from the bridge and treat any strangers I met here with respect.' He paused, took a pipe out of his pocket and jammed it into the corner of his mouth before lighting it. 'So, you lads have got to cross over to save yourselves. That's the sum of it?'

I nodded.

'Well, can't say as I'm surprised after hearing your story. Never liked that woman; never trusted her neither.'

At this the great auk had gingerly taken a step or two towards me and was now looking up at Softly.

'Well, I never. What's this then? Some kind of penguin, is it? Where did you spring from?' He bent down to look at the great auk.

'She's a great auk or *garefowl*,' I said hastily. 'She's the only one of her kind.'

'In more ways than one,' added the great auk unnecessarily. 'And by the way it's not *garefowl*. Everyone makes that mistake; it's *garry-fowl*.'

'A bird that talks too,' said Softly. 'Well, I've heard everything now.' But he didn't seem very surprised. 'You lads know what you're doing?'

Iggy nodded. 'We save ourselves then we come back for more plum pudding.'

'Ah, yes, Mrs Vetch makes a fine Christmas pud, doesn't she?'

How long ago that pudding and the Christmas dinner seemed. I looked around and then above us.

Softly was studying me. 'What are you searching for, lad?'

'A…a friend…it's quite difficult to describe her.'

He puffed at his pipe so the bowl glowed, then let a thin stream of smoke out of the corner of his mouth, and followed it with his eyes. 'A bit like that is she?'

I nodded.

'A girl? Likes to dance?'

'Yes, but she's not part of our…'

'World? You don't have to tell me, son. I know the one. A pretty young thing – I've often seen 'er in the woods, dancing alone. Once on a summer's evening I got out my fiddle and played her a tune. She seemed to like it. I wondered about her. A lost soul like so many in this place. Perhaps she'll come back to you when I've gone. Anyways, I better be off.'

'The fire keeps dying – everything is too damp,' I said. 'Have you got anything to make it go better?'

'Oh, I can help you with that.' He knocked his pipe out on the heel of his boot and went to a metal box beneath the seat on the tractor.

He returned a few moments later. 'Here are some rags. I put a drop of oil on them so they'll go up a treat.'

Iggy took them and stuffed them into the fire and lit them. Very soon the fire was roaring and snapping and the trees were lit orange.

'You'll keep warm for a bit with that,' said Softly, returning to the tractor. Before he climbed up he took his pipe out of his mouth and held it by the bowl with the stem pointing at us. 'I'll tell Tom Jebard that I've found you and that you're all right.' I moved forward a couple of paces to catch what he was saying, because as usual he was speaking under his breath. 'I'll say you're going to try to be back soon, but not to worry if you're not. I can't say much more or else folks round here will be thinking I'm touched in the head, and we don't want that, do we?' He mounted the tractor and started the engine, which turned over with not much noise. 'Right, you look after yourselves. And I'll keep an eye out for your return. There'll be snow on the ground for many weeks yet, so you'll need me to come and fetch you when you're back. Make another fire. I'll see the smoke.'

He put the tractor in gear and drew a wide arc in the snow before setting off up the track and throwing a final wave over his shoulder.

Our eyes returned to the fire.

'Did you bring any money?' I asked.

Iggy put his hand to his mouth. 'No, Brother Kim. I forget sovereigns. But I have this from father before three. He took a watch and chain from one of his pockets. 'This is gold also.'

'We'll give him the watch and say we'll come back another time to leave some money for him. Maybe he'll give your watch back.'

A voice suddenly came from behind us. We both jumped and whipped round to see the Old Man of Tarle standing with his stick and a huge bearskin draped around his shoulders.

He had made not a sound coming over the bridge.

Chapter Seventeen

The Plight of Silverfish

'Credit! Did I hear you say you wanted credit?' He said scowling at us from a great height. 'A couple of fly-by-nights like you! Credit!'

'I give you this, my watch,' said Iggy, moving quickly to the stone and placing it on top.

'Ha-ha! A watch!' He looked down at us. 'Does it occur to you that I am the very last person who needs a timepiece of any sort? Ask yourselves what I would do with a watch. I am a master of time, not its slave! Am I to gaze at the dial to know the hour in this cold, dank time of yours and think what jolly fun?' He opened his hand and I saw the gold glint dully in the light of the fire. He had already taken it from the stone. 'Ah ha! I see now why you're so desperate. Just fifteen minutes to midnight. Just fifteen minutes of life before she takes you as her own. That is what we chaps in the time business would call a deadline. Ha-ha! A deadline! You see the joke.' But he wasn't smiling.

'A watch for a Watchman,' said Iggy.

'Is that your idea of wit?'

Iggy opened his hands good-naturedly and held out the watch. 'It is made from gold and it comes from father before three.'

'It may have sentimental value to you, but you can hardly expect me to regard this trinket in the same light. And the gold, well that can be melted down and used to my advantage no doubt, but it's not enough to allow the two of you to cross.'

'Four,' I said, 'There are four of us...'

'Ah yes, the bird. I recognised her immediately. The great auk, or as the natives in Greenland called her, *Isarukitsoq*. Latin classification: *Penguinis impennis*. Probably comes from the Welsh for *pen gwyn*, in other words *white head*. She is the last of her species. I have a mind to let her pass over free of charge.'

The great auk's chest swelled with pride and she moved forward to the stone bridge.

'But not yet!' growled the Old Man of Tarle. 'Our negotiation is not over. There are certain formalities to complete. For one thing you need to specify the hour, day and year that you wish to visit. For another, you must make various undertakings. You cannot go back and change things willy-nilly to suit yourselves. You must go, find what you want and return. You are an observer, a witness, not a participant. Interference of any sort will lead to extreme retribution.'

'What's retribution?'

'Punishment, idiot boy! You will be conveyed to the darkest time in history and there left to rot.'

'Is that what happened to people you didn't like who came here – the picnickers and trippers?'

'Precisely, but do not interrupt if you want to save your life.' He extended a long blackened finger from a mitten and wiped his nose. 'And you must specify the hour and date of your return before your departure. That is a more difficult calculation to make than you might suppose.'

'No it isn't,' I said looking at Iggy. 'We come back tomorrow, 26th December, 1962.'

'You seem very confident. Are you certain of that?'

I hesitated, wondering if there was a catch and looked at Iggy again. He nodded. 'Yes,' I said, 'because the curse of the picture will no longer be working, will it?'

'Ah yes, the Master of the Fallen Chairs. You know you cannot alter events that have occurred

301

because of the painting, however regrettable they may seem to you or me. A man who has died, whatever the circumstances, remains dead.' He looked at the watch and chuckled again. 'I would advise a slightly earlier time – maybe a touch before your departure.'

'Is this possible?' asked Iggy.

'Well, if we bend the rules a little, I am sure no one will notice. And you may find that you need to return to complete some business on Christmas Day. 'Course, it's up to you. And what is your destination – at what time do you want to be set down?'

'The 25th December, 1862,' I replied, nervously looking beyond the light of the fire where things were shifting among the trees and shapes flitted from the shadows.

'Are you sure? Nothing to add?'

'Twenty-four,' said Iggy quickly, 'not *twenty-five*.'

'The twenty-fourth it shall be. And the hour?'

'Middays,' said Iggy.

'Yes,' I said, 'we will need to be there before Christmas Day.'

'And the fourth?'

'Er…? I'm sorry, what do you mean?'

'You said *four* were to cross the bridge. Who is this *fourth* person? I see no one here.'

'Her name is Silverfish,' I said.

'Silverfish?'

'Yes, er…she is dead…but her spirit is…I think she'd like to go back to a time when she was alive.' As I said it, I was aware of Silverfish forming by my side. The Old Man looked down at her without surprise.

'Ah, is *this* your little honey?' he said.

'No, she isn't; she just needs to be alive. That's all.'

'Doesn't everyone? Anyway, it's out of the question.'

'Please, sir, we will give you money.'

'Money has nothing to do with it. Conveying your wispy little sweetheart to the time when she was alive would be an offence against nature. It is forbidden to return the dead to the living. Imagine a young woman bumping into her own ghost. It's unthinkable. I cannot – so to speak – pour her back into the living flesh and blood because her spirit is already there in her body. Ask the girl if she knows the date and time of her death.'

She shook her head.

'Exactly. Few ghosts do, in my experience. It's all a bit hazy. Poor lambs. And that presents difficulties because if she got it wrong and went back later than the time of death we would have the ridiculous situation of two identical ghosts haunting the same place. You have to know the exact time of death. The very second of expiration is a minimum requirement.' He paused. 'You appear to be a bit vacant, young man. Perhaps these metaphysical problems are beyond you? Suffice to say, she's not coming.' He grinned and showed his foul black teeth.

'But I thought you said you could bend the rules and no one would notice.'

'There is a difference between rules and laws. You cannot bend laws. Laws govern the universe. Rules are what some fool says you must or must not do. I break rules as a matter of course – in fact as a sacred duty.'

I turned to Silverfish, who smiled weakly. 'After all you did for me, I wanted to help.'

'No one can help the dead, Boy,' she said quietly.

'I will never give up trying,' I replied. Then I thought of another argument and turned to the Old Man. 'If the great auk is going back and she's dead, why can't Silverfish?'

'I am most certainly not dead,' huffed the bird.

'Then what were you doing nailed to that stand for a century or more?' I asked.

'I was merely detained,' she replied.

The Old Man raised a hand. 'Exceptions are made for extinct species of waterfowl etcetera etcetera. Besides, the bird has little chance of meeting herself in the expanses of history, to say nothing of the expanse of the oceans. And if by some incredible chance she met herself she wouldn't know it, because one great auk looks much like another and they all say the same thing.' He held out his hands to warm them by the fire and considered us. 'Do we have a deal? Are you going to stand here and waste what few minutes remain to you?'

'We come,' said Iggy.

'Then you must pay,' said the Old Man with a frightening leer.

'We can only pay when we come back,' I said, thinking that was one way of making the Old Man keep his side of the bargain.

'Ah, but this little trip is worth more than a battered gold watch, and I cannot trust you to return here with the money.'

'You must trust us,' said Iggy.

'I trust no one as a matter of policy. It is impractical to go hunting down people that owe me money through time *and space*. You will work for me in exchange.'

'Doing what?' I asked nervously.

'Just a few errands,' he said, turning and placing his stick on the first stone slab of the bridge.

'But what about Silverfish? I can't leave her.' I took a step towards the spot where Silverfish shimmered in the moonlight. 'They will throw her to Firebrat and he will do his worst with her in his horrible place.'

'She knows how to look after herself, and I have no doubt that you will see her again – in another time and another place, as romantic novelists say.' He stopped suddenly, and the tone of jaunty contempt disappeared. 'Ah, she's among us again. She never gives up, does she?'

I turned to see Alba with her throng of horrors moving towards us across the frozen clearing. There was no sign of the barrier of wood spirits that had caused the ravens to crumple to the ground.

The Old Man of Tarle straightened, as though to confront her, and muttered some words that none of us heard. I looked at Alba in the moonlight, so poised, beautiful and terrifying, and saw a smile spread across her face. In the Old Man's features there was a look of familiarity. Something had passed between these two time travellers, and just for a moment, I saw them as gods, equal in their power and great heartlessness.

The Old Man nodded to himself and rasped, 'It's not finished yet – not by a long chalk.'

The moment was over. He rose to the first slab and towered above us. 'Come along, stir your stumps, or it's fried tomatoes for you two.'

'Fried tomatoes?'

'Pulverisation – a pulpy bloody unrecognisable mess is what you will be in a matter of minutes if you don't climb up here.'

The bird did not need any further invitation and hopped up. Iggy and I followed and so began our journey through time, but not before I turned to gaze at Silverfish once more and saw her put her hand up to stop a tear before she vanished for good.

Chapter Eighteen

Crossing Time

Tap-tap, tap-tap, tap-tap went the Old Man of Tarle's stick across the icy slabs of the bridge. Iggy placed a hand on my shoulder to make sure that I didn't slip and tumble into the river. The bird waddled ahead of us with the see-saw gait of a penguin, her eyes wide and darting from side to side expectantly. I hated leaving Silverfish behind and now it occurred to me that I would even miss the great auk when she swam into the vast ocean of the past.

'Keep up. Don't hang about!' shouted the Old Man over his shoulder. 'I haven't got all night.' He turned and glared at me. 'Don't tell me I've got a snivelling moper on my hands.'

'What's a moper?' I asked.

'Someone that mopes about the place when they are separated from their sweetheart.'

'I wasn't thinking of her,' I said.

'Huh…as a clever fellow I once knew remarked, "The grave's a fine and private place, but none I think do there embrace." That young lady's dead. Now forget her and keep up.'

Iggy looked suddenly interested by this and smiled to himself.

'The bridge is very long,' I murmured a few minutes later to Iggy.

'Longer than you thought?' the Old Man said, shouting out above the noise of the river, which seemed to have got much louder. 'There's a reason for that. You're not just crossing a bridge. You're crossing through time.' He stopped suddenly and turned to us. I bumped into the great auk and trod on her tail and she let out a squawk.

'We are betwixt and between times,' he said, 'the place where the great dark descends and where all that is known to man is nothing and never was. Being? There is no existence here, no meaning. Just *time* washing by. Where is the moon now? Where are the clusters of stars?' We looked up. The moon had disappeared. There were no clouds, no stars. I glanced back along the ancient clapper bridge and saw no hint of the bank. The bird mewed her anxiety, lifted her wings slowly and looked up to me.

'Now cast your eyes down to the waters, if you will, and watch the flood of time. Everything that *was* or *is* or *will be* is there. The day after tomorrow is the day before yesterday...and is now. We are betwixt and between times where all passion and dread and love and happiness are nothing. Everything felt, or seen, or heard by any man that ever lived is lost in the desolate wastes of endless time. That is the secret of the universe, the single great meaning of it all: there is no meaning, just time.'

He watched silently with one arm raised in our direction to stop us talking, then thrust his stick into the current and made the water curl up round the shaft. He grimaced with the exertion of holding it still, then withdrew it and turned to us with a leer. 'Right, follow me and keep up!'

The water roared and roared and we seemed to walk for an age along the span of flagstones. But then we came to the end and the Old Man of Tarle dropped down to a grassy bank where there was no snow or ice but merely the signs of a recent flood – a flotsam of dead reeds had gathered round the tussocks of grass. It was daytime – a curious misty morning light filled the pastures and woods all around us. And there was birdsong, more varied and louder than I had noticed before at Skirl, even during summer.

Iggy looked about, his eyes narrowing with the speculation that was always bubbling in his head.

'Here we are,' said the Old Man. 'The 24th of December, 1862.'

'Christmas Eve?' Iggy said.

'Er…yes, in principle,' he replied, wheezing with amusement.

Iggy took his hat off. 'What is principle?'

The Old Man of Tarle grinned in a way that I didn't like. 'In principle it is Christmas Eve.' He paused, searching our eyes for understanding. 'But in practice it isn't. If we were in a time when there was Christmas Day, this indeed would be Christmas Eve.' He put a fist up to his mouth to suppress a chuckle and I remembered with a shudder what he had said the first time, 'I picks them up and puts them down in another time.'

'We asked to go back 100 years to Christmas Eve, 1862,' I said.

'Yes, you specified 24th December. Yes, you specified 1862. Yes, you specified you would like to arrive at noon – that is to say in daylight. And all those requests have been met to within an hour's accuracy.' He grinned again.

312

Iggy's eyes bulged and the great auk edged behind him.

The Old Man's gaze darted from the trees to us. 'I particularly asked if you had any further instructions and you said 24th December 1862. That was all. You must appreciate that time travel is a precise business: it's not some kind of nature ramble where you decide to go first in one direction then the other as the fancy takes you. I asked for co-ordinates, which you gave me, but they were regrettably lacking in one essential ingredient – AD or BC. Was it 1862 BC, or AD? How was I to know?'

Iggy looked at me. 'Old rascal takes us back 4,000 years.'

'Mind your tongue,' he snapped, 'or you'll be spending the rest of your days here. So...to continue, I selected the one that I thought would be most interesting to us all – that is to say 1862 BC, some 3,824 years before the time you were in. And here we all are on what I think you will agree is really quite a decent kind of morning, with an almost spring-like breeze blowing up the river. It is, as you will notice, a good deal milder than the time you left, which is because the earth is enjoying a warming trend between the ice ages.' With this he prodded us off the bridge with his stick and the bird let out a wail of protest.

'So, we are your prisoners,' said Iggy, coming to the point. 'What you want?'

'I wouldn't have put it like that myself but I am, as you observe, in a strong bargaining position.'

'Will you take us to 1862 AD?' I asked.

'There's no deal. These journeys across time don't come free, you know. I am not some cut-rate tour operator. You made a mistake and you have to pay for it.'

'With errands?' I said.

'Yes, but I would put them in the *task* category rather than the *errands* category, if you know what I mean. What I have in mind may even qualify for the *labours* category, as in the Labours of Hercules, ha-ha! When you have completed them I will return you to your own time. Do I have your agreement?'

'We see picture first and save our lives first. Then we do errands.'

'You're in no position to bargain.'

'Please, Iggy.' I said with an edge in my voice designed to make him shut up.

'No,' insisted Iggy, 'picture first, errands second – or no deal.'

The Old Man's eyes became thunderous and then quite simply he disappeared.

'Now you've done it,' said the bird.

'Well, there's nothing to stop you jumping into the river and swimming down to the sea,' I said. 'BC or AD, it doesn't matter to you, does it? As long as you are in a time when there were plenty of great auks. There are probably even more great auks in this time than ever before or since.'

'But not my one and only beloved great auk!' she said.

'Oh golly, you mean to say you're hoping to find your mate?'

'Yes.' The bird's head was drooping, her wings hung limp and a tear had formed in the corner of her eye. I reflected that there was no more depressing sight than a lovesick auk – great or little. 'OK,' I said a bit sharply. 'What are we meant to do about that? We're all three of us trapped here.'

'Remember, I am the last,' she said passionately, 'the very last of a species which your kind drove to extinction. If it wasn't for me no one would know what a great auk looked like.'

Iggy nodded sympathetically. 'What you want, honourable bird? How we help?'

'Take me with you to the house. I was hoping

315

for some clue as to when I was caught and killed. That way I might be able to go back to the time before and find *him* and save *him* from that terrible death.'

'Of being tried in a court and stoned.' I said quickly, to stop her telling the story again.

The bird continued. 'There was a wild rocky outcrop in the great northern seas where we spent our time together. I will wait for him there and...and...I know he will come. I know...' Her voice trailed off and her beak dipped even lower.

'I am sure he will,' I said. I patted her on the back. 'We will get you there, if we can.'

'And then,' said the great auk, her tone brightening, 'I will bring him back to the bridge and we will ask the Old Man if we can be together forever in the distant past – during the time when our greatest adventures were had and when men stayed on land and the seas were our own.'

'First things first,' said Iggy.

'What are we going to do?' I asked him.

'We will make deal with Old Man of Tarle,' he said, raising his voice.

'Good fellow,' came the Old Man's voice, though we could not see its owner. 'We have a deal. Follow me to the centre again and I will guide you to Christmas Eve 1862.'

'AD!' I shouted.

'Agreed.'

'Picture first, errands after,' Iggy called out.

'Very well, if you insist,' came the voice. 'But I warn you that there are one or two surprises... And...er...well...you will see for yourselves.'

We mounted the first flagstone and started across the bridge. It became dark again. We walked until the noise of the torrent of time beneath our feet drowned out all voices. All we could hear was tap-tap, tap-tap, tap-tap.

It took us ten minutes to find the Old Man. He was standing facing downstream with the mist swirling round him. His face was sombre and he was staring intently into the water.

'What's wrong?' I asked, struck by the sudden change in his manner.

He turned to me. 'There's no point sucking up to me, young man, I am impervious to all blandishments.'

'I wasn't,' I said. 'You looked sad and I wondered what was the matter.'

He examined me with his terrifying eyes. 'Man is what's the matter – his folly, his vanity, his destruction. I see it all flooding past – the same mistakes, the same barbarity, the same pride, generation after generation. Man is a cliché.'

'A cliché?' I said, not knowing what it meant.

'He is a bad joke repeated.'

The great auk nodded sagely. Iggy's eyes looked sad.

'It's something you have to get used to in my line of work.' He stopped. 'All present? Good!' He thrust his stick into the water and held it there for a few minutes then removed it.

'I'll be getting along, then. Use whichever side of the bridge you like and remember you cannot change events that have occurred because of that picture. Nothing must be altered. Do I have your solemn undertaking on that?' Iggy and I nodded. 'Right, now I shall withdraw to a pleasanter time and wait for your signal. Make the fire in the same place.' He moved off then stopped and turned to us. His face was never more dreadful. 'If you do not return, I will hunt you down and take you to a time and place where you will certainly cash in your chips. The Black Death of 1347 AD has always been a favourite destination of mine for troublesome customers.' He took a few more steps and disappeared in the swirls of mist with the words. 'Do not defy me, *Flopsy.*'

Iggy shrugged. 'Old rascal!' he said and put his arm round me.

But he wasn't gone yet. A croaky voice came from somewhere out in the mist with a verse.

Oh, my darling feet,
That splendid couple
Where the ends of me meet:
Odd but symmetrical
And utterly unique
My darling and delightful,
My adorable feet!

Silence followed.

Chapter Nineteen

The Good Christmas Past

We crossed to the side where we had made the fire a hundred years in the future. It was light, and the trees were covered with hoarfrost. The clearing was still there, yet on the far side stood a broken-down cottage and nearby the remains of a cart. There were more trees in the woods than in our day and the undergrowth was denser.

'What shall we do?' I said.

'Find place for hiding, then go and see picture.'

'But we can't be seen with the bird. That means we will have to go into the house when it's dark. Shall we hide in the farmyard?' I stopped. My head was muzzy with fatigue. 'And we need food.'

Iggy put an arm round my shoulder. 'Come, Brother Kim: it is not far.'

We set off up the track. How odd that

everything we had ever done was in the future. Everything we were going to do in the next few hours was in the past.

'Do you think the house is the same with all those ghosts?' I asked.

'No, more people than ghosts. That is point, Brother Kim. Miss Alba makes kingdom for herself in the house. It is becoming larger and she draws spirits from all around.'

'How do you know that?'

'I have my profession,' he began. 'I am not just Igthy Ma-tuu Clava, Lord of Ro-Torva, brother of Brother Kim. I am artist of seashells, poet, magician, magnificent sailor, teller of stories – in own language, of course – fisher, the maker of perfumes, and investigator. That is chief profession.'

'What do you investigate?'

'Time, Brother Kim, and murders: the foul play mostly.'

'How do you investigate time?'

'I am investigating time at moment – as we say in my language, the *cracks in time*.'

'Have you seen one before?'

'I have but I not use it like with old Bony Fingers.'

'Bony Fingers?'

322

'Old Man of Tarle. Old Bony Fingers.' And then he added with a significant wink, *'Old Inky fingers.'*

It was true, the Old Man's fingers were bony and two fingers of his left hand were stained with black ink, but I didn't think it important.

The bird took little interest in our conversation and trailed behind, saying that she wished she had swam up the river, although she agreed that she would have been spotted sooner or later. I was so tired I could barely raise the energy to put one foot in front of the other, but Iggy kept me going by pointing out the difference that a hundred years made. The track was rutted with cartwheels, not tyres. Little cottages were dotted around the estate that did not exist in our time. The fields and hedges were all well looked after.

But nothing prepared us for the view of Skirl when we crested the hill and saw the house lying in the valley below looking like a palace. Smoke from thirty or so chimneys rose into the cold morning air, and the trees and bushes which shrouded the house and blocked out the light of the twentieth century had not yet seeded, taken root and grown. The courtyard, a place of such neglect in my time, was alive with activity. Several carriages were lined up and being cleaned and polished by grooms. A horseman rode up and was greeted by two men who ran from a doorway. Everywhere you looked there was something going on. Men were raking the gravel on the drive, cutting hedges, digging flower borders, washing down and leading horses, carrying supplies from wagons into the house, tending fires, sawing and stacking logs, hoisting milk churns, leading cows, ferrying piles of laundry from an outhouse. We were seeing Skirl in its heyday: the Drago family was at the height of its wealth and power.

With all these people about it wasn't going to be easy to get into the house without being spotted. Then another thought occurred to me, 'We don't know the picture's there,' I said. 'Just because it was painted in 1862 doesn't mean that it's in the house now, does it?'

'It is there,' said the great auk. 'I know it.'

We walked on a little and found a brick and timber barn, which was filled to the rafters with hay and straw. The bird and I climbed up to a loft on one side and sank into the warm, musty hay while Iggy went off to look for food, saying he had ways of not being seen. I wondered what he meant and whether an extinct bird needed food, before falling into a deep, dreamless sleep.

I woke in the same position with something

sharp digging into my ribs and turned my head to see the bird's beak pecking at my side. Voices were coming from below us. The bird's eyes were wide and staring. I crawled to the edge of the hayloft and looked down. Two farm workers were loading a wagon with pitchforks, grumbling about the weather and their wives. A horse stood steaming in the cold, having pulled the wagon up the hill from the farm. The men wore floppy hats, boots, gaiters and leather jerkins fastened up to the necks. Their faces and hands were red. One wore a beard and the other had magnificent side-whiskers that flowed outwards. Suddenly this man looked up and caught sight of me.

'What you be doing up there?' he said.

I didn't reply for a moment, then realised that I couldn't let them see the bird. I stood up and at the same time saw Iggy through the opening between the doors, making his way up the hill to the barn.

'I'm playing a game,' I said.

'Oh yes,' said the man with whiskers, 'what game might that be?'

'I am hiding from Prince Igthy Ma-tuu Clava, Lord of Ro-Torva,' I said, raising my voice so that Iggy would hear me before he got to the barn. 'We are staying at Skirl for Christmas.' Of course this was true in one sense, if you didn't think about which century.

'Come down and let's be having a look at you. We ain't heard of no Prince being at the house.'

'He's travelling *incognito* – it's a big secret that he's here. So you can't say anything.'

They looked up at me doubtfully. 'You'd better come down anyway, young master. We don't want you getting into trouble.'

'And what's your name?' asked the other.

Before I could answer Iggy entered the barn. He had taken some of his warm clothing off, so that his silk tunic and trousers were visible, and from somewhere in his myriad pockets he had conjured a little round embroidered hat which now sat on the back of his head. To keep the pretence of the game I had dropped into the hay again, and I put my finger to my lips to stop the great auk doing anything stupid. I heard him say to the men. 'Small boy – where is he? Is boy up there? I have picnic for him.'

'A picnic for him, sir! Well, I'm sure he wouldn't want to miss that.'

Iggy had begun to mount the ladder. By the way the men were laughing with him I could tell he had won them over. 'Aha,' he exclaimed when

326

he reached the top. 'I have found small boy and we have picnic. I am thanking you for help.' He beamed down to me in the hay. 'You are showing yourself, Brother Kim, and say good day to these gentlemen.'

I got up and smiled down at the men.

'What shall we say, if they're looking for you,' asked one. 'It's not long before nightfall now. Will you find your way back without a light?'

'We won't be long, will we, your Highness?' I said.

'No.' said Iggy. 'Ten minutes tops.'

The men decided that they had got enough hay and left, wishing us a Happy Christmas.

'If they only knew one of us was dead and the other two weren't born yet,' I said after their wagon had disappeared down the track. 'What would they think?'

'I am not dead,' said the bird, looking down eagerly at the bundle of food Iggy had brought.

As the valley was folded in darkness and the lights came on all over the house, we dined on pie, boiled eggs, bread, cheese, Christmas cake and ginger ale. Iggy had found some salted herring in the larder that he had raided without being seen – a fact about which he was extremely mysterious – and after poking and sniffing it, the bird swallowed her first meal of fish for well over a century. 'See, I'm not dead,' she exclaimed.

We said that we had never had any doubt.

When it was quite dark, and we were sure no one would be about, we left the barn, descended to the house and hid in some bushes near the drive. At the front door, two braziers had been set up. Their coals glowed in the dark, and footmen warmed their hands and scuffed the gravel with their boots.

Inside the house we could see hundreds of candles being lit and servants scurrying about with oil lamps. The preparations were much more elaborate than at our Christmas Eve dinner a few hours before, and it was easy to see how the Drago family's fortunes had changed from this time to our time. The house was different too. Although the building was much the same, there wasn't the air of oppression and darkness that I knew so well. Through the windows we could see the servants smiling as they helped each other, and the footmen waiting by the braziers all wore smiles. Iggy watched all this intently then said, 'This, Brother Kim, is the good Christmas Past.'

'Yes, everyone looks so happy,' I said.

About half an hour later a carriage, drawn by

a team of four, came along the drive and pulled up at the front door. Three women in long dresses, hats and mufflers stepped down and hurried up to the open front door where another two footmen stood. More carriages arrived and above the noise of the grooms shouting and the horses being turned and the carriages being taken round to the courtyard, the first strains of music reached our ears.

'They're having a party,' I said.

'With fancy costume,' said Iggy.

'No, it's just the clothes of the period,' I said.

'No, fancy costume and new faces.'

'New faces?'

'Look, there is man with new face.'

I saw a man wearing a mask step from one of the carriages. 'Oh,' I said. 'I think it must be a masked ball. People come wearing fancy dress and masks so they don't recognise each other.'

Iggy absorbed this then, without a word, slipped from the bushes and vanished. One or two more guests arrived, but the main problem now was the number of men who were standing around outside and would be there until people left several hours later. Through the gateway to the courtyard I saw that another brazier had been set up. About a dozen men were smoking long white pipes and heating irons in the fire before thrusting them into their beer mugs. Every time one of them did this there was an angry fizz and a puff of steam rose from the mug. They started singing Christmas carols, at first haltingly, but as they drank more they threw their heads back and serenaded the stars.

Soon Iggy returned, crawling on his hands and knees and dragging something behind him.

'What's in there?' I asked.

'Fancy costumes,' he replied.

'Where did you get it?'

He didn't answer, but told me to stand up and take off my coat, woolly hat and gloves. Then he wrapped me in a dark-red velvet curtain, which fell over me to cover my Wellington boots. 'This isn't going to work,' I protested, feeling foolish. But before I could say anything more, he had taken out a pot and was covering my face with a shiny ointment. Finally he placed the little round hat on my head and buttoned the flaps. 'I king, you slave,' he said, wiping his fingers.

'What about the bird?'

'Bird is dead. You pick up bird and carry it.'

'It!' exclaimed the great auk. 'I am *her* not *it*! And I'm *not* dead.'

'Pretend to be dead,' I said. 'It's only for a

short while so we can get into the house. Once we're inside no one will notice us.' I slipped the bag over my head.

Iggy removed his own coat, laid it on the ground and rolled it into a bundle with my clothes inside. We moved to some trees behind us where he hung the bundle on a low branch so we would be able to find it later.

Guests were still arriving. Our plan was to pretend that we had been set down in the drive and simply amble up to the house. Just as we were about to make for the doorway, a splendid black carriage arrived, drawn by two horses that wore red plumes on top of their bridles. Following this was an open-top carriage with two men in the back who were standing and holding on to a large white square object. A very tall man wearing a black cape, black silk breeches, and top hat and mask got down from the first carriage and started gesturing orders to the two men behind. They tried to lower the thing to the ground by themselves but it was too heavy, and another four men had to help lift it out of the carriage and bear it up the steps.

'Now,' said Iggy striding ahead of us.

The bird was standing in a dreary heap beside me. I told her to go rigid so I could pick her up.

'It won't be long,' I said, putting her under my arm.

We got to the foot of the steps. There was so much fuss over the thing they were now struggling to get through the door that no one took any notice of us. Iggy bounded up the steps. I followed but just as we reached the top, a man shouted from the bottom. 'Ere! Where do you two think you're going?'

Iggy turned.

'They're all right, Joe,' said another voice. 'He's the prince. He's staying in the house with this lad.' It was the man we had seen in the barn who was now helping turn the carriages around. His companion, also spruced up for the occasion in a groom's coat and hat, nodded vigorously.

Iggy gave them a princely bow and we entered through the door where just a few days before – a hundred years in the future – I had first set eyes on Igthy Ma-tuu Clava.

The draughty cavernous house of my time with its ghosts and mysterious noises was now exuberant with candlelight and joy. A cheer went up from the throng of guests as the tall man made his delivery, which was covered in a satin sheet and tied with red ribbons like a Christmas parcel. It was manhandled through a second door into the great hall then propped against the wall beneath the stairs. Silence fell as the man in the cape and mask stepped forward and announced that he was going to reveal his gift to the Dragos of Skirl. He cut the ribbon and told the men to pull the sheets off. 'And this,' he said, sweeping the crowd with his silver-topped cane like a circus master, 'is the fairest representation of paradise that I know. A picture fit for the noble house of Drago.' A gasp went up and the guests cheered again and clapped. The man banged his stick on the floor several times, took off one of his gloves and laid a finger against the surface. 'Have a care, ladies and gentlemen. One or two portions are still wet. The artist – the anonymous artist, ha-ha! – made the final touches this very day. This very day, I tell you.'

He stepped back. 'It may interest the esteemed assembly that not only is this a representation of the house and its lands, the exceptionally broad panels come from one of the six ancient oaks of Skirl which was struck by lightning and fell two years past. These trees are known to be over 1,200 years old. When the acorn that gave birth to this wood fell, the country was plunged into the strife, chaos and ignorance of the Dark Ages. This timber is history – the history of the great estate of

Skirl and the rise of the Dragos. Imagine that, Ladies and Gentleman. Imagine the knowledge locked up in these panels.' He stopped, took a long look at the painting then turned and bowed to the throng of guests.

And so the painting by the Master of the Fallen Chairs came to Skirl – but who was the Master of the Fallen Chairs? Was the artist this huge man with the cane or was he an unknown artist? I searched Iggy's expression for a hint of what he was thinking but got nothing in return.

We were tucked into a corner by the door and I had to peer through gaps in the crowd to see the picture properly. It was very different to the one we had studied in the light of the oil lamp. This was a portrait of Skirl bathed in the light of wealth and happiness. There wasn't a hint of the curse of the Dragos, and not a single sinister detail. The delicate white chairs were all standing upright and everything seemed set for a pleasant afternoon, a picnic perhaps, tea and sandwiches as the shadows grew long. It was summer – not winter as in the painting we knew – and you could almost hear the rustle of the leaves and the birdsong. There were no ravens, or horrified faces staring from opened windows and bridges. No dogs chasing hares, gaping holes in the ground or people falling out of trees. I almost wondered if it was the same picture.

'Come,' whispered Iggy.

I glanced down at the bird in my arms. She looked no more than a dusty, moth-eaten relic, though I did see a flicker in her eyes as someone bumped into her behind. 'But what about the man who painted the picture?' I asked. 'Who's the man in the cape? Is he the Master of the Fallen Chairs?'

Iggy said nothing but smiled lifelessly, as people do at parties when they want to seem to be having a good time and don't want to be noticed. Yet people did notice us, and one woman, who wore a tiara and a mask, leaned into my face with a smell of powder and sweet scent and asked where I had found such marvellous gold paint. I looked like a statue from Roman times, she trilled. And who was the oriental potentate? Everyone was asking; he was quite, quite intriguing. Iggy grinned, waved the sleeves of his crumpled silk tunic imperiously and ordered me about as though I was a slave, which annoyed me a bit.

Gradually we made our way to the old dining room, which was laid out with a feast the like of which I had only ever seen in pictures. There were pheasants and turkeys, salmon and huge joints of beef on silver pedestals, jellies with flowers and fruit trapped in them like amber, pies that you could build a house with and scores of dishes decorated with mayonnaise and aspic. At the corners of the room were footmen standing to attention with plates and silver trays filled with champagne glasses. Everything glittered under the light of hundreds of candles in the chandeliers.

Iggy murmured that we didn't know when we would get a good meal again and grabbed a plate and loaded it with as much food as he could, then we left by the far door, with the glances of one or two guests and the footmen following us. Most of the servants were too busy with the demands of the party to show anything but passing interest in us, and because we knew the house, it was easy to dodge those who gave us more than a second glance.

As we went we were struck by how airy and light the place was. The furnishings were plush and everywhere we looked there was new decoration and signs of money having been recently spent. It seemed to me that they had at least half a dozen people employed on replenishing candles, filling oil lamps and stoking fires. And almost nowhere did we have the brooding sense of the old house; in fact it was difficult to tell where it was because most of the stonework had been painted over. This made me wonder if in my time the old building had somehow gradually swollen inside the skin of the newer house.

We went to the first floor to try to find the second floor at the back of the house where I knew we would be able to find an empty room. As we rounded a corner we came across two servants lugging a large bucket of coal towards us.

I froze, then pushed Iggy through the nearest door. The bird made a slight squawk when I accidentally scraped her head against the doorframe. But it was not loud enough to be heard down the corridor. A few seconds later, the couple struggled past the door without looking into the darkened room.

'What, Brother Kim?' hissed Iggy. 'Why are we in here?'

I looked into his eyes, unable to find any words.

'You white in face, Brother Kim,' he said. 'You see a ghost?' His hands shimmered in the air.

'That was Bella Brown,' I said. 'I know it was her. I know the way she walks. I saw her face. That was Bella Brown!'

Chapter Twenty

Help from an Unseen Hand

I sank to the floor. This was too much for me. How could she be alive a hundred years before she was murdered and look exactly the same age?

'What's happening, Iggy? Why is she here?'

His expression had changed but he couldn't resist the joke. 'Your face white because you *don't* see ghost.'

'That's not the point. Why's she here?'

'More fascinating,' said Iggy. 'We find out later.'

'You say most fascinating in English,' I said, 'not more fascinating. It doesn't make sense.'

'But it is not *most* fascinating – it is just *more* fascinating.'

'More fascinating than what?'

'Than a piece of wood.'

I gave up after that.

Although I wasn't hungry, Iggy insisted I ate the

food we had taken from the banquet because we never knew when we would see a square meal again. 'Time travel bad for digestion,' he added gravely.

We knew that we'd have to hide out until the house fell quiet in the early hours of Christmas Day before looking at the painting again.

Iggy touched the great auk lightly on the back. She woke from her museum-piece trance with a start.

'Where we find your secrets, dear bird?' he said softly.

Her eyes fluttered and she swallowed. 'In the natural history room – where Clive has made his collection. You will find me there too.'

Iggy shook his head. I understood that he knew it was breaking a convention of time travel to take the bird into a room to confront herself. It would be like me meeting myself when I was ten years old. We had to get round that and the best way seemed to be to park her in some obscure corner and collect her after we had found everything we needed.

'You were part of Iggy's great grandfather's collection?'

'Didn't I mention that? Yes, I was the prize specimen. He paid *5,000 guineas* for me. Only later was I moved to the Long Gallery where you found me. And it was there that the desecration of my species took place when the horrid young men of the house aimed darts at me.'

'Where is the natural history room?'

The bird raised her wings doubtfully. 'It is near the other room – by the stairs.'

I remembered a door off the ancient wooden stairs, which led up to the Long Gallery, but it was empty in my time. Maybe that was where Clive Endymion kept his collection. We took some candles from one of the wall lights and hurried through the house, most of which was quiet, although there were one or two servants still clearing up.

Having left the bird in a cupboard we clambered up the stairs and found the room unlocked. We slipped in and closed the door behind us. The candles flickered in the cold air and we immediately saw the bird again on her stand. We both ignored her. Life was too short and we were too busy to get involved with two dead great auks that were in fact the same extinct bird.

All around the walls there were cases of mounted insects, beetles and butterflies. Skeletons of snakes and lizards, skulls of fish and some fossils were laid out in a glass case. Each was identified on a card with spidery brown handwriting. Hanging above the bureau was a small turtle shell and on the opened flap of the desk was a brass microscope and a finished drawing which was entitled '*Copepoda Cyclops* – the tiny beast with one eye'.

Iggy moved his great grandfather's work, marvelling at the skill it had taken to draw something that could only be seen with a microscope. There were also notebooks written between 1842 and 1862. Each was inscribed on the cover with Clive's name. I began to read them. Mostly they were observations he had made in the fields around Skirl with little drawings in the margin. But he had also recorded when he bought two fossils from a dealer in Lyme Regis. This was in brown not blue ink. Soon I found the mention of the purchase of the great auk in the book for 1853. The stuffed bird came from a Mr Turvey of Farringdon Road, London, and was purchased for 500 – not 5,000 – guineas, as the bird had claimed!

I read aloud to Iggy. 'In June, the year of our Lord 1844, Mr John Turvey's acquaintance, Richard Liggett, was sailing in the seas off the island off St Kilda. On an outcrop known as *Stac an Armin*, Ligget spotted two large black and white birds. He knew instantly that they were great auks. Liggett and his companion scaled the rock and approached the birds. The garefowls showed not the slightest inclination to defend their nest, but immediately ran along under the high cliff, their heads erect, their little wings somewhat extended. They uttered no cry of alarm, and moved, with short steps, about as quickly as a man could walk. Liggett, with outstretched arms, drove one into a corner, where he soon had it fast. The other began to flap its wings and open and shut its beak, though emitting no sound. Taking one last look at its mate, it dropped into the ocean swell below. This specimen I have purchased was in all probability one of the very last garefowls or great auks to live. No scientific record of a sighting since that day in June 1844 exists. However there may have been one bird – perhaps the bird that escaped my grasp – captured on St Kilda later that year.' Then, in underlined sentences, Clive Endymion had added. 'I honour the great auk's memory and mourn the loss of the species. I would give anything for this sad relic to be living now.'

'Little did he know,' I said.

I closed the book. 'We've got it. She has to go back to before June 1844 and she will find her mate again. Your great grandfather seems a good man.'

Iggy nodded in the candlelight. Something was going on behind his speckled brown eyes.

'I wonder why he had to leave Skirl,' I continued. 'He doesn't seem the sort of person to make a scandal.'

He did not have time to answer. I shuddered and then both candles flickered. These were familiar signs. Despite all the light and warmth in Skirl that Christmas Eve of 1862, something or someone from the other side had joined us in the room. We looked at each other for several seconds. Then came a voice so faint and hoarse that we had to strain to hear it. 'Boy, be my friend. I like the look of you, boy. Be my friend.'

'Silverfish?' I said astonished. 'How can it be you?'

'That is my name. Be my friend, Boy.'

I was about to say something, but Iggy put his finger up to his lips. 'Silverfish does not know she has seen you before because it is in future time, Brother Kim.'

I nodded. 'Why are you here?' I said to the room. 'Show yourself.'

'I have come to help you, Boy.'

At this, two carved pillars set in the middle of the row of pigeon holes in the bureau shot out towards us. Each pillar concealed a secret compartment. Iggy poured the contents onto the bureau – a small black notebook, some letters folded very tightly and keys. He pressed opened the book and asked me to read.

'Go on,' said Iggy.

Suddenly the pages began to shift under my hands. I let go of the book and allowed them to turn and turn until the book fell open at pages where the writing was very small and scratchy.

I rummaged in my bag and found the magnifying glass and gave it to Iggy, who held it about three inches from the surface of the page so I could read. 'Since this woman came to Skirl,' I began, 'neither family nor household has been content. All manner of disputes have arisen and there can be little doubt that the responsibility for the turbulence and sourness in the air lies with the governess of my brother Titus's two children, Miss A.H. But neither Titus nor his wife, Sarah, comprehend the malign effect of the woman in their employ for she is careful to disguise her true nature by offering innumerable services to them and to Father. Yet when our backs are turned, she is poisoning the love between us, corroding our trust in each other, destroying old friendships. She means us harm, but the others are blind to it and allow their suspicions and malice to grow every day.

'Today (November 15th, 1862) I have employed a Mr Poulter of *Poulter's Professional Inquiries*, Bournemouth, to act in the matter and search out this odious person's true origins. When I have the evidence I will present it to Father and we shall be rid of her.'

'It's Alba Hockmuth,' I shouted. 'She's here too. A.H. are her initials. She always uses them. I knew it. I just knew it must be her when I saw her blurred pictures in the photo album. In every frame she had moved so that she couldn't be identified.'

Iggy was unsurprised. 'Read, Brother Kim.'

There was a lot more about how she had set one brother against the other. How the wives of Titus and Rufus were estranged and no longer talked to each other. How Titus had threatened Clive when he tried to bring up the subject of A.H. Then there was a note dated 22nd December, 1862. 'Triumph! All the references that Miss A.H. supplied are false. She has attended none of the institutions and academies that she claims, nor have any of the people she mentioned as previous employers ever heard of her. After Christmas I shall confront the family with this evidence. This is good news and I have rewarded Mr Poulter handsomely.' This was followed by a coded entry, several lines of capital letters and numbers. Iggy copied them down very carefully, rolled the scrap of paper up and placed it in an inside pocket.

'Why do you need that?' I asked.

'Silverfish show us this for good reason. Maybe Silverfish know something important.'

I whispered to the room, 'Silverfish, are you there? Is there anything else you want us to see?'

We waited and then Iggy gestured to the window where our breath had steamed up the cold glass. On it was written. 'Be my friend.'

An odd thought occurred to me. *The first time I met her she already knew me. The first time she met me, I already knew her.* Then I said to the room. 'I will be your friend. I promise, Silverfish. Can you help us once more? We are looking for another book – a much older book. It has diagrams and codes in it and it's very, very old.'

Nothing moved; no answer came. We both knew she had gone.

Then, quite suddenly, the book came fluttering out of the air, as though someone had tossed it hard from the other side of the room. Heaven knows where it had been, but now it was with us.

'This is it,' I said, turning the pages quickly. Iggy examined it against the maps he had brought with the Bible. They were the same. Then he took a pen and paper from the desk and began very carefully to copy all the diagrams and coded grids. I noticed now that some of the grids contained symbols rather than letters. 'Why don't we just take the book?' I asked.

'We must leave it for father before three. We have everything we need.'

Eventually he finished making the copies, closed the book and rose. I glanced at the little brass clock on the wall. It was half past twelve.

'Happy Christmas for the second day running,' I said.

We realised that the sounds of the party had faded. The carriages had left without us hearing them. We waited another hour, during which Iggy told me stories from his island. Then we stole from the room that contained the great auk and went to collect the same great auk, but a hundred years older, from the cupboard where we had hidden her, which was all a bit unsettling.

The house was silent. Keeping to the first floor we took a longer route to the Great Hall, which went right round the back of the house.

Eventually we descended to the ground floor by a narrow wooden stairway and found ourselves in a darkened billiard room.

It was here that we heard voices coming from the wide passageway beyond. Lights and shadows danced on the walls and up into a small gallery which ran along one side. We crept forward and peeped through the door. Six men in evening dress, but not masks, were lined up. They glowed and were laughing and slapping each other on the back. Each held a candle in his hand, except for the man I immediately recognised as Clive, who read from a tablet. I suppressed a cry of amazement. They were about to play Slipcandle.

Iggy looked on amazed at seeing his ancestor so alive and in such good spirits.

'Now pay attention, you scoundrels,' Clive shouted 'Slipcandle. The rules thereof: "*One*, the game of Slipcandle shall only be played on Christmas Eve. *Two*, each man shall contribute to the purse the sum of two guineas. *Three*, side bets are permitted but shall be no less than one guinea and no more than ten guineas. *Four*, there shall be no blowing, flapping or sudden movement employed by contestants wishing to snuff out, or otherwise sabotage, a competitor's candle. *Five*, no linseed oil shall be used to grease the underside of the plate. *Six*, once a contestant's candle has been extinguished he must withdraw and remove his plate from the course. And seven, there shall be no disputes."'

The men began to send their plates skidding along the polished wooden floor. There was much laughter and joking, yet there was an edge to the remarks the three brothers, Titus, Rufus and Clive, flung at each other. Eventually they were left in the race although we couldn't see which of them was in the lead.

It was then that a slight movement in the gallery attracted our attention. The light was poor but for a fleeting moment we saw a woman move in the shadows. She was staring down with intense fascination at the game being played below her. A smile curled her lips and there was a look of lofty amusement in her eyes. I froze. I would have known that face in half the time it took to see her. Alba Hockmuth was secretly spying on the victims of the curse and plotting their death and captivity in the afterlife. Then as the candlelight slid along the wall, we caught sight of a not quite human shape beside her; a shape that did not hold itself for long, but formed ambiguously only to dissolve into the shadows after a brief moment.

'It's Alba,' I whispered.

'And the Lyncher,' Iggy added.

He had seen enough. He tugged at my arm, and we began to crawl backwards across the soft carpet of the billiard room. The bird had remained rigid all this time but when we reached the back stairs and were out of earshot, she demanded testily, 'What's going on now?'

'We saw Alba Hockmuth.' I said. 'We found out when you...er...you lost your life. You were captured in the summer of 1844 near an island called St Kilda. Your mate must have been taken that winter.'

She nodded sadly.

'We thought you'd be pleased'

'Oh I am, I am. I was just thinking...'

Iggy interrupted. 'Come, Brother Kim, we must go see painting while she is watching game.'

It amazed me how well he knew the house. He found a way through the maze of corridors and dead ends back to the Great Hall where all but two lamps had been extinguished. There was a smell of alcohol and women's scent in the air, mixed with cigars and oil from the lamps. The clocks simultaneously began to chime two o'clock all around us.

We stood in front of the painting and

wondered at its innocent appearance. There were no clues for us to work on. Iggy knelt down, and I handed him my magnifying glass.

'Is there a signature?' I asked.

He shook his head and shuffled to the right-hand side of the picture. 'Yes and no,' he said eventually. 'There is something here.'

'What?'

'Later, Brother Kim: I tell you later.'

'That's the second time you've said that. What do you mean?'

He grunted with concentration.

'There's nothing to work out,' I said helplessly. 'It's just a picture of the house.'

'No, there's magic in the wood. Big magic. This Iggy did not think of.'

'The wood from the oak trees?'

He nodded.

He was on all fours for several minutes longer before he exclaimed something in his own language.

'What is it?'

He pointed to the chairs, but I couldn't see anything.

'Look, Brother Kim. Look!'

I still couldn't see anything.

He jumped up and went to fetch one of the

lamps from the wall. With the light close to the painting and the magnifying glass held in front of my nose, I could see tiny marks on the backs and fronts of the chairs. These were not painted but scratched into the surface of the damp paint. I looked closer. 'It looks like writing but it's so small...hold on...I think they're names.

'Yes, they say Brother Kim and Igthy Ma-tuu Clava and my father before three.'

'I can see why we missed them before,' I whispered. 'They're all here – Titus, Rufus, Clive, Andrew, Charles, Richard, Francis and the rest, and here we are on the two chairs left standing in a hundred years' time.'

Iggy touched the surface of the painting and looked at his finger. Then he took the handle of the magnifying glass and rubbed it against the paint so that the scratch marks disappeared. We each looked through the glass again to make sure that they had gone, and Iggy did some more rubbing to be on the safe side.

'What about the others?' I said. 'We can't leave their names here and let them die.'

Iggy shook his head. 'For us, they are already dead. We made deal with Old Inky Fingers.'

'So what! They don't have to be dead.'

'Yes, they do.'

353

'You mean we can't change what has already happened?'

He nodded sadly.

'But what about the bird? She's already dead.'

'I'm not dead.'

'Well, how do you explain all that business in the journals about you being captured on that rock and Clive buying a stuffed bird? That was you.'

For once the great auk was lost for words.

'Come on, Iggy. Let's try it. No one will know and we will save all those lives. All that misery.'

He shook his head firmly and got up. 'I am time investigator. I know things. We do not change what already happened in our time. If these men live, we may not.'

I got up to face him. 'You mean it would change the whole history of the family.'

'And your father may never meet your mother,' he said placing a hand on my shoulder. 'And Clava never come to Ro-Torva and never meet my mother before three and Igthy Ma-tuu Clava is still a grain of sand, and nothing more, and never lives.'

'A grain of sand?'

'We were all grains of sand, Brother Kim.'

I let this go. 'Are you sure that we can't help them?'

He nodded. Just then both the oil lamp that he held and the one still in its place on the wall flickered and went out within a few seconds of each other.

'Drat,' I said, 'they must have been filled at the same time.'

We stood in almost total darkness for a few seconds and then decided there was nothing more we could do with the picture and that we should leave the Great Hall and head for the front door.

We took a few steps and then there was a noise behind us. I whipped round to see two faint shadows moving from the staircase towards us at incredible speed. The first was a physical entity for there was a rush of air as it lashed out at us with a stick. I crouched down instinctively and saw the figure silhouetted against a little amount of light coming from one of the landings above us, a tall thin shape wearing her hair in a bun with her arms raised above her.

'How dare you! Who are you? What are you doing here?' came the unmistakable, scalding anger of Alba Hockmuth.

She stopped to sense what lay in the darkness. There was a glint above her head. This was no stick but a fine rapier that was suddenly poised in the air, scenting out its prey. It came down towards us. I felt the bird dive to the left and I rolled to the right. Then I heard a moan. It was Iggy. I knew he couldn't be hurt. He was drawing her away from us. She took three steps to my right and the blade scythed through the air and connected with some wood. A voice called out and light came on up the stairs, just enough for me to see Iggy's shape crouch down and launch himself at Alba's midriff. The blade barely missed him and I heard it ripping through the fabric of a chair nearby. The blade was stuck. Alba stumbled then gathered herself, yanked the blade free and went after Iggy with several slashes. He dodged but lost his balance and had to roll on the ground to avoid the next thrust. The bird scooted around in a panic, flapping her wings. For a second or two I froze. We had saved our lives in the future but there was nothing to stop us from being killed in the past. And where was the other figure? Two assailants had rushed at us from the dark.

For the fifth or sixth time the blade rose like a scorpion's sting above Iggy, then fell and glanced across his shoulder as he rolled away again. Now he was trapped against the wall. I couldn't see him but I heard him writhing on the polished floorboards as he struggled to get a foothold. His legs were kicking out furiously. The blade glinted in the air again, scenting the blood it would certainly taste. Before I knew it, I ripped off the velvet curtain I was wearing, jumped up at Alba and threw it over her head. At the same time I kicked her with all my might and pummelled her back with my fists. Then she landed a blow, which sent me reeling. I didn't yell out because I knew she still couldn't see us, and something told me that she might have no clue who we were, and we had to keep it that way.

I was still bent recovering when one or two more lights appeared high up on the staircase. A man called out. Now we could see a bit more of Alba, but she couldn't see us because the curtain had become wrapped around her neck. I turned towards Iggy and was horrified to see him still on the floor. Around his neck was a rope. He was being dragged into the shadows by an unseen force. With each terrible jerk a gurgle escaped his throat. His legs and arms were trussed and a terrible grimace was spreading across his face as Lyncher began to garrotte him in front of my eyes.

I fumbled for the harp and started plucking the prongs for all I was worth, but it did no good at all. Instead of the notes flying from my mouth and expanding in the air to vanquish the ghost, there was a dull plonking sound.

But help was at hand. The bird had scooted into the shadows and with a banshee's cry and a snapping of her beak was laying about Lyncher; and very effectively too, for suddenly the ropes that held Iggy fast were loosened and he was able to scramble away. Choking and with one hand round his neck, he grabbed me with the other and we staggered in the direction of the front door. The bird followed and, by the time we reached the door, she was already claiming a historic victory over Lyncher, who she called 'the executioner of the underworld'.

Meanwhile, we heard Alba hastily change her act by meeting the worried voices descending the stairs with a wail of hysteria, as though she was the one who had been attacked.

Now Iggy was ripping open the bolts and turning the key. Suddenly we were out in the delicious cold air and running to the black outline of the clump of trees where our bundle of clothes was hanging. My heart was pounding and no thought was in my head but the need to flee. We pulled on our clothes and were grateful for them, for it was very cold. Iggy touched me on the shoulder.

'Are you all right?' I said.

'Yes. Come, Brother Kim, we must go. Old Inky Fingers waits for us with his errands.'

The earflaps of his hat were sticking out. I remembered the moment when I set eyes on him for the first time – just a few days ago, which was now a hundred years in the future. He looked now as he did then – outlandish and funny and mysterious. I felt a grin spread across my face as I looked up at him. With such an extraordinary friend, anything was possible. He regarded me with a humorous expression but said nothing. Then, without hurry, he tied the flaps of his hat and wrinkled his nose at the bird, who was still descanting about her heroism.

We all glanced up at Skirl. More and more lights were coming on and we could see the smoke winding from the chimneys into the still winter air. It seemed not so much like a house but a great ocean liner moored along a quayside. I thought how beautiful and sturdy Skirl seemed just at the very moment when the evil of the Master of the Fallen Chairs had taken root in the house.

We turned without a word. I picked the bird up again and soon we were hurrying across the frosted fields under a never-so-starry sky, free and alive, certain that we had mastered the Master of the Fallen Chairs and would live to tell the tale.

Chapter Twenty-One

Once More to the Bridge of Tarle

But that night in 1862 was not over for us just yet.

We trudged up the hill and found a path through the woods that would lead us to the bridge. There was a lot that I needed urgently to ask Iggy, and for once he seemed happy to answer my questions. 'Do you think she knew it was us?'

'No, Brother Kim.'

'Why not?'

'Because she never see us.'

'Yes, but she must have guessed. After all, she has seen us before.'

'No. This is Lady Alba now in 1862. She has never seen us before and she don't know us. If she see us tonight she would know she seen us in the future and not try to stop us go to bridge because she don't know that we passed over with help of Old Inky Fingers. See? So, she don't know us now.'

'Ah, I see,' I said, grappling with the complexity of time travel. 'She can't know something now that she learns in the future even though she can go between different times. So in a way she is no better than you or me.'

'Or me,' said the bird.

'This is correct, Brother Kim. You are certainly very clever.'

'But she is good at making friends with ghosts and using them to get what she wants,' I said.

He laid a hand across my shoulder and bent down. 'She has big magic in this way and she gets bigger magic in future times.'

'What about the painting? Is that how she does it?'

'Yes, she uses magic wood to make things happen.'

'How?'

'This confounded mystery, Brother Kim. Like Honourable Bird is confounded mystery and all this place is confounded mystery. Like codes are confounded mystery.'

I was about to mention the other confounded mystery – what Bella Brown was doing in the house a hundred years before she died yet looking exactly the same age as she was in 1962. But then we heard a dog baying, and soon after that the excited yelping of a pack of hounds in full cry. We stopped and listened to the night. There was no doubt about it: the dogs were making their way down the densely wooded slope towards us. I guessed we were about ten minutes from the bridge. There was nothing for it but to run, but this was easier said than done because we kept on straying off the track and bumping into treetrunks and low branches. Several times I fell over and dropped the bird into the frozen undergrowth, and Iggy had to pick us both up. We tried carrying the bird between us, but this didn't work very well because the sound of the dogs panicked her and made her flap her little wings and squawk. The pack was now above us on the winding track. And they had been joined by new sounds – horses' hooves and the clatter of a carriage being driven at breakneck speed. We glimpsed a light turning in the trees about 200 yards up the slope.

There was only one thing to do. We jumped off the road and plunged down a steep bank, tripping, falling and eventually sliding down on our backsides. The bird wriggled free of my grasp and tobogganed down on her front. At the bottom, we should have found the river but instead came to a piece of open marshland full of dead grass tussocks.

I realised that we must have taken the wrong track when we entered the woods. Panting and bent double, I broke the news to Iggy that we would be on the wrong side of the bridge. He gave my shoulder a squeeze as if to say it couldn't be helped. Hearing the dogs not far behind, we set off again, zigzagging through the tussocks of dead grass. The frozen bog crunched beneath our feet and in some places the crust of ice gave way and our feet sank into the cold slime. The faster we went the less this happened. The bird, being much lighter, was able to scoot ahead of us and call back that we were being very slow considering how many dogs were pursuing us.

We reached some lines of willow trees and pushed through the plantation with our heads bent down to avoid the icy boughs slashing at our faces. Suddenly I realised that this exact same patch was still in use a hundred years later: Tom Jebard had once pointed it out to me and explained how the willow rods were stripped and dried. Nearby there was a raised road that led to the bridge, one of the old straight tracks the ancient people had used to drive their cattle across the land – Jebard told me it was thousands of years old. I veered off to the left, shouting for Iggy and the bird to follow, and very soon we were scrambling through a clump of dead reeds and up a bank.

The majority of the pack had lost our scent and gone off in the wrong direction but a few were on our trail and, seconds later, we heard them follow us up the embankment. Iggy immediately slowed his pace. 'If we walk, they walking too,' he said. But it took more than this to stop the bird and he had to reach forward and grab hold of her.

Five deerhounds loomed behind us. They trotted up, panting, and sniffed the bird, who wailed her alarm and moved very close to me. We took no notice and continued walking purposefully towards the bridge, but then the remains of the pack sprang out of the marshes ahead of us and started baying for our blood. I was sure that it would take a bite from just one and the rest would join in.

What seemed to be stopping them was Iggy. From that first moment on the doorstep with Jebard, I remembered Trumpet, Applejack and Black showing a respectful interest in him, and whenever he was near them they rarely took their eyes off him. Now he made a high pitched clicking noise with his tongue – tee-tchick, tee-tchick, chicky, chicky, tee-tchick – and the steaming bodies of the hounds let us pass. They were very smelly and slobber dropped from their mouths.

We steadily edged forward to the bridge, but just as I was beginning to think we might reach it safely, there came the sound of a horn and the carriage, which had been careening through the woods, swung onto the track and was coming towards us. It would be upon us any moment. Iggy told the bird and me to drop down among the hounds, so that we wouldn't be seen. This confused the dogs even more. They milled around, thrusting their muzzles inquisitively into our faces, but despite several blasts from the hunting horn they dared do nothing else to us. 'Tee-tchick, tee-tchick,' went Iggy.

The next thing we heard was the carriage being driven full tilt into the hounds. I shot up to see a small black vehicle, just like the London hackney cab I knew from pictures of the period. Alba was standing up front cracking a whip over the backs of a pair of horses and yelling at the dogs to get out of the way. The unearthly, piercing fury of her cries echoed around the woods and was soon joined by the howls of the dogs that had been hit by the wheels and trampled by the horses.

Suddenly the horses had had too much and reared up, causing the carriage to swerve. Alba tried to control them with the whip, which only seemed to add to their panic. Then I heard her shriek, 'Seize them! Bind them! Hang them!' I glimpsed a very tall figure get down from inside the carriage and start wading through the pack. I couldn't see much but I knew it must be Lyncher come to dispatch us to the next world with his ropes. But the dogs liked the sight of this spectral creature moving several feet above them no more than we and they began to surge forward, pushing us along with them.

It was just then that we heard the blissful sound of the river crashing around the breakwaters of the bridge. We were within a few yards of being saved. Iggy jumped up, took a few paces in the direction of Lyncher, and threw something into the melée of dogs and horses. There was a flash followed by a very loud bang, and a cloud of smoke enveloped us. A manic laugh came from the middle of the fog then all hell broke loose. The dogs set up a terrible howling, the horses whinnied and snorted and at least one must have broken free from the harness because I could hear the carriage being dragged off the embankment and Alba screaming.

Iggy appeared out of the fog. 'Come, Brother Kim, bring Honourable Bird to the bridge.'

'What did you throw at them?'

'Modest Chinese whiz bang! Great lady in bog and Lyncher – he gone.' He snapped his fingers twice and giggled.

We stumbled blindly through the rest of the pack and jumped up on the first slab of the bridge, then without thinking ran as fast as we could across the slippery great stones towards the other side where we would make the fire and summon the Old Man of Tarle.

But it turned out this wasn't necessary. Halfway across, at the point where the noise of the river drowned out the clamour we'd left behind, we found the Old Man of Tarle contemplating the waters in a silvery grey light. We skidded to a halt, and he turned to us.

'Damned fine fellow! I like your style Flopsy, old chap,' he said with a horrid grin. 'Bags of gumption! A few tricks up your sleeve! Oh yes, you're the man for the job, I'm certain of it.' He clapped his hands. 'Oh, but the sight of her falling base over apex, being tipped into the mire with all her finery, was pure delight. A delight, I tell you!' He paused and examined us. 'There is, of course, the outstanding matter of errands I need to be completed. Are you prepared for a little light labour?'

'Not so quick, Inky Fingers,' said Iggy quietly. He folded his arms in front of him and smiled pleasantly in the mysterious light that illuminates the centre of the Bridge of Tarle. There was a no-nonsense tone in his voice that I hadn't heard before.

'What's that? Got something to say, have you? Speak up then.'

'Inky Fingers is Master of the Fallen Chairs.'

I was astonished and also more than a little worried at what the Old Man would do.

'What's that you're saying, Flopsy?'

'Inky Fingers paints fallen chairs for his lady love. Lady Alba!'

'Rot!' exploded the Old Man. 'I'll see you in court, you slandering rascal.'

'That's not right,' I interrupted nervously. 'He said he didn't paint the picture when I asked him, and he hates Alba.'

Iggy's eyes did not leave the Old Man. '*No*, he say to Brother Kim that it was *pathetic* question and he told Brother Kim to think of a better question. He *not* say he didn't paint picture of fallen chairs.'

Now I came to think of it that was exactly right: the Old Man avoided the question.

369

'Inky Fingers loves Lady Alba,' said Iggy. 'And he paints picture of her and he make songs for her. That is why he has inky fingers because he is always painting and writing for *Lady Love*.' Iggy pouted, put his hands on his hips and swayed as though he was a very curvy woman. The Old Man scowled at him, but said nothing.

By 'song' I realised Iggy meant the poem that was concealed in the painting of Ahrinnia Hecht. The last lines stuck in my mind and I recited them aloud, '"Unslave her radiance from life's distress, Make this woman for all time Time's mistress. And with this painted secret I do impart; No small measure, but my traveller's heart." It's true, isn't it?' I said. 'You are the traveller. You wanted her to be your girlfriend!'

'That's enough!' shouted the Old Man of Tarle. 'That's enough, I tell you.'

Iggy shrugged. 'But it is truth, Inky Fingers. You love her. That is why you make paintings and songs for her. And little gold earring of man is you. Like you are her prisoner – her *slaveman*.'

I stared at the Old Man and I was so angry that I forgot his power to pick us up and drop us down in the time of the Black Death. 'All those people died because of you. Iggy's great grandfather and the others died because you are the Master of the Fallen Chairs and you laid a curse on them. *And us!'*

The Old Man shook his head and took a few steps as though he meant to disappear again.

'You're a coward,' I shouted at his back. 'You planned for us to die tonight and you never had the guts to tell us. Now we've wiped out our names on the chairs and we shall live, but the others all died because of you. That means you are as bad and cruel as she is.'

He turned to me very slowly and gave me one of his most withering looks. 'Believe me, young man, there is no comprehending the scale of that woman's evil. And by the way, she added those names.'

'Yes, but you painted the picture and you knew you couldn't trust her.'

'And you takes picture to Christmas party,' added Iggy.

'That was a long time ago, when I trusted her.'

'It was tonight, ' I said.

'To you, yes. But what seems to you to come before may come after for me. But I don't expect you to understand that.' He cleared his throat loudly and thumped his chest. 'The point is that the powerful magic is contained in the ancient panels of oak wood and her evil did the rest.

I have no interest in killing strangers in the future. I would not debase myself with such a low and barbaric project. And just remember who enabled you to go back in time and fix the painting. If I had wanted you dead, I would have allowed her to catch you in 1962.'

'But what about the inscription?' I said.

'I might have suggested it to her in fonder days, but an inscription, a motto or legend, or a bit of a teaser is not the same as a curse. Anyway I do not have to explain myself to you two.'

'*Three!*' said the great auk.

The Old Man was silent for a few minutes then made a terrible snorting sound and blew his nose into a spotted handkerchief. He turned his sulphurous gaze downstream, and in a voice that was both distant and agonised – as though he was talking to himself – he began his story. 'It is true. I did love Ahrinnia Hecht. *Once!* Many centuries ago, a fragile and clever young woman entered my life. My Bohemian rose, I called her. Imagine! I met her in this exact spot. Here! Right here!' He drummed his stick. 'And she came to me possessed of such guile and beauty and grace as has ever been contained in mortal flesh. At last, I had found a companion for my centuries of wandering; at last there was an equal with whom

I could share the sacred secrets of this place, a person who could anchor my roaming spirit and enjoy with me the favours of eternity. And I resolved to make her mine forever, to fashion a love that would endure all time, a love that would not wither from age, nor shrivel with the dull familiarity of ordinary human life. But then…well that is another story.'

'Then she left you,' said the bird unexpectedly.

The Old Man groaned. 'What? Is my condition now to be summarised by an extinct feather-brain?'

The bird batted her eyelids apologetically and raised her wings so they stood out then slowly fell back in place.

'Honourable Bird is right,' said Iggy. 'Lady Alba takes secrets and laughs at Old Inky Fingers. And Old Inky Fingers send spies to see what she doings.'

The Old Man's eyes cast about him impatiently.

Iggy gave me a look. 'Bella Brown is spy for you,' he said.

It took a second or two for this to sink into my tired brain, but then everything fell into place. Bella had been sent to infiltrate Skirl as a maid at the time when the Old Man delivered the painting, then again a hundred years later for the Renewal, when the energy of the Lines of Tarle was at its height.

'You knew Alba would recognise her from a hundred years before,' I said. 'Bella died because of you!'

'Alba is not the sort of person ever to notice servants,' growled the Old Man. 'They all look the same to her. And Bella Brown's current state is by no means permanent. I should add that I did attempt to contact her but she failed to make the rendezvous.'

So it had been the Old Man watching the house before Christmas, but this interested me less than the idea that Bella's state was *not permanent*. The laws of life and death *could* be ignored for some people, so why not for Silverfish? But I kept this thought to myself because I'd noticed that Iggy gave nothing away to the Old Man of Tarle. Or, come to think of it, to me. I was amazed at how much he kept to himself about the Master of the Fallen Chairs.

'Right, to business!' said the Old Man of Tarle. His eyes swivelled in their sockets and glittered with mischief and a general contempt for humankind. Then he cleared his throat in a disgusting way. 'I can't stay here all night. It does my breathing no good at all. I suffer from Time Traveller's Lung, you know.'

'What's that?' I asked.

'A rare condition, an occupational hazard like housemaid's knee.' He coughed and spat some phlegm into the water and stamped his feet. 'You try loitering on a cold damp bridge for thousands of years.' He paused. 'Now, are you taking the bird with you or not? As far as I am concerned, she can go or stay.'

We both looked down at the great auk.

'You must go to join your mate,' I said. 'You know the time in 1844 when you were captured and…er…preserved. You just have to return and find your mate and avoid all those things that made your species extinct.'

The great auk's eyes flickered. 'But I can't leave you two here,' she said. 'You need me.'

'Um…' started Iggy.

'I owe you both and I will stay and help you,' she continued.

One glance at Iggy was enough to tell me that he thought the bird would be a hindrance wherever we were going. 'That's very nice of you,' I said. 'But don't feel you have to.'

'Oh, but I do for the honour of my kind.'

'Right, that's settled then,' said the Old Man hastily. 'Your first task is…'

'Not so quick,' said Iggy. 'We must make deal about errands.'

'We want to know what we have to do,' I added.

'Oh, it's very simple. You will travel through time to discover the origin of Alba's power. You will see how and where she uses it, and you will report back to me in readiness for the final battle, when at the point of Renewal I must challenge her power.'

'No tricks, Inky Fingers!'

The Old Man of Tarle vented his impatience with a monumental sigh. 'Look, if you don't like it, Flopsy, you can lump it.' He pointed along the bridge with his stick. 'At that end you can take your luck with Countess Ahrinnia Hecht and her unsavoury friend Lyncher.' He turned and held out his other arm. 'Or you can choose that end where she lurks on the eve of the Renewal with an assembly of ghouls that will rip you to pieces. Or you can throw your lot in with me. You have a choice, or rather no choice.'

'How can she be in two places at the same time?' I asked.

'It is not at the same time, idiot,' he snapped. 'That is the whole point.'

He raised his stick and cried, 'Welcome aboard,

me hearties.' Then he held it out and plunged it into the waters, which seemed to embrace it by rising up the shaft. The bird shuffled close to me and I clung on to Iggy's arm. As we stood shivering on the bridge, betwixt and between times, waiting to know our fate, I looked up and saw a strange intensity in Iggy's expression. 'What are you thinking about?' I asked nervously.

'Plum pudding,' came the reply.

Look out for the next story
about Kim and Iggy
and the House at Skirl

Coming soon…

ABOUT THE AUTHOR
Henry Porter lives in London with his wife,
two grown up children and a dachshund.
He has published four novels for adults,
the most recent of which, *Brandenburg*,
won the Ian Fleming prize.

www.masterofthefallenchairs.com

OTHER ORCHARD BOOKS YOU MAY ENJOY

The Cure	Michael Coleman	978 1 84616 345 6
The Fire Within	Chris d'Lacey	978 1 84121 533 4
Icefire	Chris d'Lacey	978 1 84362 134 8
Fire Star	Chris d'Lacey	978 1 84362 522 3
The Fire Eternal	Chris d'Lacey	978 1 84616 426 2
Toonhead	Fiona Dunbar	978 1 84616 238 1
Eggs	Jerry Spinelli	978 1 84616 700 3
Love, Stargirl	Jerry Spinelli	978 1 84616 925 0
The Mighty Crashman	Jerry Spinelli	978 1 84616 960 1
Milkweed	Jerry Spinelli	978 1 84362 485 1
Stargirl	Jerry Spinelli	978 1 84616 599 3 (pink)
		978 1 84616 600 6 (silver)

All priced at £5.99 except *Love, Stargirl*, which is £10.99

Orchard Red Apples are available from all good bookshops,
or can be ordered direct from the publisher:
Orchard Books, PO BOX 29, Douglas IM99 1BQ
Credit card orders please telephone 01624 836000
or fax 01624 837033 or visit our website: www.orchardbooks.co.uk
or e-mail: bookshop@enterprise.net for details.

To order please quote title, author and ISBN
and your full name and address.
Cheques and postal orders should be made payable to 'Bookpost plc.'
Postage and packing is FREE within the UK
(overseas customers should add £1.00 per book).

Prices and availability are subject to change.